Addicted

Addicted

Addicted

AMELIA BETTS

New York Boston

Copyright © 2015 by Amelia Betts
Cover design by Rebecca Lown
Cover copyright © 2015 by Hachette Book Group, Inc.

Forever Yours
Hachette Book Group
1290 Avenue of the Americas
New York, NY 10104
hachettebookgroup.com
twitter.com/foreverromance

First ebook and print on demand edition: October 2015

Forever Yours is an imprint of Grand Central Publishing.
The Forever Yours name and logo are trademarks of Hachette Book Group, Inc.

The publisher is not responsible for websites (or their content) that are not owned by the publisher.

The Hachette Speakers Bureau provides a wide range of authors for speaking events. To find out more, go to www.hachettespeakersbureau.com or call (866) 376-6591.

ISBN 978-1-4555-9297-5 (ebook edition)
ISBN 978-1-4555-3764-8 (print on demand edition)

*To all those who have ever obsessed to
the point of ridiculousness.*

Addicted

Prologue

Loneliness—real "drag your soul through the mud, with your heart trailing behind like a tin can tied to a pickup truck, capital *L*" loneliness—is waking up the morning after the best sex of your life and realizing that the man responsible for that incredible, mind-blowing sex is no longer in your line of sight. Or anywhere in the near vicinity, for that matter.

And you suddenly remember why you've avoided any kind of relationship for the past three years—because of the hurt, the physical pain that comes from the void left behind when the guy leaves. You remember why you would have been better off with plan A, which was to stay far, far away from the male species for the rest of eternity; to keep your distance and enjoy the thrill of the secret crush; to stock your fridge with all your favorite foods and find creative ways of devouring them, one by one, until it's time to restock again.

But the sad fact of it is, you went with plan B. And now your heart is the tin can on the back of the truck, and that truck is speeding along a desolate dirt road with mile markers bearing snarky reminders of all the wrong turns you've made.

Mile One: Aah, one-night stands. Can't live with 'em, can't
live without 'em, eh?

Mile Two: Well, I guess you did live without them until
now...

Mile Three: I mean, did you really think a guy who looked
like *him* was coming back for seconds?

Mile Four: But then again, you've never had much willpower, have you, Mischa?

Mile Five: I guess when someone is so far out of your league,
it's in your best interest to jump on it...

Mile Six: On the other hand, rejection is a bitch.

And so on and so forth. For miles and miles.

And still somehow you're expected to get out of bed and move
on with your day, even though your soul and your heart are being
dragged, at breakneck speed, by this unstoppable force that feels
like it will go on forever.

Some of us just weren't cut out for random flings. In fact, I
knew by now that I wasn't cut out for any of it. I was fragile, like
a baby who hasn't stayed long enough in the womb. My heart was
prone to breaking at the drop of a hat, and I'd already learned
about the crushing regret that came along with putting myself
out there, the advanced level mess-with-the-bull-and-you-get-
the-horns kind of loneliness that spoiled my days for an entire
year after my freshman-year boyfriend dumped me and never
looked back.

But it was that exact feeling, the loneliness with a capital *L*,
that I invited in, practically begging for it to walk through my
door, the moment I met *him*.

Chapter 1

Last Tuesday in May: Oceanside Rec Center Meeting
Topic of discussion: "Living in the Past"
Calories imbibed: 2,500 (ish)

Hi, my name is Jennifer."

"Hi, Jennifer," a chorus of grave-sounding voices, including mine, responded.

"Today's topic feels pretty relevant to me. I've been thinking about the past quite a bit lately. Specifically, I've been going over and over in my head all the things my mom and I went through when my dad moved out of our house. I was in kindergarten..." Jennifer's swampy, Gulf Coast accent helped give her story a little Southern flair, but beyond that, it was just like mine, and the girl's next to me, and roughly 90 percent of the women I had ever heard speak in these meetings. We *all* had absentee father syndrome, it seemed, or absentee mother, in the rarer cases. And most of us had the overcompensating single parent who showed their love by stuffing us full of junk. We were the Overeaters of the world—ours the personal tragedies spelled with a little *t*, not a big one. We weren't the twelve-steppers who had ruined other people's lives, or stolen money from family members, or driven expensive cars off of docks. We were the silent, sweet sufferers with well-meaning dimples in our chubby cheeks, allowing each other little glimpses into our otherwise clandestine, often nocturnal, habits of food stuffing, stashing, and hoarding. Except I had never even allowed anyone else that glimpse.

Despite coming to Overeaters Anonymous religiously since I was fifteen, I had never once raised my hand to share. Mostly it was shyness that held me back. I had always been a wallflower at heart, and even in this most comfortable of environments, I was only interested in hearing other people's tales of woe, not exposing my own, which centered around a diplomat father whose job had taken me and my mother to various exotic locales like Belgium and Kenya and Singapore before he had dropped us like a bad habit, jetting off to the Philippines to start a new family while she and I had retreated to her hometown of Eagle Grove, Iowa, when I was only eight years old. But today felt different. I was about to graduate from college and I had no place to live, no job prospects, and no safety net. I had eaten two trays of frozen mac and cheese and a bag of barbecue-flavored Lay's (in addition to an unknown quantity of cheese puffs) and was in dire need of intervention. But what would I say? My housing and employment problems didn't seem like the most relevant subject matter here, and if I was going to talk aloud about my food addiction for the first time in my life, wouldn't I need to go back to the absolute beginning? Start with the very first binge? Or the time I got caught shoplifting Doritos because I'd run out of allowance money and eaten everything in the house? Should I describe my one very unsuccessful (read: traumatizing) attempt at purging? Or maybe just the bizarre fact that this was my first share in spite of coming to these things for seven years?

"Okay, who else?" I heard Sherrill the moderator's singsong cadence interrupt a brief silence and froze in my seat.

"Hi, my name is Lynette," a voice that was not mine said, after a hand that was not mine was picked.

"Hi, Lynette," I managed to say along with everyone else, kicking myself for wimping out.

To her credit, Lynette had a lot to get off her chest that night. As did six other women who readily raised their hands after she had had her turn. To no one's surprise—not the least my own—I never ended up sharing. But the thought stayed with me and nagged at me for the next few days as I packed up my apartment and ate the entire contents of my fridge and pantry in an attempt to forget about my impending homelessness. Somewhere between the binging, scouring the classified ads for minimum-wage jobs, and creating a resume that somehow screamed both *under-* and *overqualified* at the same time, I got the idea to seek out a new meeting, one that would be filled with unfamiliar faces, and try again. On the OA website, I found a listing for a Friday night group at a massive Baptist church fifteen minutes from campus and decided to force myself to go.

Unfortunately, there were several fast-food options along the way and I was moved to stop at two of them—Burger King for dinner, Wendy's for dessert. Eating junk on the way to OA was the height of blasphemy, but I figured it was all in the name of getting me there. Hot Friday night plans, indeed.

By the time I drove into the church parking lot, I was ten minutes late and definitely stressed out. A thin layer of sweat had broken out underneath my white V-neck T-shirt, threatening to push my casual look into not-so-appropriate territory. I power walked to the church in search of the meeting spot, located in one of its smaller chapels. Most of the time, I preferred to be late, since

meetings usually began with boring administrative announce-
ments that I tuned out anyway, but I didn't want to draw attention to myself with a brand-new group. Luckily, this one seemed
to be just getting started as I rolled in and settled into an empty
pew in the back, trying not to double take as an incredibly attractive, out-of-place-as-all-hell, twentysomething man in tight black
jeans and a light-blue denim button-down took the stage. I had
never seen such a specimen at OA before, and because I was so
shocked by his presence, I looked around at the other attendees to
gauge if I was the only one having this reaction—which is when
I realized I was surrounded by men and only men. Men who, in a
strange twist, were all relatively attractive.

Not your mother's Overeaters Anonymous, I thought.

"Hi, my name is Liam," he said as he sat down on the lone
chair onstage.

Oh God, he has an Australian accent.

"Hi, Liam," the group responded.

"Hi, Liam," I followed suit a half second later, the singular
female voice among the crowd.

"So, tonight was supposed to be my big three-month chip. But
I fucked it up. I had to tell Ben just now that I didn't earn it this
time around. Sadly."

I couldn't believe what I was hearing. What was this man's
trigger food? Carrot sticks?

"The truth is, I had sex with an employee earlier today. At the
restaurant I own, in my office. She gave me a blow job."

And what does this have to do with your eating problems, sir? I
glanced furtively around to see if anyone else looked as confused
as I was, but all eyes were on the speaker.

"I felt so ashamed after. I'd really been trying to stay a hundred
percent sober—no touching myself, nothing," he continued.

And that's when it hit me. I scanned the room yet again and noticed the knowing nods, the pain in these attractive or, bottom line, average-looking *men's* eyes—I was definitely in the wrong place. I was surrounded by sex addicts.

In a panic, I sank down in the pew, double-checking my phone for the meeting details I thought I had gotten right.

"I spiraled immediately," his gravelly hot voice went on. "I was contacting escorts on Craigslist. I drove to this woman's house and sat outside in my car, beating off in hopes that I would skip it with her. Which I didn't…I went in right after I came. And there she was, your basic call girl, hanging out in her lingerie, the smell of vodka coming off her skin from ten feet away."

Again, knowing nods all around. I found myself doing the same, afraid that the others would sniff me out as an intruder, here to listen to their salacious stories for my own amusement. But then I remembered my general invisibility to the male species, my inherent wallflowerness—in this instance, it was like a superpower.

"And then the most fuck-all thing happened. I realized I'd left my wallet back at the restaurant. I couldn't pay her up front, and she obviously wasn't going to take my word for it. I told her I'd go and come back—now that I'd seen her, I knew I'd obsess over the sex until it was done. But the drive back had all this traffic, so I ended up stuck on the highway, just crying my eyes out like a little girl, thinking about tonight and how I had fucked it all up. Then I beat off again, in my car, probably in full view of a taxi driver in the lane next to me." He paused to look around the room, making eye contact with someone in the front pew. "Whatever I was going to say tonight no longer has meaning. I can either start all over again or not. I'm glad I'm here. I'm always glad about that. But I wish I was celebrating something. That's it."

He stood up abruptly, clearing his throat and glancing at the moderator, Ben, who took the stage as Liam hopped down and slid into the front pew. An older man in reading glasses patted Liam's shoulder.

For the remainder of the hour, I kept having to make sure that my jaw wasn't visibly agape as sex addict after sex addict spoke of their overwhelming lust and carnal desires that knew no end. It was such a different manifestation of neuroses than mine. Instead of stuffing their faces full of calories, these guys were out there burning them! Mind you, they were placing themselves in dangerous situations with fellow nymphos, sex workers, strippers—you name it—but they were involved in something extremely, wildly different than anything I knew.

I amused myself with the idea of standing up—the female intruder making herself known—and telling them about the time that Terry McInerney, my freshman-year sailing instructor, had pressed his penis against my stomach for three minutes in a bar. It was after fall finals freshman year, during my *"most-skinny-ever!!!"* phase as I had coined it in my journal, when unbeknownst to me I had contracted a tapeworm in Costa Rica on a humanitarian trip I'd taken just before school had started. For the first and only time in my life, I had felt what it was to be one of those girls who were universally desired—not just a pretty face on a "fluffy" (as my mother liked to call it) frame, but a hot girl with actual power over the opposite sex. The phase had lasted long enough for me to start dating Bradley Griffin, the cutest guy in my dorm; stop going to OA; lose my virginity; fall in love; have said tapeworm diagnosed and treated; and get my heart broken by Bradley Griffin, still the cutest guy in the dorm, by the time I'd gained back thirty of the forty pounds that I'd lost. It was when I was still in the throes of that skinny phase, though, that Terry McInerney the sailing instructor had unnecessarily crushed his body up against mine at the local pub for the entirety of our brief conversation. Toward the end, I'd felt him against my torso, a hot, hard bulge pressing into my stomach. The sensation had sent tingles through every part of my body, and all I could focus on was the tantalizing part in his lips as he had waited for me to say something else, the heaving of our chests as they had collided and fell away from each other with each anticipatory breath. In a way, it was the most subversive sex act I'd ever taken part in. *Sure felt steamy to me!* I imagined myself saying to the group of sex addicts in my midst, then explaining about the box of Dunkin' Donuts I had eaten later that night, washed down with a carton of chocolate milk. *Did I mention I'm at the wrong meeting, guys?*

Obviously standing up and talking was not a viable option, so I slumped down in the pew and waited patiently for the hour to pass. At the end of it, I skipped the serenity prayer, eschewing the handholding and inevitable reveal of myself as an interloper in lieu of a quick getaway. I made a pit stop at the bathroom in the church's main building, shaking my head at my clueless reflection and wondering where the hell the OA meeting had actually been. After a good two minutes of self-reflective hand washing in which I questioned for the millionth time that week my overall preparedness for adulthood, I moseyed out to the parking lot, trying to act as if nothing had happened.

The biggest thing on my mind now was getting to the nearest 7-Eleven for a pint of rum raisin. Would my resolve have been the same had I attended the right meeting and finally spoken as I had planned? Would I be giving in to my usual cravings, or would I be stronger from the outpouring of communal support after I finally told my story? I would never know…but the thought of going back to my apartment alone, only to drag myself through the sea of half-packed boxes and contemplate my aimlessness sans ice cream, recalling all the stories I'd just heard about the kind of hot, dangerous sex I'd probably never know in my lifetime, was too desolate to bear.

Alas, I didn't make it to 7-Eleven that night. In fact, I didn't make it out of the parking lot before the strangest, most unlikely, and luckiest thing that had ever happened to me unfolded before my disbelieving eyes.

"Hey there."

I was headed toward my car in the church's vast parking lot when my ears perked up at the sound of his Australian accent. I knew without a doubt it was the dangerously hot sex addict before I'd even raised my head and taken him in, seeing him up close for the first time. He had green eyes, lit up by the too-bright LED parking lot lights looming over us. His hair was sandy blond and messy in an on-purpose kind of way, his features all perfectly proportioned and symmetrical on his heart-shaped face. He had the look of a golden boy gone bad, like a professional soccer player with a secret drug problem or the high school prom king who'd ended up in a minimum-security prison for embezzlement. He was thin but built, like a track star, and holding a grimy hubcap in his left hand.

"I think this might be yours," he said, nodding toward my derelict Honda Accord, lovingly nicknamed "the Sloppy Jalopy" by my best friend Gracie.

"Oh my. How did that happen?" I reached out sheepishly for the car part that had been expelled without my knowledge.

"Probably one of those damn speed bumps. I'll just snap it back on, no worries." He made his way around the car and crouched down by the rear right tire like a regular pit-crew member. Simple car maintenance had never looked so good.

"Wow, thank you," I said. "My car already suffers from low self-esteem. I don't think she could handle a missing hubcap." I heard him laugh from behind the car and silently congratulated myself for having the wherewithal to crack a joke.

"Haven't seen you at the meeting before," he said, popping back up. "In fact, I'm not sure I've ever laid eyes on such a convincing transvestite." He wiped his hands on his jeans as he approached me. "That was a joke. Because you were at a men's only meeting, not that I think you look like a man. Quite the opposite. Name's Liam."

Utterly confused by the level of hotness colliding with me, I didn't notice right away when he reached out his hand.

"Oh, are you not okay with touching people?" he asked.

"No." I shook my head slowly, like someone just regaining consciousness. "I'm sorry. I'm Mischa." I held out my hand and Liam shook it, a grin overtaking his face that was both incredibly charming and devilish.

"Mischa. I like that name. How long you been in the program?"

"Me? Uhh…pfft, on and off since I was fifteen, I guess."

"Wow!" His eyes opened wider. "That's quite a thing to acknowledge at fifteen. Good on you."

He thought I was a fellow sex addict, clearly. I toyed with the idea of letting him believe it, too—that I was a reckless nympho, drifting about this crazy world in search of my next fuck, purposely attending this meeting to take advantage of the men's compromised states. But I had never been a good liar. "I was at the wrong meeting, actually. I was supposed to be at OA."

"OA?"

"Overeaters Anonymous. For people who binge eat and such." I sounded nervous and winded, like I was in a rush to get somewhere, as I looked into green eyes that seemed to know their own power. "Sex isn't a problem for me. Like at all. It's mostly just ice cream, pizza, Ruffles, Cheetos, the usual suspects…"

"Well, I wouldn't know it by looking at you. You look great." He winked again, and suddenly I figured out how this all made sense: This guy was not chatting me up because he and I were a likely match or because he really thought I looked *great*, but because he was in the middle of a sex binge, his mind a hazy blank in search of the next fix. I could have been anyone. My heart sank a little, as if I had already hung my hopes on this Liam person as a romantic prospect and those hopes had been dashed within a minute of speaking to him. It was my impossible fragility rearing its ugly head once again. I tried to wish it away, thinking, *Would it be such a bad thing to have no-strings-attached sex with a guy who could pass for a Greek god?*

"All right, well, it's time for me to go and try not to buy ice cream," I said, flashing a polite smile as I pulled my car keys from my purse. "Thank you again, for the hubcap. You really restored my faith in humanity."

Liam winked at me, then glided in even closer and placed his hand on the hood of my car. It took everything in me not to gasp. Would it be wrong if I reached out and touched his arm? Just for a moment? "Listen, I don't want to be a bad influence, but—"

"You're not," I said, hardly able to concentrate in this stranger's proximity but acutely aware of his gaze that was now, without question, directed down my shirt.

"I have the most fantastic gelato at my restaurant. Caramel dark chocolate. Served with homemade whipped cream and an almond wafer."

My eyes closed at this description of the best sounding dessert I'd ever heard of. I felt like I was in one of those ironic commercials where an unbelievably hot guy makes all your mundane

dreams come true without an ounce of judgment. Had Isabella sent me a strippergram as an early graduation present? It
seemed like a plausible explanation, but when I opened my eyes,
they registered his face again and I remembered that Liam was
a sex addict whom I had accidentally stumbled upon through
nobody's fault but my own. And he was very real, and still standing within inches of me, his hand propped on my car as he slowly
leaned into me, then backed away again. He smelled faintly of
cigarettes and cologne and danger—not a combination I would
have dreamed up before this but actually quite divine. I hadn't
been this close to a guy in ages, or felt my body straining to take
over for my head. Every physical part of me wanted to press up
against him, like I had with the sailing instructor in the crowded
bar, but my mind was contradicting, urging me to run and hide.

"Wow, gelato sounds amazing. I'll have to take a rain check,
though." I flashed what I hoped was my most flirtatious smile
and pointed an index finger into the air to signify the mental
note I was making. Meanwhile, my heart was palpitating. Lucky
thing I had a rib cage to conceal it.

"Well, then." Liam gave himself a final push off the hood of
my car and drifted back, waving at me with cramped fingers.
"Mischa, isn't it?"

"Yes! Liam." I pointed to him, overly enthusiastic. "See you
next time!" But he had already turned away, making it crystal
clear that the likelihood of a "next time" was on par with alien
abduction.

* * *

The first person I thought of on the car ride home was my feisty
eighty-five-year-old friend Isabella. She would have killed me

if she had been there. Her motto, oft repeated, was as follows: "Every man who comes into your life is an opportunity for adventure. Nothing more, nothing less." She was of the mind-set that marrying was for money (she hadn't married until her forties and, true to form, had picked a much older man with even older money), and everything else was pure pleasure principle. Of course, she had looked like a supermodel in her day and had run in circles with rich playboys whose lives closely resembled James Bond movies, so the philosophy felt a little less relevant to my particular case study. Still, I felt bad that I was a letdown to her; she was always begging for salacious tales about fraternity boys and surfers, incapable of grasping how low I was on the "men equal adventure" scale.

This would have been the story to tell her, I thought as I drove home, unable to shake the feeling that I had lost out on something big. The questions running through my head were torture. When was a guy like Liam ever going to talk to someone like me again? Why would I pass up the chance to have a story about hot sex with an Australian restaurateur? I understood why he made me nervous, but why couldn't I embrace it, just for one night? Did I think he was going to lure me back to his restaurant only so he could kill me, chop me into little pieces, and serve me to unknowing diners as part of a delicious bouillabaisse? Doubtful.

The feeling of failure was almost too much to handle, but the thought of calling Gracie, whose approach to dating didn't veer far from Isabella's, was not so comforting either. My only choice was to go back home and wallow, which I did. Lying on the AeroBed I'd borrowed from Gracie after selling my mattress on Craigslist, I closed my eyes and imagined Liam with his hand on the hood of my car, leaning into me then pushing off, back and forth, back and forth, like the ocean at low tide. Then

I imagined him naked, and my hand found its way down my body, slipping underneath the waistband of my boxer shorts. As I touched myself, I thought of Liam doing the same somewhere across town, still looking down my shirt in his mind, remembering the way my hair smelled just as I remembered the allure of his scent, his body heat, that gravelly Australian accent.

Chapter 2

Sugar. The bane and joy of my existence, the stuff of my dreams and nightmares. It was my first word, according to my mother: *"Sugar, sugar, sugar!"* I would command, my spoon dripping with pureed peas held spitefully in the air. I never specified when asking for it like other kids; I didn't say, "May I have some candy?" or "When do I get ice cream?" I knew sugar was in a variety of products and was careful not to limit my requests in case someone had, say, nothing but cough drops in their purse (still sugar!). Eventually the obsession broadened to all types of food, and the salty-sweet cycle happily replaced my obsession with sweets. But still, in my deepest, darkest moments, it was sugar that offered the most comfort.

So naturally it was a large bowl of Fruity Pebbles that managed to lure me out of bed after six hours of nightmares involving Liam the sex addict. In most of the dreams, he was laughing and taunting me as I ran away from him in various locales—his bedroom, my bedroom, a taxicab, the Baptist church parking lot. They were the kind of nightmares I used to have in high school, when I couldn't stop thinking about a particular football player who would never have looked at me twice or the menacingly attractive Goth boy who lived in my apartment complex. The difference here, of course, was Liam *had* looked twice. For some inexplicable reason, he had tried to seduce me with sweet, sweet, sugary gelato, and I hadn't allowed it.

The whole thing made me want to self-flagellate. But I also knew that to focus on last night's interaction would be a terrible mistake, given the current crisis that was my life, so I washed off the pink-tinted milk residue that had dribbled down my chin during my breakfast in bed, made a quick to-do list, and got dressed in a hurry, determined to mark off the first task ("Pick up cap and gown @ Plex"). As long as I wasn't naked at graduation or freshly knocked up by a stranger who'd offered me gelato in a parking lot, things couldn't be so bad, right?

* * *

The tables set up for cap and gown distribution were lined against a wall of floor-to-ceiling windows in a vast, otherwise empty conference room at the Reid University Student Complex, aka "the Plex." There were only three other students there when Gracie and I arrived, which added to the absurdist *Waiting for Godot* feeling of the cavernous room. The dazed, middle-aged woman manning the "J–N" table didn't even ask for ID when I gave my name, leading me to the conclusion that I probably could have just skipped the four years of tuition and endless studying and claimed somebody else's cap and gown for the same result: a diploma that I may or may not frame and mount on a wall, depending on how my future shakes out.

"This is where I leave you, boo," said Gracie in her scratchy, sleep-deprived voice as we left the room with our shrink-wrapped packages.

"Where are you going? I thought you were gonna come over and watch me pack," I whined.

"As thrilling as that sounds, I gotta go turn in my last paper," she said.

"The day before graduation? Seriously?" I lagged behind a little as Gracie hurried toward the lobby.

"Double extension, baby. You wanna know the title? I'll give you two guesses."

Like me, Gracie was a nutrition major. We had met during orientation week and quickly discovered our near-telepathic connection and our ability to share clothes, even though she was an inch taller and not a binge eater like myself. Between the two of us, she was the healthy eater, so she loathed my ability to stuff my face without adding more than five or ten pounds. On the flip side, I envied her self-control and the fact that her thoughts weren't constantly ruled by food. One thing we did have in common was our self-deprecating humor, something all fluffy girls must learn at a young age or risk becoming socially irrelevant.

"I don't know, 'Food for Thought'?" I said.

"Are you kidding? I used that one freshman year. Twice. You're never gonna guess. It's called 'Obesity Cynicism.' Isn't that good? It's catchy, right? I think it's gonna be a thing. Like I'm coining it: Obesity Cynicism."

"It's good."

"I think it's definitely a meme." She bounced down a set of stairs to the front entrance. "Is that what a meme is? Anyway, I don't care. We need to go out and celebrate! I'm thinking many drinks are in order."

I rolled my eyes. Despite having zero tolerance for alcohol, Gracie liked to tie one on. *"It's not my fault I'm Korean!"* she would argue, blaming her ethnic background for all instances of epic sloppiness.

She playfully flicked me off, backing into one of the entrance doors, which thudded into someone or something. "Oh no!" Gracie's eyes went wide as she scrambled outside, where a man was doubled over on the sidewalk, clutching his knee. "Professor Maxwell!" she cried out. "Are you okay?"

I followed her outside as Julien Maxwell, the painfully debonair African-American studies professor who had taught our Intro to African-American Lit class this past semester, righted himself and greeted Gracie with a forgiving smile. "Gracie! Fancy meeting you here."

"I'm so sorry," she said, her look of concern morphing into a shameless grin. This, I knew, was Gracie's ultimate fantasy. She had always been professor-obsessed, and Julien Maxwell her last and ultimate professor crush. "Droolian Poundwell" she called him. I could see the appeal—his big brown eyes and square jaw were of the statuesque variety, and at thirty-five, he was the youngest professor we'd had—but I was always too reverent to see male professors as anything other than authority figures. And this one in particular was a tragic case: a widower of one year.

"You excited about graduation?" he said.

"No way! Nobody wants to be birthed into the real world. Am I right, Mischa?" Gracie turned to me, generously acknowledging my presence even though she probably wanted me to scram.

I nodded and waved. "Hey, Professor Maxwell."

"Mischa! I guess all of my seniors are here, then," he chuckled. "Imagine that."

The class we had taken, English 401, aka Intro to African-American Lit, was a freshman staple for English majors, but Gracie and I had masterminded our course schedule four years ago, leaving a bunch of easy requirements for senior year and making us the oldest, most competent people in the room more often than not.

"So what are you all up to after this? Moving on to bigger and better things, I assume?"

Beaming, Gracie told him about the organic lobbying internship she'd landed in Washington, D.C., carefully leaving out the details of how she had gotten the job through her well-connected parents, pulling strings all the way from Seoul.

"Congratulations! That sounds tremendous," he said, and patted her on the shoulder.

"I actually have no plans for the future," I answered when he pointed his gaze at me, pulling my to-do list from my back pocket, "as you can see from this number two action item on my list for the day." I held it up so Professor Maxwell could see.

"'Find job slash place to live,'" he read out loud. "Does that mean you're staying here for the summer?"

"I'm not sure." I grimaced. "I applied to some grad schools. Nutrition programs. Including the one here, actually, but they waitlisted me."

He shook his head. "I don't believe it. You two were my best students, and not just because you had three years on everybody else," he said with a wink. "Hey, listen, if you're not sure what your next step is, I'm actually looking for an assistant for the summer. You'd be perfect."

"Uh…" My response was more of a grunt than anything else. Not believing what I'd just heard, I closed my eyes to run it back in my head. *Is he offering me a job?* "I don't know what to say."

Gracie elbowed me. "Say yes," she instructed.

"It's only a couple of months," he explained. "I'm doing an annotated version of *Through the Ivory Gate*, which you're familiar with from my class. All I need is someone to proofread, really, and keep me on track. Organize my research, that sort of thing."

My head slowly went from shaking to nodding, disbelief to utter elation. "I think that sounds great, if I'm qualified."

"Don't be silly. You're overqualified. Listen, the pay won't be great. Probably twelve an hour, if you can get by on it."

"Sounds good—"

"Then when can you start? The sooner the better, actually." Professor Maxwell glanced at his watch, as if he meant for me to follow him to his office right then and there.

"A couple of days? I just need to move apartments. Well, first I need to find a sublet…" I squinted, trying not to crack up at the sight of Gracie doing a victory dance behind Professor Maxwell's back.

His eyes lit up. "Don't worry, I got you covered. There's a guesthouse in my backyard. Totally renovated, just sitting there empty."

Gracie's jaw dropped mid-victory dance. She raised her hands as if thanking the gods.

"Wow. This sounds perfect, Professor Maxwell. Thank you so much!"

"You heard me say *twelve* an hour, right?" He chuckled again, an easy laugh that made him seem the polar opposite of the grief-stricken man who had lectured us on the plight of the black artist in America. "And call me Julien, please." His smile revealed a straight set of teeth with a charming, tiny gap in between the front two.

"Okay!" Gracie reemerged from behind his back. "Now that this deal is brokered, I guess my work is done here. Professor Maxwell—sorry, *Julien*," she said, extending a coquettish hand.

Playing along, Julien kissed Gracie's hand. "I have to get going too," he said. "Mischa? Give my office a call to work out details. Or drop by. Whatever works. I'm there too much." He gave a quick wave and, with a barely detectable limp from the blow Gracie had dealt him, headed inside the Plex.

"I ship you guys," Gracie said, pointing in his direction, then back to me. "If I can't have him, you can, right?"

I shook my head. "Not my style, boo. But how amazing is that? I just got a job *and* a place to live!"

"And you have my clumsy ass to thank for it," she said, holding up her hand for a high five.

"I know." Ignoring her hand, I drew Gracie in for a hug. "What am I going to do without you?"

As soon as I had thrown my arms around her, however, she wrestled away from me like an ornery child. "Ew, ew, ew! It's too hot for this sentimental crap. Save it for graduation." She waved me off and started down the asphalt path toward the Science Hall. "When is that again?" she called over her shoulder.

"Tomorrow, dummy."

"Oh yeah, we'll be the motherless children!"

"That's right," I said, remembering Gracie's recent announcement that her parents had canceled their plane tickets. Their excuse (general workaholism) was hardly as genuine as my mother's: After a bout with pneumonia in the harshest Iowa winter in a decade, my hard-working single mom didn't have any vacation days left. But I had assured her that having Gracie there was tantamount to having family with me; she was the closest thing to a sister I'd ever had. If it weren't for her, in fact, the only real friend I'd have to show for myself after four years of college would be an octogenarian, and unlike Isabella, Gracie didn't have eighty-odd years of life experience to hit me over the head with every time I did something stupid.

As I made my way toward the parking lot, it dawned on me that I had forgotten to tell Gracie about Liam the sex addict. I must have subconsciously nixed it for fear of the terrible advice she would give, probably something along the lines of "Do him! Do him now! Find that man and seduce him!" As a collector of experiences, she believed in making bold decisions as opposed to holding back, which was my way. Our philosophies on boys and sex were as different as our study habits and just about everything else, and I could predict exactly what her response would be if she knew how much I had obsessed over him already: "Actions speak louder than words, my friend," she would say. "Stop thinking, start doing."

* * *

As far as the actual commencement ceremony was concerned, I hadn't been looking forward to it, and as expected it went by in a flash. I was actually glad my mother hadn't come, even though she'd wanted to, because she would have realized how few friends I'd made, and for some reason I preferred that she think of me as something other than a social underachiever. There were about five girls and two guys in the Nutrition program who I actually hung out with outside of class, but the lot of them were anti-social types who didn't do much beyond classwork. Also, my dependence on Gracie and our sibling-like tendencies could have struck my conservative, Midwestern mother as something sapphic, which I really didn't want to have to deny or explain.

Graduation day was also particularly stressful given it was the first of two moving days for me. I had yet to stow all my furniture and boxes in a musty little storage unit before moving into Julien's guesthouse the next day, so I was still dressed in my drab graduation gown when I rented a U-Haul that afternoon, with the bittersweet melody of "Pomp and Circumstance" still stuck in my head. I had talked Gracie into helping me move the big stuff in exchange for a steak dinner, but somehow we had lost each other in the diploma-clutching throngs and I found myself waiting for her in the U-Haul parking lot for over an hour, getting intermittent texts that said things like *traffic=me* and *directions fail/there in... soon.*

Lucky for my inner demons, the U-Haul office had an extensive vending machine selection, and in the course of an hour, I had sampled not one but two bags of chips, a wrinkly yellow packet of peanut M&M'S, and a roll of Life Savers that may or may not have been there since 1995. I was actually standing against my car, graduation gown open to expose my less-than-formal T-shirt and shorts underneath, and clinging to all the empty wrappers as I foraged through my last bag of chips for edible crumbs, when a U-Haul pickup truck pulled into the lot and slowed down as it passed me. I squinted to get a better view of the driver, but the sun was in my face and I couldn't quite make him out. I went back to foraging, eventually tipping the bag over my mouth in a shameless display.

"Hey there... again," I heard a voice say as the door to the pickup slammed shut. "Long time no see."

I whipped my head in the direction of the Australian accent, in utter shock and disbelief. It was him—Liam.

"Oh, hi!" I called out faux-casually as he made his way toward me, his shoulders moving in unison with his hips in a James Dean swagger. I had never seen someone so happily aware of their own sexiness. It almost put me at ease.

"Mischa, right?"

"Yes!" How the hell had he remembered my name? If I were

a cartoon, my eyes would have been bugging out of their sockets and my eyebrows hovering somewhere above my head.

"Whatcha got there? Ruffles?" He pointed to the bag I had forgotten I was clutching.

I glanced down, my eyebrows knitted as if the chips had just materialized in my hand miraculously. "Oh. Yeah. I've been here a really long time. I was starving." Straightening my posture self-consciously, I shoved the bag, along with my other empty wrappers, into the back pockets of my shorts.

"Hey, you don't need an excuse to eat Ruffles. I fucking love those things." Liam leaned beside me against my car. "You know, I never heard of Overeaters Anonymous before the other night. It got me thinking, I probably need that too."

I gave Liam's lean body a quick once-over, doing my best not to gawk. "I doubt it," I said.

"No, I swear. All I do is eat. I own a restaurant for God's sake. Anyway, I figure food is like the fundamental addiction. If you can get over that, you can get over anything, right?"

I shrugged. "I'll let you know when I get over it." Liam nudged me, and we both smiled. For two people who hardly knew each other, we'd fallen into casual conversation like it was no big thing. Had I already been demoted to the friend zone?

"So is this the big graduation party?" he teased.

"Yeah, I'm the first one here," I shot back, determined to make him laugh if nothing else. "No, I have to move out of my apartment. What about you?"

"I had to haul some artwork to my restaurant," he said.

I nodded. "Cool." This was followed by a long pause. There was nothing else I could come up with to say, other than *So . . . how's your sex addiction going?* Which I figured was out of the question, even if posed ironically.

"Listen, I'm sorry about the other night," he said. "I was in a bad place. I shouldn't have hit on you like that."

I shaded my eyes to see him better. "No worries. I didn't take it seriously. So, no harm no foul." We shared another smile, and I allowed my heart to melt just a little.

"I appreciate you not taking me up on it, for what it's worth. Anyway…" He tossed his U-Haul keys back and forth between his hands, his light green eyes—almost colorless in the sunlight—making contact with mine. "Are you waiting for someone, then?"

"Yeah. My friend's helping me move. Hopefully sometime in the next century."

"Oh yeah? How late is he?"

"She," I responded almost giddily, flattered that he had assumed I had some strapping guy to help me instead of my diminutive girlfriend who was probably tipsy from the flask of spiked Arnold Palmer she'd brought to graduation. I checked my phone. "She was supposed to be here an hour ago. An hour and ten to be exact."

"That's no good."

"Well, we were supposed to come here together but we lost each other in the crowd. It's fine. She's helping me move on graduation day, which is a lot more than most people would do."

"So how was it? Did some famous person give you the best advice of your life?"

Shifting my weight against the car, I laughed and shook my head. "Our speaker was the Pensacola-Five weatherman. He's alumni, I guess."

"I never went to my high school graduation," Liam said. "That's the only chance I got for the whole cap and gown scene."

"It's overrated. I almost didn't go. Stuff like that just isn't very important to me."

"No?"

"Yeah, I never went to prom, for instance. I mean, not because I protested it or anything, just because I didn't have a date."

Liam tilted his head and grinned. "Aww, I would have taken you," he said.

I squinted at him, incredulous. "You don't even know me."

"So cynical!"

"Just realistic."

Liam lifted his hands as if to feel the heat surrounding us. "Hey, listen, you can't suffer out here forever. Let me help you."

"Oh, gosh... That's... I mean..." It took everything in me not to say, *"Yes! Yes! A thousand times yes!"* And why couldn't I? Here was this modelesque creature offering to help me, of all people, with whom he wasn't even having sex. I could just imagine walking behind him as he carried two boxes at once, watching his muscles strain as he lifted the heavy end of my ratty couch... But the naysayer in me argued that someone like this would never make such an offer unless he was a demented serial killer with a long line of victims, all short, round versions of myself. "That's fine." I shook my head, embarrassed for some unknowable reason. "Gracie'll be here any minute."

Liam looked up and down the empty street beside the parking lot. "Right. Well I'm gonna turn in my keys. If she's not here by the time I'm back, I'll force my services on you. How 'bout that?"

Before I could answer, he had walked away, and I found myself praying that Gracie would be a no-show. I checked my phone and saw her latest text: *Whatta nightmare. Tell u in 5 secs.* Based on the entire string of messages she had sent me, however, which had referenced multiple amounts of minutes and/or seconds it would take for her to arrive, I had come to realize that the time frames she was giving were completely arbitrary. In fact, according to her texts, Gracie seemed to be operating entirely outside of the space-time continuum as I knew it. So maybe she would be here in five seconds, or maybe five hours. Which brought me back to the concept of Liam helping me move. It felt like a daydream hallucination I had had after standing in the sun too long—a Liam mirage, complete with witty repartee. What would I do if it actually happened?

A loud car horn snapped me out of my thought-spiral as Gracie's neon-green hatchback, arguably more of an eyesore than my Sloppy Jalopy, careened into the parking lot.

"I bumped someone's rubber fender—no scratches!—and they wanted to DUI me. Can you believe it?" she screamed through the open window as she parked. "I told them no problemo, called their bluff," she said as she got out of the car. "For the record, there was one shot in that entire flask. I know that look on your face."

"I'm not looking like anything." I glanced behind me, noting that Liam was still inside. I had the keys to the U-Haul I had rented in my hands, and without speaking another word, I silently led Gracie across the parking lot. If I waited for Liam to come out, there would be an awkward pause as he realized my friend had shown up, and I'd have to introduce them, and Gracie would make some Gracie comment, telling Liam to his face how smoking hot he was, and for some reason it all felt like too much. It reminded me of high school, when I would inexplicably duck out of conversations with cute boys because I couldn't handle how anxious they made me. When faced with "fight or flight," I had always chosen flight, then kicked myself for it afterward…

"What's wrong? Are you really mad at me for being late?"

Gracie asked, climbing into the passenger seat as I turned the keys to the truck.

I shook my head, still silent. This was officially the second time I had fled from Liam in less than twenty-four hours, and the second time I was filled with regret about it.

If I see him again, I thought, *all bets are off.*

Chapter 3

So what are you gonna do with yourself this summer? Other than try, try, try, very, very hard not to suck Julien Maxwell's enormous cock?" God bless her, Gracie had a one-track mind.

"You're a sick and twisted individual. And I've told you a million times—crusty old professors are your deal, not mine." Gracie saluted me with her freshly refilled beer, which she proceeded to guzzle, and I was struck with a pang of bittersweet emotion. "I'm gonna miss you!" I said. "I wish you weren't leaving so soon."

"I don't know how you're going to survive out here without me," she said, wiping the foam from her upper lip. "Especially in the summer. This place is d-e-a-d dead in the summertime."

"Well, aside from working for your dream man, I wanna keep working on my juice cleanse—"

"There's too many juice cleanses. You should do something else."

"There are no *perfect* juice cleanses. Mine will be perfect," I said, smirking to indicate my level of seriousness. The "Mischa Jones Patented Juice Cleanse" had been my running joke of senior year, a pie-in-the-sky scheme that would allow me to pay off my student loans and start a nutrition empire. I referred to it anytime someone talked about their *real* plans for the future. Meanwhile, I had been working on it, off and on, and wasn't fully convinced it was a bad idea.

"You know what? I'll drink to that."

"You'll drink to anything!" I teased.

"Right you are." Gracie smiled as we clinked glasses, a couple of happy orphans enjoying graduation dinner sans the proud parents.

As we talked about her plans for D.C., my impending move into Julien's guesthouse the next day, and toasted all the big and little triumphs we could think of, my mind kept going back to Liam and his green eyes glinting in the sunlight in the U-Haul parking lot. Part of me was itching to tell her about it, especially after two beers and the two more shots she practically forced down my throat. I wanted to slam a hand down on the table and announce that a drop-dead gorgeous sex maniac had told me he would have taken me to prom, had offered to help me move out of the goodness of his heart, and had even remembered my name! These things didn't happen to the Mischa that Gracie knew and loved, and maybe it was time to change that. Yet each time the news started to bubble up, I stopped myself, knowing that the way I had responded to Liam *was* the Mischa we knew and loved, and that was *no bueno*. Even with a solid buzz, I couldn't handle hearing Gracie's cry of disbelief at the anticlimax.

* * *

The next day, she and I shared a tearful, hungover goodbye at the Pensacola Airport before she flew off to D.C. I hadn't anticipated how much it was going to hurt to see my friend go, and the only thing that kept me from falling into a total depression was the knowledge that I would be moving into Professor Maxwell's guesthouse that afternoon and hopefully diving into work. In fact, from the airport, I drove directly to his address, parked on the street in front of his house, and approached his front door with my rolling suitcase in tow, buzzing with the anticipation that comes along with a new job, a new place, a new chapter. The house was a nice, traditional, two-story wooden structure painted white, with black awning-style shutters. It was almost colonial, like a turn-of-the-century home in the Caribbean, but the tame green lawn with sprinklers on timers and gem-toned zinnias and hydrangeas gave it away as suburban Florida. About a minute after I rang the doorbell, I decided to knock and was relieved to hear hasty footsteps coming down a set of stairs, eradicating my fear that he had forgotten about his new assistant-cum-houseguest.

"Hi." A small voice came from behind the door as it swung open to reveal not Julien Maxwell but a thirteen-year-old girl with braces and an oversized One Direction concert T-shirt.

"Hello." I smiled, hiding my surprise. Julien was just old enough to be this girl's father, so I had to assume that was the case. "I'm Mischa. Your dad's assistant for the summer."

"I know," she said, looking me up and down, suspicious. "He said he'll be right back. You can come in."

"What's your name?" I asked.

She looked me over once again, as if her decision to disclose any personal information would be based on my appearance. "Cecile," she finally revealed.

"Oh! Great name."

"I think it's kinda lame, actually."

"I don't know," I said. "It sounds very grown up to me." I was trying not to sound pandering, but it's a thin line when you're trying to win over a thirteen-year-old girl.

"Whatever." She frowned as she led me inside with a limp-wristed maneuver that felt less than welcoming. Her attitude made sense, given she had lost her mother hardly more than a year ago, not to mention she was thirteen, so I didn't begrudge it.

On my way to the living room, I noticed a family photograph displayed on the credenza in the foyer, showing Cecile's clear resemblance to her mahogany-skinned, high-cheekboned mother. In the picture, the girl was a few years younger and quite skinny. Now she was decidedly fluffy. I wondered if her looking me up and down hadn't come from that brand of self-hate that drives women, especially teenage girls, to size each other up in comparison.

For a few painful minutes, Cecile and I sat awkwardly in the formal living room, both of us seeming to lack the necessary social skills to engage in small talk. Instead, she pretended to be busy with her phone while I glanced around at the eclectic decorations—a painted coral centerpiece on the coffee table, a massive gold-hued still life on the far wall, the Oriental rug that nearly covered the entire room. I vaguely recalled news reports from the time of Mrs. Maxwell's death saying that she was an art history professor, which explained the impeccable interior deco-ration and the overall air of sophistication about the house.

Even though we were both waiting for it, when Julien's arrival actually happened, it took Cecile and me by surprise. He gusted in through the front door and called out "hello" so loudly that I jumped a little in my seat.

"Dad, your student is here," Cecile said, eyes glued to her phone as she got up from the armchair and skulked out of the room. I heard Julien kiss her hello in the foyer and stood at atten-tion as he walked in.

He was in workout clothes—long gray shorts, a white V-neck, and slightly goofy-looking neon cross-trainers—the type of outfit that always prompts the same response in me: *I need to work out more.* "Mischa, sorry I wasn't here when you arrived. Let me show you to your new place." He was slightly out of breath as he led me through the house and explained that he'd just ridden his bike from campus. Sweat dotted the back of his shirt. "Do you ever ride?" he asked.

"Regrettably, no," I said, my eyes focused on the floor as I rolled my suitcase over various runners and rugs, following him down the hall and through the kitchen.

"I never did until last year. Now I can't live without it. It helps me clear my thoughts." Julien swung the back door wide open, and I trailed behind him with my suitcase knocking down the steps of his back porch. The backyard was unmowed but impressively green, with sweet little wildflowers rising up around the stone path that led to the cottage where I would stay. It was an A-frame structure that could have been deemed a "shed" if it were any smaller. But inside, there was a stark yet homey decor, and the high pointy ceiling made it seem more spacious than the outside let on. The walls were wood panels painted white. The bed had a simple iron headboard and a red-and-white Amish quilt. After he showed me the small bathroom and pointed out a stack of plush white towels, Julien sat down on the red-and-white quilt and bounced on the mattress slightly.

"Still good!" he announced. "This thing has been with me since undergrad. Best three hundred dollars I ever spent."

"This is perfect." I parked my suitcase by the door, dropping my purse on the small desk beside it. *Gracie would be in heaven right now,* I thought, seeing Julien on the bed across from me.

"I'm glad you're here, Mischa," said Julien with one last pat of the mattress before standing up.

I inched to the left so that he could get past me. "Me too," I said. "This is a real lifesaver."

Julien held out his hand for a firm handshake. "Glad it could work out for both of us," he said. "I'll leave you to get settled."

I smiled and let out an actual sigh of relief as he closed the door behind him. Moving had taken a toll on me, and even though Julien's talk of cycling had seemed motivational, I was even more inspired by the idea of a nap on his $300 college mattress.

* * *

My welcome dinner at Casa Maxwell turned out to be a particular form of torture. First of all, I had been lying facedown on Julien's prized mattress, drooling on his Amish quilt, when he had knocked on the door to invite me.

"Hello." I answered the door out of breath, after running to the bathroom to adjust my clothes.

"Hey, Mischa, how's Indian sound? Cecile and I are ordering in."

"Oh, no, don't worry about me," I said.

"Please. We'd really like for you to join us. Unless you have somewhere else you need to be."

"No, not at all. I'd like that, thanks."

The truth? I did not like Indian. Of my many food-related quirks, including a tendency to stuff down my feelings with copious amounts of it, was a total abhorrence of mayonnaise, eggplant, and curry. So when I sat down to dinner, which was fresh from the to-go boxes that sat atop the kitchen counter, I ate a heap of saffron rice while slowly cutting my chicken tikka masala dosas into bite-sized pieces that I pushed around my plate until the inevitable question popped up: "Do you not like your food?"

I answered with my stock excuse: "I just have a stomachache. It's really delicious, though…"

It wasn't just the food that made me uneasy. I found myself withering under Cecile's persistent glare. She probably assumed I had a crush on her father—Gracie couldn't be his only admirer—and had come to seduce him. I wanted to pull her aside and assure her that I was not a seductress (far from it!), plus I only had eyes for a certain rogue sex addict roaming about town, but that wouldn't be appropriate. Just the thought of Liam in this family setting seemed to emphasize how wrong he was…

Despite my abilities as a champion worrier and problem-anticipator, I hadn't foreseen how difficult it might be to assimilate into this little world I'd landed myself in. Not just because Cecile appeared to be shooting daggers at me from her eyeballs, but because I felt like an interloper in every sense of the word. For one, the house was much grander than the small apartment I had grown up in, or anywhere I had lived during college, and everything around me seemed valuable in that breakable and irreplaceable kind of way. Julien and Cecile possessed exotic good looks that clashed with my Midwestern-ness. They had fancy condiments in their refrigerator and expensive dinner plates, even for their Indian takeout. There was also an obvious void, a dark cloud looming over every room. I couldn't help imagining the ghost of Julien's perfect wife looking down on us at the dinner table, disapproving of my pedestrian presence.

After dinner, I pretended I had someplace to be, got into my car, and headed down the block aimlessly. It was a Monday, so I had no meeting to retreat to, and I was hungry from not eating dinner, but the last thing I wanted to do was embark on another binge, especially the first day after graduation. Coasting along at ten miles per hour, I ogled the neighbors' houses and my mind

wandered to Liam. Where was he right now? Had he fallen off
the wagon again with some other woman at his restaurant or
a random Craigslist hookup? How was I so obsessed with him
already? Didn't I know better than to go for a guy that good-
looking? Would a cheeseburger help me forget about him?

Stay strong, Mischa, I coached myself through the mach-force,
industrial-strength crush threatening to take hold. If there was
one thing that would help get me through this, it would not be
cheeseburgers but willpower. So instead of autopiloting to Taco
Bell, I resigned myself to buying groceries and ran the options
over in my head. Just like the quirky, ritualistic schedules I
adhered to when frequenting fast-food restaurants (McDonald's
for daytime stops; Burger King and Wendy's for dinner; KFC
during hometown visits; Taco Bell for all other needs), my grocery store preferences were highly specific, with Publix being
my number one choice for nighttime/weekday shopping. It was
hands-down the most popular supermarket in Oceanside, and
therefore crawling with screaming babies and young children
anytime before sundown. But after dark on school nights it was
like a safe haven. Which is why, when I heard my name called out
from the other side of a precarious mountain of bananas in the
produce section, I was especially taken aback.

"Mischa! You've got to stop following me around like this."
Liam's irresistible Australian brogue hit my ears like a clap of
thunder, and I was as stunned as if actual lightning had struck.

"Hello," I said, deer-in-headlights style. Remembering where
I was, I furtively glanced into my basket—it would have been
instant mortification had I already hit the snack aisle, or worse,
frozen foods—and breathed a sigh of relief when I saw a single,
respectable bunch of kale.

"You disappeared the other day. I'm starting to think you

don't like me." Liam's devilish smile was a little more tentative than the last time I had seen him, as if he actually cared.

"Of course not, no—" I reached out for a banana and the entire display began to tumble, prompting Liam to rush over and stop the mini-avalanche with his body. I dropped my basket and collected the fallen fruit from the floor.

"I thought this only happened in movies," Liam said as I helped him put the bananas back in place.

"My life is just that magical," I joked. Liam turned to me and smiled. What he didn't know was this moment was actually magical for me. I couldn't believe I was seeing him again, as if all my obsessing had dreamed him into reality. The thought I'd had driving away from U-Haul the day before came back to me: *If I see him again, all bets are off.*

We stood there for a moment, a Lionel Richie song and the hiss of produce misters providing a soundtrack to our awkward silence. "Anyway, I don't want to keep you," he said.

Oh no. Now Liam was the one fleeing, waving at me and sauntering away before I even had time to respond. A panic alarm set off in my brain—I had to do something. "Wait!" I called out, having no idea what I planned to say.

He turned on a dime, his eyebrow raised à la Jack Nicholson, as if to challenge me. "Yes?"

"Umm…" I was trying to recall something we had talked about, a conversation starter, but nothing came to mind. I drew a blank, too transfixed by the fluorescent-lit sparkle in Liam's eyes, visible from ten feet away. And then my food-driven brain kicked in and remembered the pivotal detail from our first conversation in the Baptist church parking lot. "Remember how you mentioned that gelato the other night? The one you make at your restaurant?"

"Yes," Liam responded with a knowing smirk.

"I've been thinking about it...," I said.

By the look on his face, Liam understood that I had been thinking about a lot more than gelato.

"It's still there," he said with an easy shrug.

* * *

Liam's sporty black Mercedes sped down Citrus Street, Oceanside's main drag, as I followed in my beat-up Honda. My fear of losing him as he zoomed through several nearly red lights kept my thoughts only partially occupied, while the rest of me questioned what exactly I was doing. Obviously we were not just going to eat gelato and share our life stories, but was I really prepared to sleep with this stranger? And would it make me a horrible person if I did, knowing that sex was Liam's drug of choice? *If it weren't you, it would be somebody else!* I heard Isabella call out from the depths of my consciousness. *Just go for it!*

He slowed down outside a gravel parking lot and pulled in past a sign that read TRIO. Suddenly, I knew exactly where I was even though I had never been there—it was the favorite restaurant of my former boss, Sasha Myers. I had booked her reservations there a million times. "The only white tablecloth establishment for miles," she liked to say when recommending it to clients at her luxe day spa. Ironically, I had always wanted to eat there but could never afford it, and now here I was with very little intention of eating.

Winding around behind the restaurant, we parked side by side in the cramped, employees-only parking lot. There were no other cars there, and only one streetlamp provided a dim, yellow beam that hovered over the otherwise dusky, moonlit lot. As I turned off my car and got out, the dense fog that had descended at the grocery store lifted from my brain and reality hit me like a smack to the forehead: What I was doing was reckless, unsafe, and above all, terribly un-me. Yet Liam looked so flawless in the moonlight.

"Is anyone even here?" I asked, timidly exiting the safety bubble that was my car.

"We're not open on Mondays." Liam sounded colder than he had when we had embarked on this little adventure ten minutes ago, and it began to sink in how absolutely strange, in every meaning of the word, this stranger really was as he rustled through his large keychain and located the key to the heavy back door. He unlocked the dead bolt and pushed inside, flipping on the ceiling lights that cast a bluish glow over the well-equipped, steel-countered kitchen.

Like Alice stumbling down the rabbit hole, I tentatively followed him in. All my life I had done the opposite of this—hiding, making myself invisible, vanishing into the woodwork—and I decided perhaps Alice really had materialized from the written word and was currently inhabiting my body.

"All right, the ice cream's in here," he said, ducking into a walk-in freezer and emerging with a stainless steel tub that gave off a little cloud of cold steam. He placed it on the counter and turned around to find me staring, clueless as to what to say or do now that I was officially alone with him. "We'll let that sit for a second. Let me show you around."

Liam smiled and walked ahead of me as I followed silently, feeling the tiny hairs stand up on the back of my neck and edges of my ears. In the dining room, he flicked on half the lights, which were dim to begin with, giving the restaurant that five-star, candlelit ambiance that people who like to pay a lot of money for their food are accustomed to. Not looking back at me, he held up an index finger, disappeared into a stockroom, then reemerged with a neatly folded white tablecloth that he draped over a corner booth.

"Is that the VIP table?" I joked, tapping my fingers on the wall beside me as Liam leaned against the booth.

"Only the best for my late-night gelato customers." He made a dramatic sweeping gesture over the table and smiled big enough so that I could see his straight white teeth for the first time. It was an earnest smile, and I felt almost at ease—what stopped me was how handsome he looked as he stood there waiting for me to approach. Hoping to calm my nerves, I tentatively explored the dining room, letting my fingertips graze the tables and chairs in the middle of the room.

"It's weird being in a restaurant with no people," I said.

"Yeah, it looks better with a crowd, I guess."

"No. It's really nice. Where did you get these chairs?" I grabbed the back of one of the white, upholstered chairs and drew it toward me, pretending to inspect it.

Liam laughed. "Really? You wanna know where I got the chairs?" He walked over and gently placed his hand on the small of my back.

I looked up at him, blushing, and let the chair go. A bead of sweat made its way down my neck. "I just like the white fabric. Anything white, really—I like the color."

"Virginal," he retorted, "like the driven snow."

"Right." I chuckled and felt my face flush. *This is flirting, Mischa. Say something sexy.* "It's hot in here," I said, plucking my shirt away from my body as I let myself lean into him, my shoulder just grazing his arm.

"Yeah, the manager has the AC on a timer. I don't know how

to change it. I'd better get that gelato, eh?" He let his hand drop and started toward the kitchen.

"Okay!" I watched him go, thinking, *This is good. This is my pace.* I didn't notice as I made my way to the corner booth, preparing myself for a little dessert before the main course, so to speak, that Liam had slowed down. By the time I reached the edge of the table, he had come up behind me and laid his hands on my shoulders.

"Just a warning, it's even hotter over here," he said.

"Really?" I reached my arms out as if to feel the air, then caught myself. I was acting clueless, which is exactly what I was. I had never been involved in a real seduction before. In fact, I had only ever slept with my ex-boyfriend, Bradley, whose idea of foreplay was the drunken groping typical of any college freshman. I decided to face my fear and turned to look Liam in the eye. "I don't know, maybe it's just you," I said, sensing his actual body heat as he pressed up against me.

"Maybe it is."

"What about the gelato?" I lowered my gaze at his broad chest in front of me. "Are you just gonna let it melt?"

"Hey, Mischa?" Liam took a step back and stared at me with his green eyes. "We're two people doing things we shouldn't be doing, right? I think the less we talk, the better."

In an instant, Liam braced my hips and lifted me onto the table so that my legs were straddling his waist. I felt myself shaking like a leaf. I had the same excited, scared sensation as being whipped around by a carnival ride, and felt like I should close my eyes like I always had on roller coasters. This was officially no longer my life. It was like I had entered somebody else's much more exciting narrative. *Wake up,* I thought. *Or don't. Let the dream play out.*

Liam buried his face in my neck, then dragged his chin down into my cleavage, which was exposed in the same ratty V-neck T-shirt I'd worn to the meeting where I first saw him. He kissed my chest and grabbed at both my breasts, growling like a predatory cat. The heat of his body against mine reminded me of the simple magic of being touched, something I hadn't experienced for so long. I wanted to give in to it, but I was also terrified by the foreignness of it all: his masculine smell, his strong hands on the small of my back, the scratchy stubble on his chin, my heart racing a mile a minute. I had no idea where I was or how I'd gotten there. When his lips, soft and pillowy, came to meet mine, I squeezed my eyes shut, and the roller coaster took its first drop. The tip of Liam's tongue slipped in past my parted lips and danced around with my own. His hand found the back of my neck and braced me as his kiss went deeper. My thighs were squeezed against his body so tightly, I could feel the seams on the sides of his jeans making an impression on my skin. Trailing his fingers from the back of my neck down my spine, Liam moved his kisses to my collarbone, then once again buried his face in my cleavage.

In an instant, I felt my elation turn to panic. Liam's touch felt so good yet terribly wrong at the same time, like the first time I ever masturbated. All the out-of-body motivation that had brought me this far dropped away without warning, and I knew I had to stop him from going any further, or I'd be lost forever. Someone like Liam—so good-looking, so experienced, so messed up when it came to sex—would crush me in a second, because I wouldn't be able to forget him.

"I can't have sex with you," I blurted, then shoved him away with a level of upper-body strength I didn't realize I had. I slid down from the table and adjusted my shirt, avoiding direct eye contact as I muttered an apology. To my surprise, Liam stayed where he was, dragging a hand across his mouth as I moved farther away. The look on his face was blank, neither angry nor relieved...just blank.

"I shouldn't have come," I said, to which he shrugged in response. Hoping to feign the same indifference, I waved and flashed a ridiculously fake smile before turning to go.

My hasty exit from the restaurant was a blur. In something close to a blackout state, I found my way back through the kitchen and out to the employee parking lot. It wasn't until a couple minutes later that I came to, registering a red light above me as I sped through it like a getaway driver. My heart racing, I glanced back at the intersection to make sure the automatic camera didn't flash my license plate and thanked God I hadn't killed anyone.

The questions swirling around my head were overlapping each other and therefore hard to discern, but the one that kept popping into the foreground was, *Why? Why did I just leave that incredible-looking man wanting more? Why didn't I want him back? Am I so afraid of having any semblance of a life that I have to run from every opportunity?*

The truth was—I realized after I'd talked myself down from the ledge—that I felt unsafe, first and foremost, which made sense because Liam was a sex addict whom I'd hardly spoken to. But his looks did confuse things. He was just the right amount of hot to be forgiven most trespasses, the kind of guy who could actually get away with murder. Which, I suppose, justified my actions, him being a potential homicidal maniac. And then there was the obvious darkness about him. He had demons that he was fully aware of and battling, one day at a time. Although the same could be said about me, my food addiction seemed like a silly, light affair in comparison with this man's lack of inhibition on the highway and weakness for anonymous Craigslist sex. We were as opposite as opposites could get—on one level, it was probably why I was so attracted to him.

But I had gone as far as following him inside an empty restaurant and he hadn't even threatened me. When I walked away, he didn't chase me with a knife or promise to haunt my dreams. Perhaps the only reason to believe he was a killer was to alleviate my disappointment in myself. The harsh reality was that a girl like me would probably never get an opportunity to sleep with someone like him twice. I'd blown my chances at one of those unbelievable one-night stands that people store in their minds and revisit for years to come—those who are wise enough to seize that kind of fleeting moment.

Without thinking, I drove back to my dreary apartment complex before I remembered I no longer lived there. My mind still a million miles away, I turned around in the parking lot and reluctantly steered my car back in the direction of Julien's.

Chapter 4

Upon waking the next morning, I spent a good ten minutes convincing myself that the events of last night had actually taken place and were not just another elaborate anxiety dream centered around Liam. If they had been part of a dream, I rationalized, things wouldn't have ended so unceremoniously. Liam would have pointed and laughed at me, or morphed into my ex-boy-friend, or forced himself on me while a crowd of dishwashers watched. But none of the above applied. No, I had walked right up to the edge of something unbelievably exciting and run away like a scared little girl.

Almost an hour had lapsed before I stopped lamenting my nonheroic actions long enough to remember it was my first day working for Julien. Luckily my anxiety had woken me up pre-alarm, and for a split second I imagined myself partaking in my favorite morning activity: dragging into the kitchen, pouring a bowl of cereal (sugary junk on bad days and flavorless, fiber-laden pellets on "good" ones), and traipsing back into my nest of sheets and pillows, mentally suspending the start of the day by another fifteen minutes or so. Then I remembered where I was—Julien's kitchenless guesthouse—and realized that from now on I would have to dress like a civilized person and go to the main house any time I needed food. Perhaps it would work out as a new diet plan.

A quick shower and primp session helped me shake off just a little of last night's regret before I made my way through the backyard and entered the Maxwell breakfast scene, not knowing what to expect. Oddly enough, what I found was Cecile in a very good mood, parked by the coffee machine. "Can I get you cappuccino or a latte?" she asked in a strangely magnanimous tone. "This thing does everything."

Well, if you're taking orders, I thought, *I'll have some eggs, a couple strips of bacon, and a bowl of Honey Smacks to smother my general feeling of failure.*

"A latte sounds great!" I said, accepting her offer with an excited nod. I knew from being one myself, teenage girls felt especially empowered when they were allowed to imbibe and/or prepare the morning coffee, and I was happy to indulge Cecile as my barista.

"Do you take regular milk?"

"Sure." I tucked my hair behind my ears and took a seat on one of the barstools by the island. As she moved around the kitchen, I continued the inventory of the Maxwells' well-appointed home that I'd started upon arrival, noticing that even the kitchen tools were fancy, and here and there were artful little flourishes like the turquoise, crackle-glazed vase holding the cooking utensils or a woven pot holder with a bright pink flamingo against a lush green backdrop.

"So, my dad says you're a Nutrition major," said Cecile, making the small talk we were both too awkward to manage yesterday.

"I was, yeah. Just graduated."

"So you probably know a lot about what I should and shouldn't be eating." She avoided eye contact as she made the statement, popping a coffee cup under the nozzle of the elaborate silver machine and cranking a dial that sent the apparatus into a quiet fit of noises and spurts. "I haven't always been fat like this. Do you think I could be allergic to some kind of food without knowing it?"

Oh dear. I could remember my teenaged self having similar thoughts. "Well, first of all, I hate the term *fat* and I don't think you are. Second of all, the allergy thing—probably not. The only advice I ever give, based on what I've learned, is pretty basic: stick with whole foods, avoid anything processed, high fructose corn syrup, sugar in general, and caffeine." I said the last one with sarcastic emphasis, prompting Cecile to roll her eyes and stick out her tongue. I laughed knowingly. "Yeah, if only I followed my own advice."

"Do you eat healthy?" Cecile's eyes were on me now, eagerly awaiting my response.

Unsure how to answer, I decided to go with a safe, somewhat honest response. "I go in and out of phases."

Cecile's head bobbed once in approval as she turned her back to me and continued foaming the milk. Although I felt a slight urge to tell her the truth, admit that I had been addicted to food since I was her age—even younger—in the hopes that I might make her feel less alone, I knew better than to disclose that much to a girl at such an impressionable age. And who knew what kind of eating habits or problems she might have? All I could tell was that she had a negative body image, which was more common than not for teenagers. In the vague, cloudy depths of my memory, I could just barely recall how intense my own warped self-image and food obsessions were during puberty, and the thought made me shudder.

"Good morning, lovely ladies!" Julien bounded into the kitchen seemingly out of nowhere. "Are you prepared to work?" he asked, flashing his winning smile with the boyish gap between his front teeth.

I nodded and smiled back, caught off guard by his total ease and familiarity. It was as if I had always been sitting at his kitchen island at breakfast time, like I was an old family friend.

"You sure you're up for it? It's gonna be a big day!" As he addressed me, he playfully sidled up to Cecile at the coffee machine and bumped his hip against hers.

"Dad, stop it." She sullenly inched away from him, stirring my latte before handing it over.

"Thanks," I said, despite my desire to hit a pause button and shake this girl's shoulders, telling her how lucky she was to have a father like Julien, to have a father at all, and how she should relish these moments because he wouldn't be here forever. And then I remembered that her mother was dead, and I stopped with the petty judgments.

Julien made us eggs and toast, and a half hour later, I was following him out the front door. Everything seemed a little strange, like I was observing what was happening from a distance. The impromptu arrangement we had made less than a week ago—me working for him all summer and living in his backyard, chatting up his daughter at meal times—was catapulting the three of us into this "just add water" level of intimacy I'd never had with anyone. It was one of those odd situations that overtakes your life every once in a while and in one fell swoop changes everything. Before you know it, you are sucked in by a current that drags you out into the unknown. Sometimes you recognize it at the time; in other cases, you wake up weeks or months later, after the waves have washed you back ashore, to process the unusual chain of events that just rocked your world. In this case, I was aware of the strangeness as it was happening when Julien suggested we bike to work and offered me his dead wife's teal-green beach cruiser to ride.

Julien's cheerfulness seemed slightly over the top as he handed over the bicycle, as if he was overcompensating for the unbearable sea of grief the bike prompted inside him. Nevertheless, I smiled as I took it from him and hopped on, awkwardly positioning myself on the tan leather seat. I couldn't remember the last time I had been biking.

Julien raced onto the street without much warning. In a matter of seconds, I broke into a sweat. I wasn't sturdy, or fast, but I managed to stay a few paces behind him, and after a couple minutes of riding, realized what Julien had said yesterday was true—biking really does clear one's thoughts. As we coasted along the flat, sleepy streets, I started to feel wistful and carefree, something I hadn't been in a long time.

Reid's campus was located in the absolute center of Oceanside, a beach town whose main business was the college. Even though Julien's house was only a couple of miles from campus, I noticed we were taking a long, circuitous route that wound in and out of several beachside neighborhoods. He seemed to be in no rush to get to the office, but I didn't mind. Every once in a while, he would glance over his shoulder to make sure I was keeping up, and I would smile in assurance.

When we passed my old apartment complex, I slowed down, craning for a glimpse of Anjuli, the exchange student who was supposed to have moved into my place the day before, but saw no trace of her. Surprisingly, the sight of the old apartment conjured very little emotion, as if I hadn't lived there for the better part of two years. One of my neighbors, an older lady whom I'd never formally met, caught me staring as she retrieved a newspaper from the bottom of the stairs and cocked her head quizzically. That's when I looked back to the road and realized Julien had already turned a corner. I pedaled fast to catch up to him, losing my breath in the process.

It became clear that we were officially avoiding campus when he cut down to the shoreline. We passed by a patch of mangrove trees that tainted the air with their overwhelming smell of sulfur, and I breathed in heartily. A line from *Cane*, one of the books Julien had assigned, popped into my head and I desperately wanted to impress him by reciting it, something about the sunshine striking a woman's "mangrove-gloomed face" like rockets. I made a mental note to mention it later, but first I would have to come up with some reasonable context. In the meantime, I examined Julien from behind, noting how neat and fresh he looked, like just the kind of person who would live in his well-decorated house: He had on muted coral linen pants, rolled up at the ankles; an easy white button-down; and seemingly unworn white canvas sneakers. Meanwhile, I was wearing my favorite frayed jean shorts, a faded purple tank top, and flip-flops. If someone had stopped us for a picture, we would have resembled exactly what we were: the dapper professor with a book deal and his sloppily dressed undergrad intern—aimless, desperate for a future, fleetingly entangled with a sex addict.

* * *

Every Monday, Wednesday, and Friday of spring semester, Gracie had unabashedly studied the face of Dr. Julien Maxwell while he had lectured and I had taken notes for the both of us. She would never shut up about what a "specimen" he was, but until now, I hadn't bothered to take notice. His face was the perfect balance of round and oval with the large forehead of a thinking man; a medium-sized nose, perfectly centered; and big, sleepy eyes that seemed to have something behind them. His skin was a beautiful, warm brown, and the stubble that covered his upper lip, chin, and cheeks a dark black with flecks of silvery gray to match his close-cropped hair. Definitely not my type—professors, as I saw them, were all surrogate fathers of some sort, no matter how young—but I could see the appeal.

The day we took our bike ride to campus, we didn't end up on campus at all. Instead, Julien led me to a beachside dive bar called Salty Sal's, a derelict structure somewhere between roadhouse and shack that I hadn't stopped to notice in my entire four years of living here. He hadn't explained where we were going at any point, and I hadn't bothered to ask. We arrived sometime before noon, after an hour-long journey that left my thighs feeling wobbly and unstable.

"No need to panic. Procrastination is a part of my process," he announced, putting a hand out for the beach cruiser after chaining his bike to a rusted white railing that ran between the parking lot and the beach.

I followed Julien inside the bar and found the kind of scene one would expect to find at a small-town dive at noon on a weekday: two sloppy, middle-aged men sitting at opposite ends of the bar, drinking the same beer out of cans, and situated between them, a fifty-something bartender who looked like she knew her way around an eighteen-wheeler. Harsh shafts of sunlight snuck in through a couple of high-set, rectangular windows, but the space remained ironically dark and depressing for being practically *on* the beach. I couldn't believe Julien actually liked this place, but it was apparent he did. I imagined him spending a lot of time here since his wife's passing, a likely guess according to the bartender's somber yet empathetic greeting: a knowing wink and a shot glass filled with tequila.

Julien winked back. "One for my friend, too, please."

Without looking at me, she poured the shot and, although I scrambled for my driver's license, served it to me without question. I whispered to Julien that it was the first time in my life I hadn't been carded.

"Thanks, Arlene." Julien smiled as he raised his shot glass and nodded for me to do the same.

"Thanks, Arlene," I repeated, eliciting a snaggletoothed smile from our stoic host.

Clinking glasses, Julien and I downed the shots, grimaced in unison, then picked up the mugs that Arlene had wordlessly placed before us and chased the fiery liquor with cold beer.

"You ever been here?" he asked.

"No. I'm not sure I knew it existed," I said. I was trying not to make a face, but my throat burned badly from the shot. I glanced around at the framed photographs of caught fish on the walls, the inoperative jukebox collecting dust in the corner, an abandoned checkers game set up on one of the small tables. I was as intrigued by my surroundings as if I had been viewing the Coliseum for the first time and realized the effect Julien had on this commonplace, foul-smelling bar just by walking into it. Much like the smelly mangrove trees had struck me this morning, for the first time, as magical literary references instead of rotten-egg purveyors, Julien's scholarly presence turned Salty Sal's into some sweet little place Hemingway might have frequented.

"The truth is, I brought you here because I think a little bonding is in order if we're going to be working together all summer. That and, like I said, my process involves a necessary amount of procrastination. Don't tell Cecile."

I whipped my hand past my lips as if I was zipping them shut. "Of course not!" I said.

"I don't want to be a bad influence. I've got future professors of America to impress here." He gestured to me before taking another swig of beer.

"Oh, I don't know about that," I demurred.

"Really? You strike me as an academic. Didn't you say your parents were professors?"

"No, not in the least!" I could feel myself beaming at the mere suggestion. It was entirely off base, but also possibly the most flattering thing I'd ever heard. Suddenly, I wanted to be Julien's vision of me: the budding professor, hailing from a long line of the same.

He sipped his beer and trained his eyes on me. "So tell me about yourself. Where are you from? What's your story?" He punctuated his questions with pursed lips and an intense stare, and I couldn't tell if he was being sincere or ironic. Actually, it was a mystery to me whether or not he possessed a sense of humor at all—I certainly hadn't detected it in his lectures.

"I'm not that interesting. I'd rather hear about you," I deflected.

"No, no, no. Tell me. This is part of your job."

"The hard part, I hope."

"You don't like talking about yourself? That's strange. I find most of my students are particularly fond of that pastime." He smiled and cocked his head just so, and I decided that yes, he had a sense of humor—albeit a subtle, professorial one. He also had a way with words; everything he said sounded premeditated, direct, precise. It made me self-conscious about my own way of speaking, which was clumsy and stilted in comparison.

"I don't like talking about myself…to a fault, probably." I blushed on cue. Simply being honest about that fact made me feel shy—the mark of a true introvert.

"Well, what if I guess where your family is?"

"Eagle Grove, Iowa. And the Philippines. And that's where my story ends." I patted the bar in a demonstrative way that accidentally signaled Arlene to get us more shots.

"Brace yourself for another round." Julien raised his eyebrows as she poured more tequila into our shot glasses. He raised his second shot and waited for me to do the same. "Cheers," he said, but not until after he had downed the liquor.

"Cheers." I tried to match Julien's enthusiasm but balked at the smell of the tequila as it neared my nose. I took a tiny sip and set the shot down.

"You know, this spring was my first semester back since being on leave, and I worry it was too soon. Everybody seemed tuned out, like I was boring them."

"No way!" I said, even though the truth was Julien's lectures had had their ups and downs. Some days he had seemed on the verge of tears, and not because he was so moved by the literature. But on others, I could glimpse the kind of teacher he really was—passionate, insightful, engaging. "Your class was the most interesting lit class I've ever taken," I assured him, my hand held up in oath. "I swear."

"Did you know what happened? About the accident?" Angling to face me, he propped his elbow up on the bar and rested his cheek on a tightly balled fist. "Everybody seemed to know."

"No, I didn't," I said. "At first I didn't know. But Gracie knew about it. She told me. I'm so sorry." I started to reach for him but stopped myself.

"It's okay." He shook his head, as if trying to shake off the unshakeable memory that his wife had been senselessly murdered by a drunk driver. "I needed to get back to work. I needed that structure. What I didn't need were all the pained looks on people's faces when they asked me how I was doing, all the reminders that they were there if I needed a shoulder to cry on. I think grieving people are like cats, you know? We don't want to talk if you show the slightest interest."

Taking another sip of tequila, I thought of the Toomer quote I'd wanted to recite to Julien earlier but realized it had zero relevance here. What could I say that would make me sound erudite and compassionate all at once? "What was that Toni Morrison quote?" I said. "Something about there being no words for pain..."

Julien looked both happy and sad. "Exactly."

Two hours and three beers later, he had all but told me his entire life story while I had sat stoically, peppering in a literary reference every once in a while and trying to mask my incredulity at this level of confidence he had bestowed upon me. Again, it was the just-add-water intimacy that had made me feel like some not-so-distant relative at breakfast that morning, come to stay with her uncle and cousin for the summer. He shared the story of how he and his wife, Renay, had first met as teenagers, explaining that she came from a wealthy New Orleans family while he had been raised by a single mother in D.C. who, like mine, had worked late hours in a low-paying job. They had been married at twenty-four and had Cecile even younger. He had gone to Brown on scholarship, then NYU, and had been slightly disappointed when forced to take tenure at Reid instead of somewhere more prestigious, because it was the only school that had offered professorships to both him and his wife. He had described to me his own version of the stages of grief, which went something like denial, inexplicable laughter, explicable rage, depression, anger, depression again, and, finally, a slight upgrade to general melancholy. He had seemed on the verge of tears when he had gripped my wrist for a brief second and insisted that life was too short for anything but absolute truth. Then suddenly, regaining his inhibitions, he had bummed a cigarette from one of the barflies and led me across the parking lot in the direction of a taco stand he'd promised was "hands-down the best."

I tried to make sense of what had just happened as we stood before the RV on the other side of the parking lot with two taciturn Mexican women inside awaiting our orders. Julien puffed on his bummed cigarette and pointed out his favorite items on the menu painted on the side of the truck. With my blessing, he ordered for both of us and paid in cash before leading me to a bench on the sidewalk where we ate our tacos while looking out at the ocean. The food was almost too spicy, but I relished it. Again, the Julien effect. I felt like I belonged here, sitting on a bench with a true mentor, someone open and honest and as smart as I could ever hope to be, who would steer me toward a better future.

"Thanks for listening in there," he said after a bout of silence.

I nodded once, my eyes on the ocean. "Thanks for trusting me," I said.

Sitting up straight, his energy shifted back to intense enthusiasm for the day as he clapped his hands together, crumpling his empty taco wrappers and rolling them into a ball. "So! We need to stop by my office for a couple of minutes at least. That way, we have an alibi." Julien stood up from the bench and I saluted him, prompting him to laugh heartily, as if it were an inside joke we'd already established: Julien as drill sergeant, me as devoted recruit. He either thought I was very funny or the tequila shots were still working their magic.

As we headed back across the parking lot, he reached out and patted my shoulder, a chaste, fatherly gesture that somehow turned my thoughts to Liam, who had touched my shoulders the night before in quite the opposite way—lustfully, proprietarily.

At the spa where I had worked up until the fall of last year, my jet-setter boss Sasha Myers was always repeating clichés about men. "Creatures of conquest," she would call them. "Once you've kissed, barring any major mishaps, they will not stop until they've sealed the deal. A man once tracked me down from Alaska because our one-night stand had been interrupted. Five thousand miles he flew! I'm telling you... they will find you and they will finish you off," she would tell single customers, throwing an extra sample of eye cream into their bag with a wink and a thumbs-up. She liked to repeat this story in particular; over time, I had realized that it was really just a pep talk for herself, a twice-divorced woman still chasing the thrill of romance. However, thinking about Liam, I wanted to believe that Sasha had been right. Deep down, I wanted him to find me and, whatever the emotional fallout might be, finish me off.

Chapter 5

The rest of the week flew past in a haze. Every morning I awoke, joined Cecile and Julien for breakfast, then biked with him to the office, where we spent seven or eight hours working diligently, Julien typing away at his computer while I filed, sorted, collated, stapled—monotonous tasks that were oddly soothing. Every night before going to sleep I noticed whether or not his light was still on, as his bedroom window was visible from mine. If it was on, I imagined he was still working, keeping his mind off the empty half of his bed. I tried to take a page from his playbook and work hard enough every day so that I was too exhausted to lie awake and think about Liam at night, but I failed. A community of butterflies had taken up a permanent residence in my stomach, and any downtime that I had was devoted to rehashing that night at the restaurant, wondering what would happen if I ever saw him again.

I came to see Julien's office as a protective bubble, the only place where thoughts of Liam couldn't penetrate my mind. We mostly sat in silence—him hovering over his laptop and me alternating between the uncomfortable wooden chair across from his desk and a patch of floor, reorganizing and flagging piles of research. Sometimes I found myself staring at one of his packed bookshelves and dreaming of what it would be like to be a respected professor like him but finding it impossible to envision myself that way. The more I witnessed Julien's quiet, brilliant, sequestered life, the more the idea of working in the rarefied world of academia became. The best I could hope for from this experience would be to come out of it a little more culturally astute, if just by osmosis.

Our bike rides to and from work were also quiet, as were shared mealtimes at the house, when Cecile did most of the talking. The lack of conversation was refreshing to me, because whenever I did speak, I caught myself trying a little too hard to please, sometimes bordering on pretention with my attempts to sound perceptive and well read. However I was coming across seemed to be working, though. At the end of my first week, Julien granted me the privilege of reading the first chapter of his book and I did so under his watchful eye, my red pen hovering over the printed pages but finding no errors to mark. When I was done, I only offered one criticism—to strike the last line of an annotation— and he thanked me so profusely, you would think I had carefully edited the whole thing.

"I wish I were you," said Gracie when I called her that Friday after work. "You should see the middle-aged bums in my office. Julien Maxwell puts them all to shame."

"I see what you're saying, objectively. But you know me—I'm working on making him the father I never had. I'm even warming to the idea of having a bratty little sister. Did I tell you she makes me coffee in the morning?"

"Yes, it's a real blended family scene you've got going over there."

"Maybe I'm just trying to fill the Gracie-sized hole in my heart since you left. So how's D.C.?"

"So far so good. I mean, aside from the irony that I'm working for an organic foods lobby and microwaving half my meals. But it's good to be in a city. You should come visit!"

"You know me, Oceanside's got all the excitement I can handle. Plus, I'm broke."

"Yeah, yeah, yeah. Well, do me a favor. Give Julien a big fat sloppy father-daughter kiss for me?"

"Ew, ew, ew."

"Or find somebody to crush over. I need to live vicariously. I got nothing doing here."

" 'Kay, I'll do my best," I said.

"Love you, gotta crash."

"Love you too." I heard Gracie sigh on the other end as we hung up. She still had no idea about Liam, and at this point, I wasn't sure why I hadn't fessed up. Perhaps because I knew she would only fuel the fire, when I really should be forgetting all about him. Of course, as someone great once said, *Best laid plans and all that…*

* * *

"You need to eat," I instructed Isabella as she rocked on her wicker patio chair, puffing the new e-cigarette she had spent the last ten minutes extolling. The first time I had met her had been on this very same porch, when as a freshman I had come to her retirement community with one of my Nutrition professors who was running a gardening program there. I had helped Isabella start a thriving tomato garden on her porch, which she had proceeded to neglect that summer when I had gone home to Iowa.

When I got back, it had made me secretly happy to know how much I was needed. Ever since, I've made weekly visits in which I cook her a week's worth of meals.

"These are the best crab cakes I have ever made." I propped up my empty plate as evidence, trying to coax her to put down the nicotine. "They have capers! You love capers!"

"Just let me have this first. You know I'm very excited to try your food, always," she said in her heavy Austrian accent.

"If I had to guess, I'd say you haven't been eating enough."

"Not true! You saw—everything you made me last week is gone. *Fertig.*"

"How do I know you didn't just throw it in the trash?"

"Because I can describe to you in detail just how succulent and perfectly seasoned the roast beef was and tell you all the ways in which I ate it—in sandwiches, heated up with the savory mashed cauliflower, in a box, with a fox."

"I'm just saying, you seem like you've lost weight."

"That's your opinion."

"Isabella, I worry about you," I said. And I did. Just as I had a penchant for gaining five or ten pounds every once in a while, she tended to lose that much, and whenever she did, she got a little wild-eyed and defensive. I had to think there was a history of disordered eating behind all of her jokes about having a "discerning palate" and needing to get ready for bikini season.

"Tell me more about this nymphomaniac," she said, eyeing me mischievously.

Even though I hadn't planned it, I had broken down and told her about Liam the minute I had walked in. "Well, he's bad news, obviously," I said.

"You don't sound so convinced. There's something about Australian men, the good-looking ones anyway. I knew an Australian years ago. Race car driver. Formula One. Biggest *schwanz* I ever saw."

I rolled my eyes and noticed Isabella's next-door neighbor, Melvin, waving from his own screened-in porch. I waved back and nudged her to do the same but she ignored me. "Why aren't you nicer to Melvin? I think he likes you."

Isabella closed her eyes and shook her head. "No way."

"Why? Is it because he's Jewish?" I said.

"Ha!" Isabella took a long drag from her e-cigarette and blew out a cool wisp of steam.

"That's what it is. You're somehow devoutly Catholic and I never knew it. Can't date a man outside the church?" I was mostly teasing, but after four years of knowing her, I had learned that Isabella was a walking paradox, a sort of deranged mash-up of Elizabeth Taylor, Jackie Kennedy, and Miss Havisham; the likelihood of her being a Freedom Rider or part of the Hitler Youth were about the same.

"Darling, I've sampled the rainbow—race, religion, creed, whatever that means. Don't be a twit. What's the Australian's name again?"

"Liam."

"Oh yes, Liam. He's got the restaurant I like"—not surprisingly, Isabella was a big fan of Trio, just like my old boss—"and your little rendezvous was interrupted by the waitress?"

"Well, sort of." I had lied to Isabella about running out of the restaurant. It had been hard enough for me to talk about in the first place, and certainly the truth—that I had aborted the mission the minute we kissed—was not going to impress her. So I fudged the story a little, saying that a waitress, there to pick up her paycheck, had interrupted our tryst.

"Then I think you have to see him again, no? He sounds like a good time. And very good-looking."

"He is good-looking. He's about eighty thousand miles out of my league good-looking."

"Pfft." She shook her head. "You kissed, it was good, who cares?"

"I just don't think getting involved with a sex addict is a good idea. I'd feel like a drug dealer giving heroin to a junkie…low-grade heroin. And then one day he would wake up and realize how much better he could do when the supermodel down the street offered him way better stuff, and then I'd be screwed. He would change dealers, break my heart, end of story."

"Nonsense! You just graduated college. Live a little. Here, have a puff." She held out her little white tube as if it promised emotional maturity in addition to smoke-free nicotine.

I took the e-cig to oblige her. Isabella was obviously proud of herself for adopting this cutting-edge vice, and who was I to shatter her illusion of coolness? Nicotine had never really done it for me; when I had dabbled with smoking as a teenager, I had found it supremely less interesting than eating lots of food and determined my money would never have to be wasted on such an expensive trifle.

After a quick drag, I handed it back. "I don't know."

"Does he make you feel comfortable? When you're with him?"

"Strangely enough, yes. I mean other than the butterflies."

To this, Isabella pretended to face-plant on the patio table, hovering her nose inches from its dusty surface. "Young lady, have I taught you nothing?"

"What?"

Isabella groaned as she straightened back up. "This is not an opportunity you pass up, my dear."

"But I'm not like you." I smiled, hoping I didn't sound too judgmental. "I don't just jump at opportunities. I'm too afraid of the consequences."

Isabella responded with a bitter laugh. "You'll learn."

"What is that supposed to mean?"

She shrugged and turned her head, eyeing one of her female neighbors as she passed on a golf cart. "Ugh, tell me I don't look that old."

* * *

That night, I tossed and turned, unable to sleep with Isabella's words still ringing through my head. What did she mean, "You'll learn"? How was she so convinced that I was letting something important pass me by? Usually I took her life advice with a grain of salt. She came from such a different world than me that most of her axioms ("Never wear red lipstick before five o'clock," or "Flatware sets should be six pieces, not five") did not apply. But her attitude about Liam had been markedly assured. Despite eighty-five years of life experience, she wasn't warning me to steer clear of him, even though I had painted him as a potential train wreck. I had even told her the part about the Craigslist prostitute, to which she didn't bat an eye. Not that I had always considered her a mentor per se, but I listened to her input at least as much as I listened to my own mother's, who represented the exact opposite of the spectrum, always encouraging me to protect my heart above all else. Between the two of them, I had probably developed quite the Madonna/whore complex without even knowing it. The problem this time was that I had only confided in Isabella, so she was the only voice in my head—or devil on my shoulder, depending on how I looked at it...

* * *

Friday, second week after graduation: Ocean View Baptist Church
Overeaters Anonymous Meeting
Topic of discussion: "Lost Causes"
Calories imbibed: approximately 1 billion

My second week at Julien's had been more of the same—bouts of intense work and distraction followed by persistent daydreams of Liam. Actually, for the better part of the week, I had been working by myself in the library, making copious amounts of photocopies at a finicky Xerox machine and tempering the boredom with even more copious amounts of vending machine snacks. By Friday, I was feeling pretty isolated, not to mention bloated, and decided I needed to have at least the illusion of a social life. So after work, I wiped the Snickers smudges from the corner of my mouth and changed my clothes, determined to find the OA meeting I'd been looking for the night I had crashed the sex addicts' group at Ocean View Baptist. *This time, I will get my details right,* I promised myself on the way there. The last thing I needed was another dose of sex addict confessionals, not to mention the sight of Liam's golden boy face mocking me for denying his sexual prowess.

Once I got there—to Chapel B, *not* A—the meeting itself went by slowly, and I felt myself itching to leave several times. My secret binging had been almost nonstop for the past week, while most of the people in the room were reporting great success with sticking to their meal plans and avoiding trigger foods, accepting a higher power, and taking it one day at a time. I could usually find inspiration in these intrepid twelve-steppers, but not tonight. Moving into Julien's was supposed to mark a new start for me, health-wise, yet I had bungled it in a matter of days.

This particular group, I discovered, liked to end their proceedings with a "gratitude share," in which everyone in the room names something for which they are thankful. My opposition to public speaking—especially on bad days—was such that even this made me anxious, and by the time it was my turn, a couple of tears had already welled up in the corners of my eyes. *What is wrong with me?* I thought, glancing around nervously and kicking the pew in front of me as, one by one, the women seated in my row named the reasons they were grateful that day (things like "serenity," "a week without chocolate," or my personal favorite, the ever-cliché "my cat"). My eyes searched for the moderator and I raised my hand halfway, wanting to opt out of the gratitude share the way I had opted out of high school gym with a doctor's note so I wouldn't have to change in the girls' locker room. But when it came time for me to speak, the moderator hadn't seen my hand, and I was too cowardly to dissent.

"Hi, my name is Mischa," I said in a shaky voice.

"Hi, Mischa," the sympathetic crowd responded.

"I guess…today…I'm thankful for…" I glanced around at the waiting faces, annoyed with myself for not preparing an answer. *Do not say pizza. Or ice cream. Especially not ice cream.* Each second that passed made me feel like more and more of an ingrate. Which is perhaps why I answered the way I did. "My father," I said.

Wait, wha…? I almost shook my head in time with the words as they came out of my mouth, having no idea what I thought I was talking about. When asked to name one thing I was thankful for, I came up with the derelict parent who had opted out of my life fourteen years ago, the one my mother and I now laughingly referred to as "the charismatic cult leader." Was this opposite day? Why couldn't I have thanked my mother, who had toiled and sacrificed and been there for me through thick and thin? For some reason, she was not who my subconscious came up with in the heat of the moment. Instead, I named my father, who had ghosted on me when I was eight years old. *Okeydokey, Mischa. I guess you've finally lost it.*

Regardless of my answer being haphazard and basically wrong, I was met with smiles of encouragement during the gratitude share. A big-haired, blue-eyed woman named Dawn, who smelled heavily of rose perfume, came up to me after the meeting to thank me for mentioning my dad and lament how much fathers tended to get a bad rap in these meetings. Of course I had no words to respond. I couldn't explain why I'd said it or burst her bubble with the truth that my father was a deadbeat just like everyone else's here. As Dawn started talking about her third step and how much difficulty she was having turning her life over to God, the room started to close in on me a little bit. I knew nothing about the Twelve Steps, beyond having them memorized. I had never worked them—had never even considered it, really.

"Hey, Dawn?" I grasped her padded shoulder lightly, not wanting to abandon her but unable to stay in that room for one more second. "I'm sorry. I've gotta get to a bathroom. I'm about to burst."

She nodded sweetly as I gave a perfunctory wave goodbye and snuck out the door, fully aware that I was acting like a coward. Befriending a person like Dawn could have been the best thing for me at a time like this, but I was in no mood for reform. That was the thing about me and OA—we had a complicated relationship.

The church's vast parking lot was the same one where I'd first spoken to Liam, and pathetically enough, I had parked in the exact same spot. I had done it subconsciously, out of the desire to run into him again no doubt, while telling myself I was going to avoid him at all costs. In keeping with the latter, I made a direct beeline to my car, eyes on the black asphalt that smelled like it had been freshly paved.

I allowed myself only one glance in the direction of Chapel A as I cut through the lot and saw a small group of men gathered on the sidewalk, smoking cigarettes and talking. I noticed the uniform posture they all seemed to have, with their backs arched and butts jutted out in a slightly vulgar way, the exact opposite of the slouched-over OAers, who were always trying to make themselves smaller by rounding out their shoulders and drawing their arms in tight. On the first glance, I didn't see Liam, but as I got closer, I looked once more and made out his silhouette—he was wearing the same black jeans as before with a fitted, black leather motorcycle jacket. His back was turned, allowing me to take in his lean, perfect figure. A full-body longing to run to him, tell him how much I'd thought about him over the past two weeks, overcame me, but I did the opposite and veered away like a coward. When I had almost reached my car, I heard footsteps but shook off the hope that it could be him. I was better off if it wasn't, right?

"Well, well, well. What have we here?" the person belonging to the footsteps called after me, his accent unmistakable. "Were you just gonna walk past me and not say anything?"

My heart pounded wildly at the sound of his voice. I turned to him with a guilty smile that gave me away. "Hi. I didn't see you. I was just at a meeting," I said. "The right one, this time."

"Oh yeah? You sure you're not a crazy Baptist? I hear they guard the crucifixion here, like in twenty-four-hour shifts."

I laughed, remembering that on top of being beautiful and successful, he was also naturally funny. "Yeah, no. In my four years of living here, I haven't found Jesus. Probably never gonna happen." I bit my lip self-consciously, trying not to smile, but Liam's own smile made it hard. A quick flashback to me running away from his restaurant made me shudder and I shook my head, hoping to physically remove the thought from my brain.

"What?" he asked.

"Nothing. Umm…" I searched for something to say, unsuccessfully, as footsteps scuffled up behind me. I turned to find an older man in reading glasses whom I'd seen patting Liam's shoulder at the meeting the week before.

"Hey there," he said. "I'm Bobby." He touched his chest to identify himself, sounding chipper but stern.

"Hi, I'm Mischa." I reached my hand out, but Bobby ignored it. Something told me it wasn't the reading glasses' fault.

He established himself at Liam's side and gripped his shoulder, Bobby's proprietary palm making a subtle squeaking noise against the leather jacket. "I'm Liam's sponsor. How do you two know each other?"

"We don't really," I said, getting the feeling that I was in trouble for some unknown trespass. It was like the high school hall monitor had asked to see my bathroom pass, and the answer was I most certainly didn't have one. Perhaps this was fate stepping in—fate in the form of a punishing older man with bad style. When Liam didn't immediately come to my defense, I announced that I should be going. "It was nice to see you!" I said, my eyes on Liam. "And nice to meet you, Bobby," I added, my real smile quickly warping into a fake one. Bobby responded with a smirk, then ushered Liam, who looked a little dumbstruck, back to the smokers' circle.

I turned to my car, my cheeks burning with embarrassment. If there were a wall handy, I would have knocked my head against it. Liam's sponsor, that glorified hall monitor of a man, had clocked me from who knows how far away and decided I was some random slut threatening to end his sponsee's latest streak of sobriety, and now Liam was probably convinced of the same thing.

Nachos and ice cream will fix this, I promised myself as I turned on the car. *Nachos and ice cream.*

Chapter 6

In the many hours of television I'd watched growing up in Eagle Grove, I had been exposed to multiple viewings of a local commercial for the Fort Dodge Fast N' Furious Family Fun Center. It was the kind of establishment that had laser tag *and* go-karts *and* batting cages *and* arcade games, and also the kind of place that had filmed one commercial back in 1987 and saw fit to use it for the rest of eternity. In said commercial, there was a young boy who flitted from one activity to another, shouting at the top of his lungs, "I CAN'T BELIEVE THIS IS MY LIFE!" After the first few times I had seen it, I had been certain that something horrible was bound to befall this boy—that nothing was ever that good, and if you can't believe your life, then you're most likely on the precipice of some terrible tragedy. Although I hadn't really thought about it until now, I'd been buzzing the last couple of weeks from the promise of Liam, in that "I can't believe this is my life!" kind of way, when really, I should have suspected that it was too good to be true. Even as a television-addicted child, fully steeped in the imaginary worlds of my favorite shows and movies, I had innately known that life is not all go-karts and batting cages.

The streets were quiet as I drove home from the meeting at the Baptist church. To ensure I would spend the least amount of time possible in the Maxwells' kitchen, hoping not to get caught by body-snarking Cecile or, worse, Julien, I planned my nacho-making in advance, envisioning where all of the ingredients were and in what order I would add them before nuking them in the microwave. The gallon of strawberry ice cream I had shoved behind Julien's frozen peas and berries was already half eaten, so I would be able to finish that without having to return it to the freezer. Sadly, these kinds of thoughts were the nitpicking obsessions that had taken up the better part of my brain for as long as I could remember: what I would eat next, where I would get it, how I would make it, when and how to dispose of the evidence.

Only when I was a few blocks from Julien's did I stop building nachos in my mind long enough to notice a speeding car coming up behind me. It followed as I turned onto the dimly lit residential street that I now called home, and when I pulled over and parked by the curb, it stopped directly behind me, headlights flickering in a bright flash before turning off. My heart began to race. I fumbled for my cell phone and swiped at the screen. When the emergency call button illuminated, I let my thumb hover over it. Then, in a matter of seconds, I recognized Liam's black leather jacket in my side mirror as he emerged from his car.

I gasped. He had somehow broken away from the watchful eye of Bobby, and more unbelievable than that, cared enough to pursue me after our conversation had been quashed. After all the missed opportunities, it felt like an actual miracle to see his reflection coming toward me. Of course a disapproving voice popped into my head, arguing that it was no miracle at all, that he was a sex addict and this is what addicts do, but that was no longer enough to deter me. My desire for him was unstoppable, unlike anything I'd ever felt before. I got out of the car to intercept him, not wanting him to glimpse the crumpled fast-food bags that littered my passenger seat, and asked incredulously, "What are you doing here?" even though the answer was obvious. Without a word, Liam kept walking toward me, and I nervously looked down and tugged at my shirt hem, simultaneously scared and excited because I knew this was it—this time I wasn't going to run.

The minute he was within arm's reach, Liam was backing me against my car, planting his hands on the hood to trap me in. It was like a plane crash, the way it happened all of a sudden, as if our bodies were set to collide and our minds had nothing to do with it. Without warning, I felt his mouth on mine, his tongue moving past my lips. Excited prickles nipped along the surface of my skin as I kissed him back, grabbing at the back of his neck like I was hungry for him. His mouth tasted faintly, deliciously, of whisky, and the day-old scruff on his chin tickled my face. He started to lift me up against the car, but I struggled to keep my feet on the ground.

"Maybe we should go somewhere," I said halfheartedly. But when he backed away, I reached out and drew him in again.

"Tell me you want me," he said, his pelvis grinding into mine. I could feel his half-formed erection against my hip bone, reminding me of the time the sailing instructor had pressed himself against me at the bar.

"I want you," I said, hardly able to believe that the Liam of my daydreams was now here, in the flesh. I pulled him in for another kiss, relishing the taste of him, our tongues teasing into each other's mouths. Finally, I became conscious of the fact that we were right in front of my boss's house. "Not here," I said, glancing at Julien's car in the driveway.

Liam kissed my neck ravenously, and I responded by planting my hands against his hips to hold him back. "Then where?" he said.

"Uh…" I looked over, surveying the scene at Julien's house. There was a gate around the side that would take us to the guest-house, but I didn't want to risk being seen or heard. I searched my brain for alternatives while Liam reached his hand inside the waistband of my jean shorts and over my underwear.

"I wanna fuck you so hard."

Wait, fuck? Already? For a split second, I had forgotten the reality of who Liam was. Things were moving fast, but I didn't want him to stop either.

"You want me, don't you? I got your lacy panties all wet." He spoke at half volume into my ear as he began to move his hand against my sex, lifting my entire body up as he brought his hand forward, then inching me back down. I let myself give in, for-getting where I was. My head dropped back and I gazed at the stars as I felt his hands, cool against my skin. His touch was per-fect, like he knew my body through and through. I had dreamed about this, awake, asleep, semiconscious, but the real-life version was better than anything I could have imagined. Liam was obvi-ously an expert—capable, determined, in control—but he was also soft, intuitive, familiar.

"Not here," I said again, even more halfheartedly.

"Shhh…" Liam had found my clitoris and was circling it with his index and middle fingers. He expertly danced around it, hov-ering above it, only hitting the spot every few strokes.

I wanted to make noise, moan with delight, but I was too afraid of anyone overhearing. The only thing I could think to do was bite down on my right hand to muffle the inevitable noises that would escape. *This is how it feels when someone knows what they want and how to get it,* I thought. He kept the circling up with his right hand while the other found my right nipple through my shirt, plucking at it lightly.

I stayed, head tilted back, as Liam's hand slipped inside my shirt and bra and grasped at my breasts. I was so focused on his touch, his every move, that I had to remind myself to breathe as one of his fingers navigated the wetness between my legs and pushed inside me. I felt a little spike of pain and drew in a sharp breath. Then there was another finger inside me, his hand still moving back and forth, back and forth.

Nothing is ever quite like we expect, but in this moment I felt as if I were watching the movie version of my life—real and unreal at the same time. Liam and I were in perfect sync. Our bodies moved like one and every time we looked into each other's eyes, it was clear how much we both wanted this. Nothing about it felt strange or dangerous, the way it had the other night at the restaurant when I had felt so wary of him. And it wasn't just physical, whatever was happening here. His longing was written across his face, and I'm certain he could see mine. I had been thinking about him nonstop, and he had been thinking about me too. We were two lost souls finding a momentary refuge in each other, breathing a sigh of relief as our bodies came together.

He kissed up and down my neck and my cheeks, then zeroed in on my mouth again. We parted our lips at the same time, and when our tongues met, I shivered. Added to the sensation of Liam's mouth and fingers penetrating me in perfect unison was the warmth of his legs as mine squeezed against them. The thrill of it all made me come faster than I ever had in my life.

"You feel that?" he asked as I gulped a swallow of air and whimpered.

"Yes." I nodded, my eyes fluttering open.

"The muscles in your pussy are fucking insane," he said, pulling his fingers out of me as I pulsed and contracted around them, my body not ready to let him go.

"Can we get in your car now?" I asked, a hint of begging in my voice. I had turned a corner. All I could think of now was Liam inside me. I wanted him right away, not to mention later that night, the next morning, and every day for the rest of my life—the thoughts of an addict.

He didn't have to be asked twice. The headlights of his car flashed as he pushed a button on his keychain and we hurried inside. The leather interior smelled new. I found the scent arousing as I smoothed my hands against the seat.

"Drive around the corner," I instructed.

Liam blindly followed orders as I studied him from the side, trying to memorize the chiseled jawline and slightly imperfect nose that looked as though it may have been broken once or twice. In the time that I had noticed his car in my rearview mirror, my infatuation had intensified by a thousand, and I knew I couldn't fight it. I was wired for obsession, and Liam, in this moment, was the perfect object of desire. As he shifted in his seat, I wanted to dive out of mine and plant myself on top of him, recklessly straddle him like some girl in a music video. I had an undeniable need bubbling up inside me to have him right then and there, in my mouth, between my legs, on top of me, behind me, wherever I could get him. Not since freshman year, in my skinny phase, had I felt so sexy and turned on. Despite a nagging awareness that he was light-years out of my league, the incongruity of his hotness with my relative frumpiness was almost liberating. No one would have placed us together in a lineup, but whatever it was, it was working.

He pulled over on another neighborhood street and parked in a dim spot between the streetlights.

Instant panic set in the minute I considered the reality of our surroundings—that this was where Liam and I were going to have sex. The idea didn't exactly sit well in my prudish brain. "Hey, I've got a better idea," I said, remembering the one secret getaway I had in this town. "Do you know where Oceanside Plaza is?"

Liam looked at me with an eyebrow inadvertently raised as he turned the car off. "That's ten minutes away. I want you now."

His green eyes had turned dark, serious. I glanced around, unsure where or how we planned to do it in his tiny car, and heard his seat belt unclick. Silently, Liam got out and walked around to my door, swinging it open wide. Although I was apprehensive about what was coming next—would we do it in the grass? Against one of the bulky stucco-housed mailboxes?—I trusted him enough to take his hand and follow him around to the back of the car, where he pinned me against the sloped trunk.

I had never had sex in public. Nowhere near it—never even outside of the bedroom. If someone had asked me two hours ago whether I'd even be capable of such an act, I would have said absolutely not. But I was operating outside of reason at this point and falsely comforted by the fact that none of this felt quite real. My hands found their way to his belt buckle, but they weren't doing the job fast enough. Liam shoved them out of the way and ripped the jeans down his legs.

Underneath, he had on black boxer briefs that bulged with a massive hard-on. My jaw practically hit the floor at the sight of it. I shouldn't have been surprised, but I was. Unabashed, I stared as he pulled down his boxers to reveal the biggest male organ I had ever encountered, both long and wide but also smooth and perfectly shaped. Of course, I didn't have much to compare it to, given it was only the second one I'd ever seen in person, but I sensed that by general standards it must be in the top one percentile. Which was confirmed when he removed a magnum condom from his jacket and tore at the package with his teeth. I imagined myself detailing this to Gracie, trying to think which little tidbits would make it into the retelling. She probably wouldn't believe me no matter how realistic the account.

It was around then that I felt my knees start to buckle and my vision blur. Too bad we weren't in Victorian England, with smelling salts at the ready. *If you miss this, I will kill you!* I thought, coaching myself to remain conscious and counting backward from ten. Liam undid my jean shorts and let them drop to the ground, along with my lacy panties that were steeped in my wetness. Sliding his hands back up my sides, he kissed me hard, then grabbed underneath my butt and lifted me against the car. I wrapped my legs around his waist as he rocked his hips to and fro, teasing me with the tip of his erection. The sensation revived me as a new wave of yearning took over. I wanted him so badly I could taste it, but when he finally started to thrust inside me, I tensed up, scared it wouldn't fit.

Liam seemed to be thinking the same thing. "Are you a virgin?"

I shook my head no.

"But this isn't something you do a lot, is it?"

I shrugged. "Why?"

"Because I want to know that you want this."

"I do. I want it," I said, clenching his shoulders for emphasis.

"All right. Just tell me if it's too much. I don't want to hurt you."

"You won't," I promised, even though I knew Liam was quite capable of hurting me in more ways than one. "Please, I want to feel you."

"Good," he said, then growled playfully, ramming into me

with a force I wasn't prepared for. I yelped in pain but quickly felt the warmth of him spread throughout my body.

"Stay there a second," I pleaded, reeling from the fullness of his cock piercing through me like a fleshy sword. I groaned as quietly as possible as he began to move in and out, at first slowly and then faster and with more force.

"You're so tight. Like a wet little glove," he said, his breathing heavy with effort. I could feel the little hairs on my neck rising and falling in time with his exhales.

Seconds passed that seemed like minutes and vice versa. I lost all sense of time with Liam inside me—there were no worries about the future or the past, just this moment. Again, I gazed at the stars, then down at his beautiful face, which was twisted into a grimace but still undeniably handsome. My body ached with desire. Even as he plunged my depths, I wanted him farther in. If he could overtake me entirely, it wouldn't be enough. I wondered if anyone had ever wanted someone as much as I wanted him right now. Or if it was at all possible that Liam wanted me just as badly, which—unbelievable though it was—it seemed like he did. For those few, ecstatic moments, we were forces of nature, dipping into each other like two desert-worn nomads diving into a pool of pristine water.

"I'm gonna come," he said into my ear, his voice gruff and insistent.

"No, please. Not yet," I begged. Desperate for more, I clenched the muscles inside me around his pulsing erection.

But Liam didn't slow down. He pushed again and again and smashed his face into my neck. I felt speared, owned, like I had no control but I wanted it that way. I could have died right then and there. Every inch of me was tingly and numb at the same time. Buzzing. Liam panted against the base of my neck and groaned.

He kept moving, but slower and slower. I felt him release, but he didn't stop. Neither of us wanted it to end.

"Mischa," he said, as if reminding me of the name I had forgotten.

No! Too soon! I panicked, feeling him shudder, then gently pull out. My quick, shallow breaths reverberated against his leather jacket. I wanted to rewind the movie to five minutes ago and pause it forever. I had the same sad helplessness that overcame me whenever I reached the bottom of a bag of potato chips, but multiplied. For a moment, we stood there motionless and expectant, as if someone was about to arrive and tell us what came next. Liam knelt down to face me, looking into my eyes as if they held the answer. I smiled and searched his face in return.

Then, as if he'd just remembered he had somewhere to be, he yanked the condom off, tossed it into a storm drain, and put his pants back on in a hurry. My self-consciousness returning in full force, I did the same, tugging my jean shorts back over the tops of my thighs. Buttoning them took an embarrassing amount of effort.

"You want a ride back?" I heard him ask, his eyes averted as he headed for the driver's side of the car.

"Sure," I answered, frowning at the notion he would even ask. I glanced around at the surrounding houses, down the sidewalk toward the dark end of the street, to make sure no one but myself was witnessing this pathetic aftermath, and got back into the car.

We drove the short distance to Julien's without talking. I was utterly confused that things could turn so quickly after what we had just shared and clung to the hope that maybe I was just missing something, that things were actually okay. From the side, I studied Liam's face but saw nothing of the determination or resolve that had been there earlier. Instead, there was shame and emptiness, and then I got it. Just like I loved a slice of pizza before it went into my mouth and hated it once it was down my throat, Liam felt that way about me now that I had been consumed. I had been to enough meetings to get it, even if I didn't want to. The shame he felt came over me too. I wanted to curl up into a ball, make myself invisible, the way I'd toss out an empty pizza box so I didn't have to look at it anymore. This was not a feeling I wanted to experience in the presence of another person. It was a loneliness that demanded aloneness. As he turned the corner onto Julien's street, I glanced one last time at the stars through his sunroof and noticed the harsh, impersonal scent of leather that pervaded the car.

* * *

By Sunday afternoon, the reality had settled in that Liam was not coming back for a do-over. He wasn't knocking down Julien's front door demanding to see me or following my car in traffic, even though I kept checking for him in the rearview mirror. He hadn't magically procured my phone number. He had probably forgotten my name, for all I knew. It was exactly what I had feared when he had so unceremoniously dropped me off at Julien's house on Friday night: The most amazing, unforgettable, mind-blowing night of my life was, for Liam, just another empty one-night stand.

I hadn't slept at all the night it happened and didn't fare much better on Saturday. So when the time came for my weekly trip to Isabella's, I seriously thought about canceling. Then I remembered how skinny she had looked the last time I saw her, and the half pound of grass-fed butter I had purchased last week for the express purpose of sneaking it into her food, and made haste to her condo.

"What is wrong with you?" she asked for the fifth time as I overpeeled a carrot, barely holding back tears. "You're infusing my food with sadness! I will die if I eat this!" she exclaimed.

"I'm sorry. I'm fine, really. I must have PMS," I said.

Isabella winced at the crack in my voice. "Don't try that with me. I'm too old. What happened?"

I looked across the counter into her large brown eyes, which appeared haggard under her penciled-in eyebrows. Instead of saying anything, I just shook my head until she walked over and removed the peeler from my hand. "Let's take a ride, shall we?"

In her retirement community–issued golf cart, Isabella drove me to the eighth hole of the golf course, otherwise known as her "thinking perch," just down the street from her house. It was early afternoon, hot and muggy and bright enough that nobody was outside. As the cart came to a stop at the edge of the green, we were surrounded by nothing but silence and an endless stretch of crisp, pristinely mowed grass.

"Did somebody die?" she asked, sounding grave.

"No." I sounded as if I wished someone had.

"Then what, darling? You have my undivided attention."

I sighed, knowing she would get it out of me sooner or later. "I slept with someone."

"Well that's cause for celebration, is it not?"

"It was a one-night stand."

"Even better!"

I shook my head. "I feel horrible."

"That will pass," she said. "Are you in love?"

I shook my head again. "That's the pathetic part. I mean, I hardly know him." I shifted in my seat to face her. "It's Liam. I told you about him. The sex addict."

Isabella coughed out a laugh. "Ha! There's no such thing."

"I think it's pretty real. He goes to meetings for it."

"Well, if there's meetings for it, I guess that makes me a sex addict too. Except I've been in severe withdrawal for the past ten years. And look! I haven't died!"

She got out of the cart and crossed her arms, walking onto the golf course in her prim white ballet flats. I followed her out, wishing I had a hat as the sun beat down from directly above. "This is the Australian, no?" she asked, raising a bony hand to block the sun from her eyes. I nodded in response. "So how was it, Fluffy?" She had co-opted my mother's nickname for me ever since I had told her about it. She tended to use it whenever she noticed I was down, which seemed counterintuitive, but I don't think Isabella had ever fully grasped that it was a reference to my weight.

"It was good," I lamented.

"You don't do that very often, do you?" she said.

I shook my head, wanting to cry for the millionth time that weekend as I stared into the distance, cursing my weakness. I thought of grief-stricken Julien and how he managed to drag himself out of bed every morning and put on a brave face for the day, raising a teenage daughter, writing a book. In comparison, my problems were trifling. *What was I even so sad about?* I hardly knew Liam, yet he had gotten under my skin more than anyone I had ever met. I wanted to know him and desperately wanted him to know me. Half of me believed we were kindred spirits. The other half thought that must be a sham if he could walk away so easily.

"Well, I'll let you in on a little secret," Isabella said, and sauntered up to me, playfully grabbing my elbow. "You got the best of him! That's all he's good for."

I sighed, inconsolable. "I know you think like that, but I don't."

"This isn't opinion I'm giving you. It's fact. There's only a few people on this earth—only a few men, I should say—who will ever really care about you and whom you will care about. And even then, it probably won't last. But this one? He doesn't sound like he's on the short list. So you got the best of him. See?"

I nodded, mostly to appease her. As much as I wanted to think like Isabella, or Gracie for that matter, there was no changing the fact that my heart was highly breakable, prone to unrealistic flights of fancy. Still, I continued to take in her words, even after I'd coached her through every last bite of her dinner, stowed away the rest of the red beans and rice and chicken étouffée I had made in Pyrex dishes, and driven home. Just before bed, after eating a grotesque combination of snacks in what must have equated, calorie-wise, to an eight-course dinner, I repeated her assessment of the situation like a mantra—*I got the best of him... I got the best of him*—then collapsed from exhaustion into a (mercifully) dreamless sleep.

In the morning, for a few blissful hours, I felt magically recovered. With Cecile's blessing, I brought my juicer in from the trunk of my car and made a large batch of "Rise and Revitalize" juice—something I was in the process of perfecting for my cleanse—with organic produce I had rushed out to buy first thing. Although she turned up her nose at the ingredients (dandelion greens, beets, ginger, and bee pollen among other things), Cecile drank the concoction without gagging.

"Is this gonna make me skinny?" she asked after gulping down all eight ounces of it and examining the greenish-red sediment left behind in her glass.

I hesitated before answering such a loaded question. "Well, not in and of itself, but once I have my whole cleanse perfected, yes. Weight loss will definitely be one of the benefits."

"So what else do you have to do? For the cleanse, I mean?" Cecile was now hovering over the juice pitcher and sniffing the drink as if she was still forming her opinion on whether or not it sucked.

Oh no. This is dangerous territory, I thought. I wanted to say that a teenage girl shouldn't be cleansing at all, but I didn't want to make her feel bad for being curious. "It's just a mixture of juices and healthy foods. I haven't finished working it out yet," I said. In truth, like most other cleanses, it was an agonizing, ten-day, liquid-only affair, the goal of which was to rejuvenate your insides and outsides and do the work of three months' dieting in a fraction of that time. The difference between mine and the other ones out there, I hoped, would be the "illusion of fullness." I wasn't quite there yet…

Cecile lowered her voice and leaned across the counter in my direction. "I wanna lose fifteen pounds. Can you help me?"

No, no, no, no, no. "You need to wait until you're done growing to worry about that," I said matter-of-factly, taking it upon myself to act as an authority. On the one hand, I knew exactly how she felt, having wanted the exact same thing at her age, but I could guess the right and wrong ways to answer. "Eat healthy, stop when you're almost full, and get involved in physical activities that make you happy. Do you play sports?"

"I swim. I used to play tennis with my mom too. Do you play?"

"No, I wish I did."

"That's okay. I wouldn't want to play with you anyway." She looked me up and down. "You're probably too slow." With that, she picked up her bejeweled iPhone and shuffled out of the room.

I winced in a delayed reaction to Cecile's comment, which was an obvious dig at my weight. I had forgotten how mean teenage girls could be. The tiniest part of me wanted Liam to magically appear so that I could drag him into the house, point him out, and say, "See this? Look who I slept with the other night! A god among men, that's who! So keep the body snarking to yourself!" But my affiliation with that god among men was not one that currently filled me with pride, and his "approval" of my body, as I now understood, was no more than a transient, passable attraction to a willing and available subject.

The fact was, I cared whether or not Cecile liked me, accepted me, thought of me as attractive, because I needed her and Julien more than ever now. With every passing day, they felt more and more like family, and I'd always wanted a sister or a brother, even if that meant enduring her adolescent mood swings.

Alone in the kitchen, I cleaned up the mess from my juicer and thoughts of Liam popped into my head like pernicious little fruit flies. I reacted by swatting at the air, as if something so simple could make them go away.

Chapter 7

Julien and I had driven to campus separately because he had a meeting or somewhere else to be that afternoon—I couldn't remember. When I got back to my car in the parking lot by the lit building, there was a note tucked under one of my windshield wipers that read: "I need to see you. Meet me at Trio @ midnight. I'll leave the back door open—L."

My initial reaction was to crumple the paper in my hand and search the parking lot for a trash can. Then, on second thought, I uncrumpled it and read it over again, studying the precise block letters. It surprised me that Liam had nice penmanship. It surprised me, too, that he knew where to find me, not to mention that he had recognized my car and written me a note in the first place. He should have forgotten about me by now. Realistically, a girl like myself was a dime a dozen in his world. But somehow this had happened. Out of sheer curiosity, I had no choice but to follow Liam's trail of breadcrumbs back to the fancy restaurant he owned across town.

When I got there hours later, the back door was ajar as promised. I made my way quickly across the darkened parking lot, noting that there were two other cars there, not one. When I entered the kitchen, only half the ceiling lights were on, and I almost tripped over a mop handle that had tipped over from its resting place on the wall, but I caught myself just in time. Putting the mop back upright, I heard a faint sound, like a tiny squeal, and moved into the dining room, taking smaller and smaller steps as I heard another, more intense squeal. As I got closer to the sound, I determined that it was coming from a woman. For some reason, at first I worried that Liam was hurting her, but then I came to my senses and realized they were having sex. Someone else had gotten to him first. How was this possible? Had he left fifteen notes exactly like mine lying on other car windshields around town? *Probably,* I figured. Liam, of all people, must be aware that successful booty calling was a numbers game. Apparently, I had become jaded overnight.

Liam's office was down a short corridor, past the bathrooms. The door had a large glass pane that offered a view inside, only somewhat obstructed by wooden blinds hanging on the opposite side of the door. Like the hero in an action movie, I slid my back against the wall and craned my neck to peek through the glass pane. In a strange twist, I felt curious without being angry or upset. More than anything, I just wanted to see.

"Oh shit! Fuck me!" the woman cried, her bare buttocks buoyed up against the edge of his desk as Liam propped his hands on her shoulders.

Shoving aside a laptop and stacks of paperwork, Liam, who was fully dressed except for the pants dangling around his ankles, repositioned the girl so that she was lying on her back. I could see her muscular legs and arms reaching up for him, begging him to take her. This was not the lithe model type I'd pictured him with. She was more like a stocky personal trainer with small, pert breasts that sat atop her sternum like pectoral muscles that had been slightly inflated.

"Fuck me, fuck me, fuck me, fuck me," she demanded as Liam's massive cock came into my view before disappearing inside her. She was tan, her muscled body slick with perspiration. I watched in awe as she groped him, then touched her own breasts as he thrust inside her, gritting his jaw.

I couldn't believe what I was seeing. I'd never been witness to real live sex before—I had hardly even watched pornography. The sights and sounds of it were titillating. My self-awareness melted away as I plastered myself against the glass door, nose practically smashing against the glass as I drank in the scene.

Pulling out, he slid his hands up the back of her legs, pushing them up so they rested against the length of his body as he went at it again.

Don't stop, I thought, then, *Holy shit! I am a voyeur. How did I not know this?* I inched forward for an even better view. I didn't want to get caught, but at the same time, I couldn't stop watching. Is this why he'd invited me here? Had he assumed I wouldn't be able to resist the sight of him doing what he'd done to me to someone else? Did he instinctively know that I'd be turned on?

I could see his erection now that her legs were pinned back. It was moving in and out of her in time with her own thrusts, like they were two parts of a well-oiled machine. The force of him pushed her farther and farther over the edge of the desk so that her head was hanging back now. Lost in the peep show, I let out a little sigh, which prompted Liam to whip his head around and catch a glimpse of me through the blinds.

Panicked, I hurried back toward the kitchen.

"Hey!" he called to me as he emerged from his office. I froze in place, feeling terrified and culpable, as if I had done something really wrong. I had almost forgotten it was Liam who had asked me here in the first place.

Liam held his unbuttoned pants at his waist as he sidled up to me, his eyes squinted. My heart was pounding as he leaned in and gently kissed my cheek.

"Hi. I'm sorry you had to see that," he said, his lips trailing down to my neck.

"I liked it," I said, just as surprised as he was to hear the words come out of my mouth.

"Oh yeah?" He looked me in the eye, a little flicker of excitement in his own.

I nodded and Liam did the same, biting his grinning lips as he grabbed my hips and led me into the darkened dining room, back to the table where he'd first tried to seduce me. There was nothing to do but let it happen. He was like the undertow and I was the reckless beachgoer who had swum out into the surf zone. As he stripped off my shirt and jeans and laid me out on the table in nothing but my white cotton panties and mismatched black lace bra, the other girl, completely naked, appeared behind him.

"This is Hadara," he said.

I looked at the girl, who greeted me by tickling the inside of my knee that was bent over the edge of the table. "Nice panties," she said. "I'd like to take them off of you."

I wasn't sure where this was going, or if I was really prepared for it, but I did nothing to protest. She was so muscular, almost manly in her physique, and she possessed a forceful, sexual energy that, much like Liam's, seemed undeniable. Liam moved to the side of the table and stroked my hair as Hadara spread my legs using the length of her forearms. Hovering over me, she pulled my bra down and pushed up my breasts as she sucked at each nipple, biting at the tips of them gently with her teeth, then licking up to my neck.

I turned to Liam, beckoning him with my eyes. He reassured me with a smile. Even though I was in over my head, his presence lulled me into a kind of trance. He leaned in and kissed my forehead, whispering into my ear that I was beautiful, that he'd been dreaming of watching me. Meanwhile, Hadara's hand slipped inside my underwear, her fingers expertly maneuvering between my legs.

"Have you ever been with a girl?" she asked.

"What?" I exclaimed, suddenly confused by her presence, as if I had imagined her this whole time.

"I said have you ever been with a GIRL?" Her voice became incredibly loud, as if she were yelling into my ear. I heard a knocking sound, faint at first, then louder and louder.

"Somebody should get the door," I muttered. "There's somebody outside."

Liam looked at me like I was crazy. "What door?"

"Somebody's knocking!" I said, louder this time.

"But there is no door. Look around you." He spread his arms wide, and I saw that the room was a pitch-black void.

* * *

The knocking was insistent. I woke up in a sweat. Unlike the morning after Liam and I had had sex, I now had to convince myself that nothing had happened, although I was in a similar state of disbelief. The dream had been so vivid, so real. The woman even had a name, Hadara—did she exist? I wanted to call him and ask, to fact-check my own subconscious as if I were writing a term paper about superfoods and needed to make a footnote.

Becoming aware of the actual knocking at my door, I realized this was why I woke up. Someone was really knocking. It was probably Julien. *Yikes.*

"Mischa?" Sounding insistent, he called to me from outside as I scrambled out of bed. Despite my efforts not to, I was squinting at him like a mole when I opened the door in my ratty boxers and T-shirt. Julien, of course, was looking put together in dark jeans and a pale blue button-down.

"Listen, I'm going ahead into the office. You wanna meet me there?"

"Oh no, I overslept." I rubbed my eyes, barely awake. "I'm so sorry."

"It's fine, really. I'll just see you when you get there, okay?"

"Okay." I waved goodbye as Julien hurried off, then shuffled back to the bed and checked my phone—it was nine o'clock already. My alarm should have gone off at seven-thirty, but I had no recollection of waking up. I'd probably turned it off mid-sex dream. My heart started to race a little as I worried about what Julien must be thinking. Of course he had to see me in my worst sleeping outfit, a pair of too-tight boxers and a paint-splattered Dolly Parton concert T-shirt; I probably had the look of someone recovering from a late-night bender. The only thing I could do was pull myself together and make it to the office as quickly as possible.

In the shower, I tried to get my mind clear, but images from my dream kept running through my head. After seeing Julien, the fantasy threesome I'd been having seemed particularly wrong, like my father had just caught me making out with a juvenile delinquent. I thought about how Julien would view Liam if they ever met, almost certain he would disapprove.

My innocent, romantic side didn't understand how Liam still

had such a hold over me. Couldn't I see that he had used me and thrown me away? Then again, I was only human. My brain was bound to run wild with all sorts of thoughts and sex dreams about him because he was beautiful, and dangerous, and had an Australian accent, but most important, because I had slept with him *in real life*, making him one of only two people I could honestly say that about. The only way I was going to stop thinking about him was by sleeping with someone else, and the odds of that were exceedingly low. Nobody wins the lottery twice.

* * *

I rushed to meet Julien at his office, but it still took me forty-five minutes. When I walked in, he was absorbed in a book. A few seconds passed before he realized I was there.

"Hey, sleepyhead," he finally acknowledged me with a wink. *You're not in trouble,* said the look on his face.

Thank God, mine replied.

"I'm so sorry, I must have turned my alarm off in my sleep—"

"Judging by the sound of it, you were having some kind of dream."

Oh no. I blushed what I'm sure was a garish shade of red, then tried to cross my arms over my chest in the most casual way possible. "Really? I don't remember. I think I was dreaming about flying or something…" Lying had never been my forte, and I could tell from his face that I was only digging myself deeper. He had heard me moaning, or saying something dirty in my sleep, if not both.

"Listen." He leaned forward, holding out the book in his hand for me to take. "Can I get you to xerox this? Make two copies. In one of them, highlight all the quotes about race. Anything on the topic whatsoever—food, modes of dress, personal hygiene, nothing's too boring. It might take a couple days."

"Okay, no problem." I took the book and studied its title, something overly long and dryly academic. At least it would be a new distraction, albeit one that sounded pretty boring.

"You haven't had any problems with the copy machine at the library, have you?"

I shook my head. I did not elaborate that spending eight hours in the corner of the library hovered over a copy machine with a traveling beam of light that blinded me each time I forgot to put the cover down sometimes caused me to question my sanity.

"Good. Hey, Mischa, I really appreciate all the grunt work you're doing. I'm gonna find a way to make it up to you, I swear." Julien smiled, baring his trademark gapped teeth. The smile was infectious; I had caught it by the time he turned his attention back to his laptop and started typing away again. On my way out I saluted him, referencing our little in-joke from that day we had eaten tacos on the beach, and he brought his hand up to salute me back.

* * *

"Yo, sexy secretary! You pregnant with the old man's child yet?" Gracie greeted me with her usual onslaught of provocations when I called her at lunchtime, sprawled on the concrete steps in front of the library.

"No, but I might be impregnated by the Xerox machine before the summer's over, depending on how many copies of *entire* books he wants me to make." *Or by Liam's love child,* I thought, realizing I could no longer hold back on telling her the news. It was bubbling inside me like pressurized fizzy water, ready to spew all over the kitchen counter after a bumpy ride home from the grocery store.

"Well, if it makes you feel any better, I have been given the task of reorganizing the supply room here. How these people can fill an entire room with office supplies, I have no idea. The natural foods lobby is more powerful than we think. And in need of many, many highlighters. Anyway, listen, I gotta tell you about this junior senator I met at a charity brunch this weekend. Did you know it was possible to meet someone at a brunch?"

Before I could stop her to get the Liam news off my chest, she was off and running, detailing her latest boy-chasing exploits. Gracie was almost as bad as me with her obsessions; the difference was she usually managed to ensnare her objects of desire. She was persistent and confident where I took no for an answer before the question was even posed.

"Gracie, I hate to interrupt—" I cut in.

"You wouldn't believe it if you saw him, in his three-piece suit. He's got like seven names that end with a Roman numeral. So yeah, he's basically a blueblood nightmare. Did I say he was from Rhode Island? Well, he is. So why am I surprised?"

"Gracie—" I tried again, to no avail.

"Junior senator from Rhode Island, look him up. Anyway, we've been e-mailing. I predict a *very* patriotic Fourth of July in my future."

"Gracie, you've got to stop talking, I have something to tell you!" I practically shouted.

"What?! I thought you said nothing was happening with him. What are you not telling me?"

"It's not Julien. It's someone else. And I have to tell you because I haven't told anyone but Isabella and it's killing me," I said.

"Well, give me the goods, gringo!" she responded in haste.

"Ok…" I squinted up at a puffy white cloud that was temporarily shielding me from the sun and drew in a breath of air. "I slept with some guy," I said, scrunching my face as if I had just ripped off a Band-Aid. The irony of my word choice did not escape me. *Slept with some guy.* Could it really be called sleeping together if it takes place against a car?

"Who?" Gracie said, in deep and utter shock. "Frank? Michael? Charlie? Samuel?" She named every guy from our major, as if they hadn't decided against me four years ago.

"No. No one you know."

"Seriously? Who is it, then?"

"It's kind of embarrassing."

"Cough it up, sister. This is landmark. You haven't gotten laid since Bradley!"

I winced at the sound of his name: Bradley. The guy from freshman year, the one who had broken my heart and ripped it into tiny shreds without the slightest hint of remorse. "Hey!"

"I know, I know. The name we shall not speak, I'm sorry."

"It's okay," I said, recalling the pact that Gracie and I had made spring semester of freshman year to never speak Bradley Griffin's name again. At first, we had done it so as not to get caught talking about him, because that's all I had done for a solid nine months (aka the human gestation period—we had called it my grief baby) right after he had dumped me. After that, the pact had remained in place so that I would finally get over him, because somehow just his name had the power to bring it all back at once—the pain, the rejection, the embarrassment. He had been a premed student, super smart and just cute enough for me to fall for him instantly when we had met in Intro to Psychology, an elective we were both taking in an attempt to figure out our own messed-up psyches. But the minute he had realized the extent of my eating problems, he had decided "we were no good for each other," which really meant that I had been no good for him. The epiphany had come right around the time I had gained back thirty of the forty pounds that I had lost from the tapeworm. Needless to say, it had been a harsh pill to swallow, and though I had mostly recovered from the heartbreak, I still thought of him in times of weakness.

"Listen, I'm gonna have to go any second now. They want me to take 'meeting minutes,' whatever that means."

"I think it just means take notes."

"Right. Anyway, speak now or forever hold your peace, because these assholes are on a strict deadline to give me carpal tunnel syndrome before the summer's over."

"Ha. I'm glad we both resent our basic duties," I said, examining my fingernails, still a little thrown by the B-word.

"I know, it's very postcollegiate of us. Now spill." I heard a crinkle of paper and the undeniable sound of my friend smacking on chewing gum.

"Okay. He's a stranger. I met him at a Sex Addicts Anonymous meeting. He's from Australia and he looks like a male model. I know these things sound untrue, but they aren't, I promise. Oh, and he owns a restaurant—Trio, the expensive one on the west side."

A voice piped in the background on Gracie's end. She muttered a hurried "okay" before whispering into the phone. "Oh. My. Holy. Fuck," she said. "Sex Addicts Anonymous? Australia? Model? Expensive restaurant? These sound like buzz words from some fantasy role-playing scenario. Are you delusional?"

"I swear I am not lying. Delusional? Perhaps. But I did sleep with him."

I heard a knock and more muttering on Gracie's end.

"Ugh!!!" she finally groaned. "I gotta go! Send me a link to his Facebook, okay?"

"I don't have his Facebook. I don't even know his last name!" I shouted, but Gracie had already hung up. As a younger student brushed past me, a dial tone kicked in.

* * *

At five o'clock, I made my way back across the quad and into the old brick Lit building where Julien's office was located on the second floor. In the middle of a typing spree, he glanced up distractedly as I placed the book and the clean copy I'd made on his desk and told him I'd be done with the highlighted version by end of day tomorrow. I had secret plans to reward myself for the monotony of the day with a trip to Damiano's, the only place in town that sold pizza by the slice, so I unintentionally sounded a little clipped when asking, "Is there anything else you need before I go?"

"Uh, yes, actually. I need your company tonight, if you're available," he said.

Oh no, I'm going to be trapped in this office, my pizza-driven brain fretted. *He'll probably want to order Indian.*

"Here's the deal—today is Cecile's birthday eve. Tomorrow we'll celebrate at her grandmother's house, but tonight I made reservations somewhere special and I'd like for you to join." Julien finished typing something and glanced up at me with a formal smile.

"Really?" I said, doubtful that Cecile would want me there.

"Why not?"

"Oh, I don't know. I don't want to spoil Cecile's special birthday dinner. She hardly knows me." I imagined myself alone in the house when they went out for dinner, free to binge comfortably in the kitchen—something I hadn't had the luxury of doing since moving in—and prayed he would see the logic in my argument.

"Please, I bore her to death. She'll be happy to have another girl around." He winked. "We'll leave at seven."

Chapter 8

I didn't realize the restaurant was Trio—Liam's Trio—until we were pulling into the parking lot. That's when my heart began to palpitate like I had just snorted excessive amounts of cocaine. The possibility that Julien was taking Cecile for such an expensive dinner on her fourteenth birthday hadn't even crossed my mind. And yet, here we were. At least I had worn my good dress—a black silk shift that slimmed me as much as any garment on God's green earth was capable. Still, it took me nearly a minute to follow them out of the car, trailing like a reluctant third wheel. The questions running through my mind were the obvious ones: Would Liam be here? If so, would he see me? What would he say? How would I introduce him if he approached? What would Julien think?

Inside the restaurant, my mind continued to whirl as Julien and Cecile waited at the hostess stand and I lingered behind them awkwardly. A nervous scan of my surroundings alerted me to two framed articles on the wall by the front entrance, which I immediately backed up to read. The article on top was from one of Oceanside's local magazines, *Surf & Turf*. The story was titled

"Chef Rock Star," and within the first paragraph, the author revealed Liam's last name—Harrison—and the decidedly more interesting fact that he had been lead guitarist for an Australian band called the Sad Sacks. There was even a picture of him onstage set inside a larger picture of the dining room at Trio. *Holy. Shit.*

I couldn't believe my eyes. I knew the Sad Sacks. I had to look them up on my phone to remember the name of their hit—"Ginger Snap"—but it wasn't hard to find. Later on, I realized I'd attended a music festival back in high school, and they had been on the roster. I couldn't remember seeing Liam perform, but I might have. In any case, it was breaking news that made me want to call Gracie from the bathroom with a bragging report: *"In addition to sex addict/Australian restaurateur,"* I would say, *"you can now add rock star. I slept with an* actual *rock star!"* It wasn't something I would normally broadcast, but Gracie kept a sexual bucket list and I'm pretty sure a roll in the hay with a rock star was in the top ten. But a call from the bathroom was out of the question given my general paranoia that someone (perhaps one of the incredibly good-looking waitresses that were flitting about the dining room in button-downs and ties) might overhear me. Thus, for now, there was no one with whom I could share the news—unless, of course, I wanted to simultaneously corrupt the newly fourteen-year-old Cecile and repel her father.

* * *

"Flat or sparkling?" I heard the waiter address Julien and was surprised when he turned to me instead of Cecile for feedback.

"What do you think, Mischa? Flat or bubbly?"

"I'm sorry, say that again?" I was still reeling over "Chef Rock Star" and therefore confused by the simplest of questions.

"I want sparkling!" Cecile chimed in.

Oh, right. Water.

"Sounds good to me," I said. My eyes darted around the room as if I were a Navy SEAL on a reconnaissance mission. The dining room was full but not too loud, and our table was smack in the middle. It felt like our little threesome had been put on display for others to stare and comment—*Look at this strange little group! What do you think the story is there?* Meanwhile, the question of whether or not Liam was there was killing me. Before reading that article, I hadn't assumed he was the chef in addition to being the owner. Instead of the back office that had appeared in my dream last night, Liam was probably in the kitchen, looking implausibly sexy in a white apron.

"This was my mom's favorite restaurant," Cecile announced, her eyes on me. "Have you ever been here?"

I shook my head in a knee-jerk reaction but refrained from speaking.

"You're acting weird," she observed.

"Cecile!" Julien shot his daughter a glaring look of disapproval across the table.

"No, it's all right," I said. "I was just having a déjà vu moment. Do you ever get those?"

"Doesn't that only happen to people who do drugs?"

Oh great. Here we go, I thought. The honeymoon period was officially over between Cecile and me, ever since she'd insulted me the day before. As I'd suspected, she hadn't wanted me at this dinner at all. So much for her being the little sister I'd always wanted.

"Cecile!" Julien reprimanded her again, then smiled at me apologetically. "She's in a mood today, don't you think?"

"It's my birthday. I can act however I want."

"Cheers to that!" I said, almost admiring her brazen, adolescent stubbornness, and raised my empty water glass just as the waiter appeared with our bottle of sparkling water. Taking my raised glass as a not-so-subtle hint, he poured mine first. Another waiter emerged behind him, carrying a long, rectangular white plate.

"Compliments of the chef," he said, setting it down.

My eyes bulged as Julien inspected the artful presentation of the tuna tartare we had just been gifted.

"Dad? Did you tell them it's my birthday?" Cecile sounded annoyed.

"No, honey. I promised I wouldn't, and I didn't."

Staring at this artful plate of food, "compliments of the chef," my head was off and running, interpreting the surprise as a direct message from Liam to me. I pictured us tucked away in some dark corner of the restaurant, stealing a moment together:

"How did you know I was here?"

"I would know if you were in the neighboring building, Mischa. You have a magnetic pull."

"So do you."

"See me again?"

A thoughtful pause. I glance past him, pensive. "The tuna tartare was really spectacular."

"Please. I can't function without you."

The sound of the flash on Cecile's iPhone snapped me out of it. She was taking a picture of our food as Julien stared at the plate, a wistful smile spread across his face. "They loved Renay here," he said. "Sometimes they'll send a little something out. It's a nice gesture."

Oh, yeah. Right. I should have guessed that the ghost of Renay Maxwell could trump my own, less innocent affiliation with the chef. I'm more forgettable alive than she is dead. *Ouch.*

But then, when the salad course was served, everyone got a little shot of gazpacho with crab, "compliments of the chef." And with the dinner course, we were presented with an extra side, a scrumptious cauliflower risotto with bacon. When it came time to order dessert, Cecile warned her father not to surprise her with anything because she didn't want to feel "like a fatso." So he didn't. Yet that didn't stop our waiter from returning five minutes later with caramel dark chocolate gelato, served with toasted coconut whipped cream and an almond wafer—the very dish Liam had used to lure me here in the first place. It was the final deciding vote in my mind that yes, indeed, this was about me. But what was he trying to get across by sending all of this free food to our table? *Thanks for the quick fuck?* Or, *Hey, I'm a mind-reading wizard who planted that sex dream in your head last night to see whether you'd be up for a threesome; here's some tuna tartare and soup and stuff while you think it over…*

"Would you mind asking the chef to stop by our table? I would love to thank him personally," Julien told the waiter, after he'd delivered our desserts.

"Absolutely! I'll send him right out," he promised, at which point, it took everything in me not to face-palm. I looked up at the ceiling, having the sense that it was somehow lowering down on me and only me. Why hadn't Liam sent out copious amounts of booze along with all the free food? I could really use a shot of tequila right about now.

"You're acting weird again," Cecile said, taking notice of my silent meltdown.

I shook my head. "Just more déjà vu." There was an audible tinge of panic in my voice. I needed a plan to get away from the table pronto, and for as long as possible. The thought of facing Liam for the first time since our mind-blowing, yet ultimately empty sex, with Julien and Cecile as my audience, was unbearable. But where could I disappear? To the bathroom? Maybe forever? "I need to use the ladies' room," I said.

"Me too," said Cecile when I stood up, and off we went together.

"Are you dying? Having to sit through this extremely boring dinner like you have nothing better to do?" she asked as she soaped her hands at one of the sinks. I was still in the handicapped bathroom stall, trying to manage the mounting anxiety that was shaking me like a mini-earthquake.

"Umm, not at all," I answered in a purposely strained voice, pretending to be ill. "Sorry, I'm just feeling a little off."

"It's probably from all the rich food. I bet we both just gained five pounds," Cecile said, her blatant, adolescent self-consciousness a good reminder that my inner voice too often sounded like hers: self-hating, judgmental, joyless. On an up note, her comment had placed us in the same boat, seemingly indicating that the pendulum had swung back in my favor, and she and I were comrades yet again.

"I'm sure we didn't gain five pounds. Maybe one," I conjectured, an honest estimate. "Listen, I'm gonna be here for a while. You should go ahead without me."

"Are you gonna force yourself to puke?"

"No! That's terrible!" My voice rose, more than a little frantic. "I don't do that! Never do that!"

"Fine, fine, fine. Jeez," she said.

I heard the door swing open dramatically and waited until it latched behind her, then exhaled forcefully as I entertained the questions that were running through my head. Had Liam already made it to the table? If so, what were he and Julien talking about? Would Liam mention me in my absence? There was really no telling, because I didn't know him. It had just now come to my attention that he was a famous (enough) rock star; that alone probably pointed to a level of recklessness and narcissism I could barely comprehend.

What could he be saying, though? How would he explain his acquaintance with me, if he chose to do so at all? Did he have an angle, or was he just winging it? Considering the worst-case scenario—something along the lines of Liam rehashing our rendezvous in vivid detail—I panicked. Whatever it was, the mystery was almost too much to bear. I decided I had to see it for myself.

Careful not to break into an actual run, I burst out of the bathroom high on adrenaline and snaked around the crowded dining room as quickly as possible, one hand on the back of my little black dress to make sure the hem wasn't riding up. Upon first glimpse, the scene at the table was weirder than I had expected: Liam was seated in my chair, leaning in as if he and Julien were the closest of confidants. I cleared my throat as I approached and caught my reflection in a mirror on the far wall. I looked utterly confused, horrified, and not as thin as I'd hoped.

I corrected my frazzled demeanor just slightly by putting on a fake smile and greeted everyone with a wave of the hand that went entirely unnoticed. After a few painful seconds of me standing by my occupied chair, however, Liam glanced up and greeted me cheerfully, seeming very pleased with himself. "There you are, girl of the hour."

"Mischa, you could have told us you knew the chef," said Julien in a jovial tone.

I smiled, relieved to find that the conversation was an amicable one, or, at least, politely awkward.

"Mischa's always been very private. Ever since she was a little girl," Liam said, his eyes on me, conspiratorial.

"I didn't…" I started to speak and realized I had no idea what to say. How the hell was I supposed to play along with some lie Liam had made up while I was in the bathroom? "I mean…I forgot—"

"It's true, we haven't seen each other in a very long time. And the family's so big, second cousins, third cousins, half of us in Australia. It's a wonder we even know each other. A testament to our mothers, I'd say, very tight-knit."

My eyes felt like they were leaping out of my head. I squinted to correct the problem, then glanced at Liam pointedly, trying to communicate my disbelief without words: *You told him we were related?* His eyes spoke back to me: *Yeah, what's it to you?* He was probably one of those compulsive liars who tells untruths just for the fun of it. But the blood relation part I found particularly insulting; for some reason, it signaled to me that Liam wanted nothing more to do with me sexually, because who has sex with even the most distant of relatives in 2015? I mean, yes, we were in small-town Florida, but we weren't *from* small-town Florida.

"I knew you had family in the Philippines," Julien chimed in, "but not Australia."

"Yeah. It's strange we both ended up here," I said, too baffled to elaborate.

"The world is ever so small!" Liam rose from my seat and gracefully ushered me into it.

"Thank you again for the dinner. It was wonderful." Julien jostled Cecile's knee under the table.

She forced a polite nod. "Thanks."

"Yeah, thanks, Liam," I said, attempting to sound casually familial.

He bared his teeth in a wide grin and leaned in, placing his hand proprietarily on the table in front of me as he addressed

Julien. "I'm happy to set you up. Anytime. Hope to see you again soon."

I tried to breathe in the scent of him as he hovered in front of me but couldn't get past the smells of various foods and burning candlewicks scattered about the dining room. As he moved away from us, his hand left the table and revealed a folded piece of paper he'd left by my napkin. A secret note—oh dear God! I wanted to grab it and open it right then and there but worried that Julien would notice. So I waited, aware of each second that ticked by as Julien paid for the bill, hiding the note in my palm for safekeeping.

Unfortunately, plan A, which was to read it quickly at the table after Julien and Cecile had gotten up to leave, was thwarted when Julien pulled back my chair and motioned for me to walk ahead. After that, the three of us walked outside to the parking lot together, which is when I implemented plan B, announcing that I had left my phone back at the table and running back inside. In the front lobby, I tucked myself into a corner and unfolded the note, which simply read: "Meet me out back in five. —L"

It was like the note from last night's dream but this time it was real. It was even signed with his first initial the way I had dreamt it, as if my subconscious could predict the future. The whole thing reminded me of middle school, when boys would pass messages like this to the girls they liked. I never got one, but every once in a while a friend would show me hers, and we would pore over it after school, analyzing the wording, the handwriting, the way he'd signed his name. Of course, my folded-up paper from Liam was far from some innocent love note, but my heart skipped all the same as I reread it a second and third time, searching my brain for excuses to give to Julien. *Liam's asked me to stay and chat after he's off work...My cousin needs some advice on family matters...I owe Liam some money but he's agreed to let me work it off...*

"Hey, did you find your phone?" The sound of Cecile's voice startled me as she dipped her head into the lobby.

"Oh yeah." I hid the note in my palm as I held up my clutch to indicate that the phone was inside.

"Let's go, then! I'm gonna miss my hour!" She was referring to the hour of television she was allowed to watch at night, prior to eleven p.m. Cecile propped the door open behind her as a prompt for me to follow her outside, and I did so obediently, in spite of myself.

Watching Liam's restaurant fade into the distance through the rear window of Julien's car was a mild version of torture. I hated myself for letting a bossy teenager ruin a second-night stand with a former rock star turned chef. Why couldn't I have stood my ground and used one of my bad excuses? He was probably in the back parking lot right now, standing under the one dim streetlight in his white chef's coat that somehow looked sexy despite obscuring his perfect body, wondering what the hell was wrong with me to turn him down *again*.

* * *

The ride home was strangely silent. I wasn't sure if there was a heaviness to it or if it was simply one of those comfortable silences that family members fall into after a big meal. Either way, the lack of conversation allowed me plenty of time to obsess over my missed connection.

In truth, I only had myself to blame for not staying behind, although it was easy to feel like something of a prisoner while riding in the backseat of Julien's car. I found myself wondering (and not for the first time) why I was even there. Did Julien expect me to be a confidant, or a mother figure, to Cecile? Was I supposed to bring light back into his dark and depressed house of grief? Was I the comic relief? And had he really bought Liam's story about being my cousin? Was it possible for someone to be so smart yet gullible at the same time?

When we got home, the quiet followed us inside as Cecile made a break for the living room, dying to watch her coveted hour of TV. I had a similar burning desire to be alone and had decided on an early bedtime after the promise of Liam's note had officially expired. In the kitchen, I filled a glass with water as Julien sorted through a pile of mail.

"All right, good night," I called from the back door, water glass clutched in both hands conscientiously. "Thanks again for dinner!"

"No problem, Mischa," said Julien, seemingly absorbed by the task of opening his mail.

Back in the guesthouse, I paced around like a madman. Usually I opted for rolling around in bed as I stewed, but tonight I was fired up. I took Liam's note from inside my clutch and read it again. Just the thought of the secret parking lot rendezvous he'd suggested made me sigh with disappointment. Unfortunately, he was probably cursing my name at this very moment, thinking I had stood him up. I needed to do something—at least tell him I would have stayed if I could— but I didn't have his phone number. The only option would be to swallow my pride and call the restaurant, though it took all of a few seconds to realize I had such little pride left to salvage, a desperate phone call to Liam's place of work wouldn't make much of a difference. I looked up the number and dialed, my heart fluttering nervously as I took a deep breath.

The hostess answered too soon, after only half a ring. When I stuttered out my request for Liam, I got a predictably unwelcome response. "Liam is not available right now. May I take a message?" she asked, her voice clipped.

Desperate, I threw out a little fib. "Actually, this is his cousin, Mischa. I'm calling about a family emergency."

"Oh no!" It turned out the stick-thin, doll-faced hostess whom I'd eyed suspiciously in the lobby was an easy mark. "Can I tell him which family member this is regarding?"

"Oh, he'll know." I sounded oddly confident. In truth, my hands were clammy and I was pacing the room even more frantically than before.

A flourish of classical piano hit my ears as she put me on hold, and my heart went from fluttering to pounding. Although it felt like I was calling a guy I hardly knew to ask him out on a date, I tried to remember that *he* had passed *me* the note, not the other way around. Also, we had already had sex, lest I forgot. The cat was rather removed from the bag at this point.

"That was a nice black dress you were wearing," Liam's voice chimed in on the other end of the line in a low, sexy hush.

"How did you know it was me?" I said, taken aback and flattered at the same time.

"You said you were family. I haven't got one of those. So, how'd you like the food?"

"Umm…it was amazing, actually."

"I could eat that gazpacho all day—"

"Oh my God, that was my favorite!"

"I wish I could have seen you eat it. I don't get many professional addicts in my restaurant." He chuckled in a way that seemed overly familiar, as if I really was his cousin, or an old friend.

I searched my brain for what to say next, but talk of food had totally derailed me.

"All right, well, good talking to ya," he said. "Hope that family emergency works itself out!"

"No, wait, Liam—" I raised my voice in a panic. "Can I see you later?"

Liam let out a long sigh. "I don't think it's a good idea. You were right to avoid me."

"I wasn't avoiding you! I was just…stuck with my boss and his daughter. I'm kind of like an indentured servant right now."

"Yeah, well, I think it's for the best anyway. I mean…it *is* for the best."

A loud crash interrupted, followed by a muffled male voice shouting expletives. "Listen, I gotta go," he said, distracted. "Goodbye, Mischa."

And that was it: click, dial tone, end of call. He was over it. He hadn't even said "good night"; he had said "goodbye," as if one of us were dying or heading off to Mars. And all I could think was *if only*…If only he wasn't over it. If only I had stuck around. If only we lived in a parallel universe where Liam wasn't a sex addict and I never ate high fructose corn syrup. I spent the next couple of hours tossing and turning before drifting into a restless sleep plagued by more nightmares revolving around him. The one I remembered after waking up involved a reunion of our pretend family, at which Liam revealed that we had slept together to everyone's disgust. He'd even gone into detail, telling mutual aunts and uncles about where we'd done it, what kind of bra I was wearing, the kinds of noises I made. Through it all, I stood like a pariah in the middle of the group, methodically eating the entire contents of a picnic table loaded with hot dogs, potato chips, and grocery store sheet cake. Naturally, I woke up ravenous.

Chapter 9

There was a note on the kitchen counter when I came in the next morning—*Gone to campus early. See you at my office!*—but I wasn't alone. Cecile was seated on a stool in her swimsuit, completely transfixed by something on her phone.

"Don't you have swim practice?" I asked, rooting through the refrigerator for the leftover juice from yesterday's batch.

"I'm leaving in a sec." Her voice was the distracted drone of a child sucked into a video game, and I realized she was probably lining up rows of candy or catapulting little birds at evil green pigs. I heard my own phone vibrating where I'd left it on the edge of the counter but ignored the buzz as I foraged for other snacks.

"Your phone," she said.

"I know."

Hoping she wouldn't notice, I turned my back to Cecile as I served myself some Greek yogurt from a large container that wasn't mine. I was waiting for her to ask me to give her some, too, but instead I heard her hop down from the stool and felt relieved that she was leaving.

"Droolian Poundwell?" I heard Cecile mutter, almost too softly for me to hear.

I whipped around and saw her clutching my phone, jaw agape, as my mind caught up to what was happening. *Oh Lord.* "Cecile, put that down!"

"Says Gracie: 'How goes it with our favorite lover, Dr. Droolian Poundwell?'" She leveled her eyes at me. "Is that some stupid nickname for my dad?"

I shook my head and hurried around the island, snatching my phone back from her loose grip. Cecile's expression morphed from one of disgust to a sick smile. "It's my friend's weird sense of humor," I said. "It's nothing."

"Oh, I understand. You want to have sex with my dad is what that means. You're blushing, by the way."

Instinctively, my hand found my cheek and confirmed the accusation. Only a taunting teenage girl could make me feel nervous over something as pointless as a misinterpreted text. "Cecile, believe me, your dad is not my type. My friend on the other hand…Gracie had a crush on him, okay? But she doesn't even live here anymore—"

"Oh, this is too good," she said, continuing to reel over her discovery. "You're freaking out right now."

"No, I'm not!" I stomped my foot, losing my cool. Even though she was completely off base, I knew Cecile thought I was lying, and I really didn't have the energy to convince her otherwise. "Please, just don't—"

"Don't tell my dad? Is that what you're gonna say?" She crossed her arms in a way that made me want to crawl into a hole.

"There's nothing to tell. Just please don't make this into something it's not," I said.

"You're way too young for him! And you're not his type at all. He likes thin. Like, model thin."

Letting her barb sink in, I glanced down at my phone and saw Gracie's text on the lock screen. If only I could go back in time and get to it before Cecile. But no, I had been too busy stealing Greek yogurt. "Listen, I wouldn't lie to you. I have a crush on someone but it's not your dad."

"Then who is it?" She dropped her arms and locked eyes with me.

"Remember the chef? From last night?"

"Ew, that guy's your cousin!"

I shook my head. "No, he's not actually."

Her One Direction ringtone interrupted. Cecile picked up the phone. "Hey, yeah, I'm coming. One second." She leveled her eyes at me. "You're lying. I can tell. Obviously this is a two-part episode, to be continued!"

With that, she disappeared into the hallway and out the front door, leaving me annoyed and even hungrier than before. I headed straight for the pantry and started raiding it like a dog in the trash, hoping that the right mix of foods might help me forget the nonsense that had just happened. Careful not to make too large a dent in any one thing, I pinched a couple of granola bites, a handful of cranberry nut mix, sesame sticks, Cecile's favorite chocolate chip cookies, the kettle-fried potato chips in jalapeno and barbeque flavor that I'd noticed Julien snacking on before dinner. There was also a bag of marshmallows I dared to open, then removed from the pantry entirely, thinking it was better to steal it outright than to leave the evidence. Only after I'd had enough to make my stomach hurt did I feel relieved enough to respond to Gracie, telling her what had happened with Cecile.

"Oh my God," Gracie greeted me when she called, sounding slightly panicked. "Do you want to kill me?"

"No! Are you kidding? She's just being a stupid teenager. She has this love-hate thing with me. It's really starting to get old. Anyway, I think I might just tell him, as a preventative measure." I had retreated back to the guesthouse and was pacing the short length of it. "Would you mind if I outed you?"

"Not at all. Plus, my heart has moved on."

"I just hope he believes me; otherwise it'll be awkward, and I really don't need that. Maybe I shouldn't even bring it up. It might sound weird."

"You worry too much, boo. Calm down! Breathe!"

I followed her orders, taking in air through my nostrils like I had learned in the one and only yoga class I'd ever forced myself to endure. "It's just this Liam stuff has got me so wound up."

"I know, getting laid is really complicated sometimes. Listen, regarding that, I have to tell you something," she said. "Remember the junior senator I told you about?"

"Who?"

"Junior…from…island!! I told you…Richard?…Dreamy?" Gracie's voice cut in and out, finally coming back. "We struck up an e-mail friendship after a particularly fated charity brunch?"

"Okay, yeah," I answered.

"Well don't get overexcited, but me and said junior senator had—drum roll, please—a platonic sleepover last night!" Her raised voice and subsequent pause signaled that it was my time to respond.

"That's good. I mean, no, that's great!" I said. "How old is he?"

"Thirty-six. Which is like twenty-two in D.C. years. Anyway, listen, I know what you're thinking when you hear *platonic sleepover*: friend zone. But let me tell you, this sleepover was like no other sleepover I have ever experienced. First of all: same bed. Second of all: I wore his pajamas. Third of all, and this is the most important of the alls: middle-of-the-night spooning! I pretended

I didn't wake up when he did it, but I did. And he was clearly awake; I could hear his breathing change. Anyway, it was like electric spooning. I could hardly sleep after that. We didn't wake up that way, though. Do you think if we didn't wake up that way, that he was like trying to erase that it had happened? Or do you think it's just because people move in their sleep?"

I had been trying to listen and knew from Gracie's rising inflection that she had just asked a question. However, I had been distracted by the menacing text I'd just received from Cecile: *How much is my silence worth to you?*

"Mischa?" Gracie prompted.

"What?"

"What do you think?"

"Uh…about what?"

"About the spooning!"

"Oh, I think it's great."

"Did you hear my question, though? What are you doing right now?"

"Sorry." I collapsed onto the bed. "I'm having a hard time thinking straight, between the Liam thing and Cecile now threatening me over text…"

"Right."

"Oh my God!" I flipped onto my back, remembering the big news from last night. "I didn't even tell you—we had dinner at Liam's restaurant! And guess what? He's a rock star. Can you even believe?"

"Uh-huh." Gracie's voice dropped. "I'm gonna go." She sounded angry, which surprised me because I knew from personal experience that it took a lot to make my best friend angry.

"Oh no, wait!" I said. "Ask me your question again! I'm all ears."

"No, you know what? This is what happens when you have a guy anywhere near your orbit."

"That's not true!"

"Mischa…you obsess to the point of absolute ridiculousness. I mean, we talked about Bradley for like two years straight."

"Shh, don't say that."

"Bradley, Bradley, Bradley, Bradley! I'll say it whenever I want! You dated the guy for three months!"

"Three and a half."

"Whatever! My point is, you're a much better person when there's no guy, because you're crazy when there is and there's no room for anything else. Or anyone else! You can't even listen to *one* story about my life."

My heart plummeted, knowing that her accusation was, in fact, more than a little true. I defended myself nonetheless. "Gracie, of course I can. Please, tell me."

"No, Mischa. I'll talk to you later."

"Gracie, wait! I'm sorry!" But my final pleas were met with a dial tone. She had already hung up. I texted her another *I'm sorry* and pounded Julien's old mattress in frustration.

* * *

When I showed up at his office thirty minutes later, Julien didn't seem fazed by my tardiness. In fact, he seemed mildly amused when handing over two more books for photocopying. A ridiculously unfounded fear made its way into my head: *Does he have a nanny cam trained on the pantry? Did he see me eat all his food?*

"Thanks again for last night's dinner," I said, pausing at the doorway as I contemplated whether or not to mention the

"Droolian Poundwell" text so that the non-news wouldn't come from Cecile.

A wry smile came over Julien's face. "Hey, was that guy really your cousin?"

"Pardon me?" I'd heard exactly what he said. What was I supposed to tell him?

"The chef from the restaurant? Is he really your cousin?"

"Oh…umm…" I shifted uncomfortably. I couldn't very well lie to Julien's face, especially since he already seemed to know the truth. "No," I admitted. "I don't know why I didn't say anything after we left. I felt bad that he lied to you."

Julien chuckled, and I relaxed a little. "That's okay," he said. "I don't expect you to share the details of your personal life with me. I just had a hunch. Wanted to make sure my bullshit radar still works."

"Well, he's not my boyfriend, either," I told him with an exaggerated roll of the eyes, unintentionally revealing my insecurities around Liam.

"Mmm-hmm, one of those." Julien lowered his laptop screen and leaned on the edge of the desk. "Not that you're looking for my advice, but ever since I had a daughter, I started looking at guys a whole new way, and he seems like one of those I would ban from my house."

I nodded, thinking, *You don't know the half of it.*

"You're a smart girl to be single at this age, Mischa," he said, making the false assumption that I had loads of options. "I got married young, but if I hadn't found the exact right person at such a young age, I would have waited longer. A lot longer. And you've got so much ahead of you. Grad school. Possibly a PhD if you decide to go that route—"

I tried to hide the look of confusion on my face as Julien

described this future for me. I had never thought of myself as a potential PhD candidate, although I found it flattering that he could envision it.

"And then your fate is entirely dependent on which school hires you, and believe me, relationships are mostly doomed when it comes to that. But I digress." He sat back in his chair, folding his hands across his chest. "I just think you're better off if that guy's not your boyfriend. He's got that sparkle in his eye, and it's not the right kind of sparkle."

I nodded, taking in Julien's fatherly advice like a spoonful of sour milk. He was right of course, but it was painful to hear Liam described as the guy with the wrong kind of sparkle. It only confirmed my fear that I'd imagined the underlying connection I'd felt with him. That Liam had duped me, the way he must dupe every girl.

"All right, well these books aren't gonna copy themselves!" My voice broke a little as I turned to leave.

"All right, Mischa," said Julien, and flipped his laptop screen back up.

I gave a quick wave and trudged out into the empty hallway, where I got out my phone and started to call Gracie before I remembered how our last conversation had ended.

* * *

All the copy machines were taken when I got to the library, even the one hidden behind the fourth-floor study carrels, so I decided to wait it out for a while in the drab, windowless computer lab, where e-mail and Facebook checking quickly devolved into shameless googling of Liam Harrison. As much as I wanted to take Julien's advice to heart, I hadn't been able to get Liam off my mind, and now that I knew his full name, not to mention the name of his *famous band*, I couldn't resist the Internet vortex that was calling my name.

First came an image search, which sent me to various obsessive fan sites with a seemingly endless supply of concert pics. Then there was the band's website, which taught me what kind of guitar Liam learned to play on (a Dove acoustic), his absolute favorite electric (Gibson Les Paul Junior), and his Beatles-inspired middle name (George). Then there were the album reviews, which pointed out Liam's songwriting contributions, including the fact that he'd written the music *and* the lyrics for "Ginger Snap," meaning he'd probably made a good chunk of money off that one song alone.

Who cares? The angel on my shoulder tried to talk sense into me as I scrolled down to yet another music magazine profile of Liam's old band. Gracie had been right, and the more links I clicked, the more I was proving her point. My obsessiveness was my Achilles' heel. As I typed Liam's name into the Google search box one more time, I could feel it in my bones: Self-destruction was imminent.

* * *

Tuesday, June… ?: Oceanside Rec Center Meeting
Topic of discussion: "Falling off the Wagon"
Calories imbibed: ??? (no attention span = no idea)

I hadn't seen Liam in almost a week when I showed up to my regular meeting on Tuesday night. Needless to say, I had spent the entire weekend dreaming up ways of running into him and rewarding myself with snacks whenever I actively refrained from calling the restaurant. I could think of nothing but Liam, actually, and was therefore newly grateful that my job entailed little more than flattening books against a glass surface and pressing a copy button one hundred thousand times per day. Because otherwise, I would have been completely and utterly useless. When not copying, I was eating and avoiding scales at all costs, but my ill-fitting wardrobe indicated I had gained at least five or ten pounds. I was also avoiding mirrors. The only clothes that looked halfway decent were my tentlike maxi dresses that made me look like an inflated bowling pin roaming around in search of its natural habitat, and if I so much as caught myself in the reflection of a window, it was enough to send me right back to the trough.

Yes, I felt like a literal and figurative pig. Which is why the day's topic of discussion, "Falling off the Wagon," hit a little too close to home. I contemplated leaving, but I didn't even have the willpower to manage that. When it came time for the "main share," a regular contributor named Meghan took the stage.

"How much time would you like, dear?" Sherrill, the moderator, said as she leaned forward from her perch on the side of the stage, glancing over her bifocals at Meghan while fumbling in an NPR tote bag for the stopwatch.

"Eight minutes, please." Impressively cool and collected, Meghan sat down on the chair that she'd brought up to the stage and crossed her legs. She was around my age, although I didn't recognize her from campus, and she had the accent of a local. Despite being a little overweight, she always looked put together at the meetings and knew how to dress for her shape (she was an apple, like me), which I admired. Somehow I never seemed to achieve the most flattering look, even in my skinnier phases; everything was either a little too tight (*aspirational* would be a kind word for it) or a little too frumpy (*defeatist*).

"Hello everyone. I'm Meghan, and I'm an overeater."

"Hi, Meghan," the group chanted in unison.

"I'm happy today's topic is about falling off the wagon, because it's something I'm very familiar with. In the past year, I'd say it's happened to me four or five times."

Oh please. I wanted to roll my eyes and stomp on the floor and shout, "I fall off the wagon four or five times a day!" But that would have been terrible, and of course I didn't do it.

"The last time was just this past week. I've been dealing with a really hard breakup, and it was on a night when my ex had been calling and texting, trying to get me to come over and sleep with him. The first few months after the breakup, I would answer his booty calls because I felt so lonely. I missed him all the time. But I knew he didn't want me beyond the sex and it made me feel terrible afterward. Now that I think of it, probably every binge this past year has come after one of our hookups."

Food and men, men and food. In so many of our stories, they were two interchangeable entities. One would replace the need for the other, and vice versa. Right now, I was battling the urge to eat everything in the state of Florida to fill the gargantuan void that I so desperately wanted Liam to occupy.

"It's funny," Meghan continued, "the best relationship I've ever had was with my high school boyfriend. He was also a binge eater. And a football player, one of the big guys on defense, and we would just eat and eat and eat together—that was our favorite thing to do. I mean, I know that's not healthy or whatever, and it's not what I want for my future, but in terms of, I guess, mutual respect and understanding...I just felt like we were in the same boat, he and I."

I found myself nodding along and considered the similarity between falling for a fellow binger and falling for a sex addict.

I was reminded again that my attraction to Liam wasn't just physical, even though it seemed like it on the surface. Things went deeper with him because I knew he had vices like mine. There was a humanity there because of his addiction to sex, and although I didn't fully understand Liam's fixation on it, I could certainly relate. Not to mention I was becoming more and more fixated on sex myself, after he had entered the picture. Well, that and food. Food and sex, sex and food.

Straightening up in my chair, I forced myself to listen to the rest of Meghan's share with rapt attention but became distracted, as usual, for the remainder of the meeting, drifting in and out of thoughts about Liam and my concerns about how mad Gracie was. Luckily there was no gratitude share with this group, so I was able to coast through without saying a word—besides the serenity prayer, of course.

"God, grant me the serenity to accept the things I cannot change, the courage to change the things I can, and the wisdom to know the difference," we all recited, holding hands in a crooked circle. Then the die-hards, as they always did, jostled the hands of their neighbors and raised their voices with the coda "Keep coming back! It works if you work it!" I never joined in on the last part, mainly because it would have been disingenuous. If I was going to be falling off the wagon more than once a day, I certainly wasn't going to be shouting about how well the program was working for me.

Chapter 10

Certain meetings sent me straight to the drive-thru, depending on how happy and together the night's speakers had seemed in contrast to myself. Tonight's meeting, however, had made me want to see Liam more than ever. For some reason, when Meghan had described her relationship with her overeating, football-playing high school sweetheart, it had stoked my infatuation with him to the point where I found myself driving to his restaurant without even noticing what I was doing. My car had seemed to steer itself, and before I knew it I was coasting in to the employee parking lot behind Trio, headlights turned off preemptively like I was planning to rob the place.

As I parked, I heard my phone ringing in my purse and scrambled to answer it, hoping whoever had called would talk me out of what I was doing. Then I saw that it was Isabella—no such luck.

"Darling, how long do I heat up these potatoes?" she greeted me, sounding frustrated.

"In the oven or in the microwave?" I said.

"The microwave, you silly rabbit! You think I have time for the oven? It's ten o'clock!"

"Why are you eating so late?"

"I fell asleep at six. Don't ask."

"Try two minutes on medium power," I instructed, checking my rearview mirror for any signs of life in the parking lot.

"Okeydokey, and how are you?"

"Oh, I'm okay. I'm just sitting in the parking lot of Liam's restaurant, wondering how I got here."

"Oh, well I'll let you get back to it, then!"

"No, wait! Isabella—what do I do?"

"About what? You're having a nighttime rendezvous. It sounds very romantic. I am brimming with envy."

"But he doesn't even know I'm here. Am I gonna look crazy barging in on him here?"

"Darling, nothing is crazy. And don't you want to have a story for me next time you see me, other than"—for this she employed her best whiny voice—"'Oh no, I'm such a *schlappschwanz*, I drove home and cried into my pillow. Woe is me.'"

"Okay, okay. Enjoy your potatoes."

"Thank you."

"And don't forget the horseradish sauce!"

"I would never. *Auf wiedersehen*," she said, and hung up.

Isabella's counsel had left me feeling no more prepared for what I was about to do. For a few minutes I just sat there in the darkened car, noticing my pulse as blood hummed through my veins at a faster and faster clip. No option sounded like a good one. Knocking on the door at the tail end of the dinner rush? Calling the hostess and faking another family emergency? Walking in and asking for a table when I could barely afford an appetizer?

No. Answer D: None of the above. While the tiny speck of rationality left inside my brain was urging me to heed Julien's good advice and drive home, that speck had nothing on a head full of delusion. I got out of the car and paced the parking lot. A minute later, I was rapping on the back door that led to the kitchen, lightly at first, then harder, to no avail. The bustle inside the kitchen was probably drowning out anything on a lower register than human shouting, so I was going to have to get more creative. This meant turning the knob and pulling on the heavy door, only to find it locked. Now what? March through the restaurant to the kitchen and get tackled by security guards along the way? Of course, I knew that wasn't going to happen— there were no security guards. However, there were some very territorial-seeming waitresses, and who did I think I was to go up against them? Wonder Woman?

And then, *boom!* Something just short of a Biblical miracle happened. The door slammed into me and I stumbled backward as a rubber-gloved, apron-clad dishwasher busted outside with a large bag of trash. He didn't see me as he kicked the stopper behind him so the door stayed ajar. Eyes on his back, I bent my knees in a slight crouch, thinking that, in this moment, all that separated me from an action movie starlet was a black catsuit. Then thinking, *Thank God I'm not wearing a black catsuit.*

Frantic and unprepared, I bolted into the kitchen, where the steely bright lights seemed to amplify how ridiculous and disturbing my entrance must have looked. Everyone—not just some of the kitchen staff but *everyone*—turned to look after the first head whipped around at the sight of me standing in the doorway, head down, eyes scanning the room, arms outstretched as if I were surfing. Ignoring them as best I could, I surveyed the room in search of Liam, hurrying down the middle aisle in my billowing tent of a maxi dress until I spotted him in a cramped corner, concentrating over a large sauté pan. Catching him unawares, I took a split second to appreciate his classic profile, the strong, tanned forearms exposed under the rolled up sleeves of his chef's coat, the pert little bump of his ass just visible in his loose black pants.

"Excuse me? Can I help you?" I heard an annoyed line cook bark at me from behind.

Ignoring my pursuer, I called out Liam's name. He glanced up from a sauté pan in a blasé manner, but when our eyes met his tripled in size. "What the hell?" he said.

"Can I speak with you outside for a second?" I was short of breath from the bolting around and the general panic.

"Uhh…" He looked around, not sure how to react to the onslaught of me. "Give me a minute. I'll meet you out there."

Retreating, I waited by the door for a couple of minutes that felt more like hours, my sanity slowly returning to tell me what a fool I was for doing this. I became convinced that he was never going to come and started back to my car, stopping only when I heard the swing of the kitchen door. I turned to find him standing there like a vision in his white chef's coat, his furrowed brow indicating that my intrusion was just that—an intrusion.

"You got the wrong night, Mischa. Shoulda been here yesterday, same time. I was standing here like an idiot." He moved toward me, and I met him halfway until there were only inches between us in the middle of the parking lot. There was a hint of a smile detectable on his face, but I couldn't tell if he was actually happy to see me or just vaguely amused. I, on the other hand, felt like I was finally scratching an itch just being near him again. My hands wanted to grab his waist to make sure he was really there.

"I know, I'm sorry. I don't know what I'm doing." I stumbled over my words; my head was swimming. "I just had to see you. I know that sounds stupid."

Liam studied me with a straight face. There seemed to be a glint of sympathy in his eyes. "That doesn't sound stupid. Not to me."

I smiled. His words were reassuring, but not his actions. He hadn't reached out to touch me. In fact, he seemed to have taken a tiny step backward. Was he just telling me what I wanted to hear? "I'm sorry, I shouldn't have come," I said.

Liam shut his eyes and shook his head. "No. It's…you're fine. I wanted to see you too." Again words only but they sounded heartfelt. Also, his accent was particularly sexy when spoken in hushed tones. He had been whispering, probably out of concern that one of his workers could interrupt at any minute, but it lent our interaction a conspiratorial air, like we were two people with a secret. I closed my eyes for a moment and clung to that feeling.

"It's just not a good time for me to be doing any of this." His words snapped me back into dismal reality. "I didn't mean to sound harsh on the phone last night. It's just that I'm supposed to be avoiding sex, Mischa. It's not that I don't want to; it's that I can't…in my right mind."

"Oh." I knew this already, so why did it hit me like the worst bit of bad news I'd heard in all my life?

"Why are you looking at me that way?" he said.

"What way?" I straightened my posture, remembering some TED Talk I had seen about mimicking superhero stances in moments of self-doubt.

"Like that. Like a lost puppy or something."

"Lost puppy? Ha." Whatever look I had had on my face turned into one of defiance: curled lip, one eye winking shut. I suddenly felt angry and embarrassed, indignant at the way Liam had torn through my world like a tornado, touching ground only a couple of times before leaving behind his trail of destruction, then calling me a "lost puppy" when I had a perfectly viable emotional reaction. The push-pull reminded me of the way Bradley had treated me; one day I was his favorite person, the next a pariah. I had no response for Liam—all I could do was shake my head and slowly back away. As usual, my actions betrayed my lack of experience in this life. I was behaving like a scorned teenager, but I didn't know any other way.

"Mischa, wait," Liam called after me, but stayed planted in the middle of the parking lot.

"Forget it! Forget I was here. Please." I fumbled with my keys. Finding the right one, I swung my driver's side door open so forcefully that it knocked the car beside mine. Flustered, I checked the other car's door to make sure it was fine, then fell into the driver's seat.

Starting the car, I shifted into reverse when suddenly Liam appeared outside my passenger door and swung it open, plopping himself onto the seat. "All right, where are we going?" he asked, loud and a little manic.

"What? Nowhere. Don't you have food to cook?"

"Nah, they got it under control. Let's get outta here." Like a thief in a getaway car, he glanced in the side mirror.

"And go where? I thought you were avoiding—"

"I am. That doesn't mean we can't go for a joyride, keep each other out of trouble, right?" He found the reclining knob on the side of his seat and tried to lean his seat back to no avail.

I laughed at the sight of Liam the Mercedes driver in my crappy little car. "That doesn't work," I said.

"Even better," he said, and patted his knees eagerly, like he'd been waiting all his life to ride around in a decades-old, half-broken Honda.

* * *

We drove aimlessly for a while, Liam floating his hand in the warm breeze outside the passenger window, me trying to figure out what was actually happening here. Were we buddies now that he had sworn off sex? Would I be able to handle that?

"So where's your spot?" he asked.

"I don't know, what do you mean?"

"Like where do you go for fun? What would be on the agenda if you were out on the town with your girlfriends?"

I shook my head. "I hate to disappoint, but I'm not that exciting. I mean, I go to the same two bars everybody else goes to, but I don't even like them really."

"Let's not go to a bar. Alcohol lowers the inhibitions. Where else? C'mon, there's gotta be something."

I searched my brain, wishing I had a "spot" as Liam had suggested. Then I realized I did—I had mentioned it to him the other night. "There is one place," I said.

"Terrific. Surprise me." Liam placed his hands over his eyes and stayed that way as I made an abrupt U-turn and drove the short distance to Oceanside Plaza, a vast outdoor shopping mall by the beach where Sasha Myers's spa was located in a three-story building separate from the others. The only other time I had snuck in after hours was on Gracie's birthday when she had insisted I take her after a night of bar hopping.

"If I were you, I'd do this all the damn time," she had said, arms outstretched on the marble ledge as she had drunkenly luxuriated in the hot tub.

"She doesn't even know I kept the key," I had told her, guilt-ridden.

"Exactly, Holmes!" Gracie had rolled her eyes at me, infuriated as ever by my squareness. She was the kind of person who got her thrills from breaking the rules, whereas I had spent that entire night checking the clock on my phone and peering into the parking lot for security guards.

When I took Liam there, the parking lot attached to the mall was closed. They had recently started charging for parking and the ticket machine shut down at nine, so we parked on the street outside and hopped the measly two-foot stucco barrier that surrounded the place.

"Oh, fantastic, are we getting the couple's massage?" Liam feigned a snobby accent as I unlocked the front door and disarmed the alarm system, using the code that Sasha had never changed from the manufacturer-provided 1-2-3-4. I slipped in and waved him inside, noticing my hands slightly shaking as I fumbled for the key and locked the door behind us. There had been too much silence between us since we had gotten out of the car, and the awkwardness persisted as we rode the elevator to the rooftop.

In fact, I was still auditioning various conversation starters as the elevator door opened and I led him out onto Sasha's "splashy sundeck." This was the pride and joy of the spa and probably my favorite place in all of Oceanside—there was a saline pool and a hot tub, and every inch of the roof was marble tiled. The minimalist deck chairs were all oriented toward the ocean, which was visible from three sides, and the waist-high railings were made of glass so as not to obstruct the view.

Slipping behind the elevator structure, I switched on the pool lights.

"Wow." Liam walked around the periphery and stopped to lean over the railing. "This is some spot."

"I know, right?" I sidled up next to him, fighting the urge to touch his shoulder or grasp his hand. There was a slight breeze but the air was still warm, left over from earlier when the temperature had reached 100 degrees in the middle of the day. The bright, silvery moon hung low in the sky. "This night is perfect," I said.

Liam grasped the railing with both hands. "I fucking love the ocean, man. It reminds me of home."

"Not me."

"Where you from?"

"Iowa."

"Yikes. I was there once."

"With your band?" I asked the question even though I already knew the answer from my extensive online "research."

"Yeah, with my band—" For a second it seemed like he was going to say more, but he stopped himself. Something had come over him at the mention of his past. I glanced at the side of his face to see how he looked, which seemed like a combination of sad and angry. Careful not to stare, I peered down at the ocean and followed the sleepy little waves with my eyes as they snuck onto the shore and quietly receded.

"Hey! Last one in the pool's a rotten egg!" Liam shouted, tearing away from the railing and ripping his jacket and shirt off on the way to the pool. At the edge, ready to jump in, he dropped his pants and boxers, and I saw the entire back of his body, naked, just before he dove. *Now that's just unfair,* I thought.

"C'mon! This feels great!" Treading water, he ran his hands through his wet hair and nodded backward, beckoning me.

I shook my head as I approached the pool, kicking off my flip-flops to dip my feet in. From there, I stared at his body, illuminated by the lights in the pool, but the water moved too much for me to get a clear picture.

"Stop staring and get in already," he teased.

"I'm not getting naked in front of you. We're supposed to be keeping each other out of trouble, remember?"

"Who said skinny-dipping was sexual? I find it quite chaste, actually. Back to nature, and all that." He smirked and held up an index finger, curling it toward him in the same sexy come-hither maneuver he had used the first time he tried to seduce me.

Sticking to my guns, I sat down on the pool ledge, pulled my dress up to my knees, and dropped my legs into the tepid water. I couldn't tell what was more refreshing, the saline pool water coursing around my legs or the fact that I'd denied Liam's request. Maybe I could handle being "just friends" after all.

He waded up to me and grabbed my ankles, pretending to yank me into the pool.

"You'd better not!" I warned, half of me wanting him to pull me in, the other half envisioning him climbing out of the pool and on top of me, smothering me with his slick, wet, naked body.

"Hey, thanks for bringing me here," he said. Stretching his arms out wide, he fell backward into the water and swam a lap of backstroke while inadvertently presenting his muscled torso and legs for me to peruse. By the time he reached the other end of the pool, I'd unwittingly let my mouth fall open, something I only realized after he had flipped around to face me and mimicked my expression.

Oh God. "I used to work here," I said, averting my eyes to avoid any further humiliation. "It's probably my favorite place in Oceanside, up here on the roof."

"I can see that."

"What's yours?" I glanced back at him as he waded toward me, slicking back his hair again.

"I don't know, I've never thought about it…"

As Liam got closer, I noticed his green eyes sparkling in the blue glow of the pool lights. It reminded me of the first time we met, when the church parking lot lights had lit up his eyes so that they looked almost iridescent.

"Probably my restaurant," he finally said. "It's the only place I feel totally fulfilled, you know? I don't think about my problems when I'm there." He chuckled to himself. "Which is odd, because the restaurant has plenty of problems of its own. But you know what I mean. Who you are, your personal life, it all goes out the window when you have a business to run, food to cook."

"Is that how you used to feel when you performed? Like you forgot all your problems?" I was doing the thing where I asked all the questions to ensure we didn't start talking about me, afraid of what I might reveal.

"No. It wasn't the same. I mean, I liked it when we were young. But later on, I ended up hating it…being onstage. I felt like everybody was looking at me."

I laughed at his seemingly obvious statement. "Well, they kinda were."

"Yeah, that's not what I mean. I don't know. It felt intrusive. I didn't really like myself. It makes it hard."

I nodded. I couldn't imagine having to stand onstage in front of thousands of people. "I guess I always just assumed the myth about rock stars, like you're living everyone's biggest fantasy."

"Well, there's that too. I definitely lived the fantasy, at least part of the time. Hey, is that a hot tub?" He pointed to the other end of the pool.

I nodded, trying to curb my enthusiasm at the thought of Liam making the journey from pool to hot tub naked.

"Do your lower legs want to come join me in the hot tub, then?"

Without waiting for an answer, Liam hoisted his drenched, naked body out of the pool directly beside me. Trickles of water dropped off of him and onto my shirt. The urge to stare was maddening, but I kept my eyes to myself, a wicked smile threatening to creep across my face. *No!* my inner voice chastised. *No looking, no flirting, no touching.*

Poker-faced and decidedly not staring at Liam's ass, I followed him to the hot tub and, once again, sat on the side, this time as far away from him as possible. Inwardly, I gave myself a heartfelt congratulations for keeping my dress on and staying the course. If I had gone in the pool, all I would have thought about was whether or not he was looking at me, whether or not he was still attracted to me, or if somehow he had magically changed his mind about having sex with me again.

"So, how's it going with the eating?" he said, seemingly out of nowhere.

"Pardon?" I responded with arched eyebrows, immediately on the defense. Whenever I felt offended, I made a point of saying *pardon* instead of *excuse me*. For some reason, it seemed to convey more anger.

"You said you do the Overeater meetings, right?"

"Yeah, well, anonymously I do."

"Well, friend, I'm not trying to pry. It's just that you told me about it." He flashed a crooked smile, something that probably got him out of trouble more often than not. "I figure it's probably all in your head, though. I told you, I think you look great. I like a girl with a little meat on her."

"Ugh, please don't say that!" My cheeks reddened.

"Why are you so insecure?"

I shook my head and redirected my attention to the stars, my feet nervously kicking back and forth underwater. "I don't know.

Anyway, OA is not about weight. It's about food ruling your life. Some people who go are totally average. Some are even thin."

"So why does food rule your life, then? C'mon, be real with me. My mother committed suicide when I was three. What's your excuse?"

"Oh my God, I'm so sorry." I looked back at Liam, whose expression had turned serious.

"It's not your fault," he said. "She threw herself off a bridge. When I was eighteen, I tried to do the same. Same bridge even."

"Wow," I said, at a loss for words. Liam's abrupt confession had snapped me out of my insecure pity party, reminding me this was a troubled soul I was dealing with, even if he did come disguised in the body of Adonis.

"I didn't do it anyway. I came this close—" He held up his index finger and thumb for emphasis. "But I didn't do it. So there's my most intimate fucking secret. Now what's yours?"

"I don't know, nothing like that. Here's the thing—I don't really like talking about myself," I said.

"Why not? You don't trust people?"

I shook my head, trying to find the right words to explain my unwillingness to share personal information.

"You don't trust men?"

To this I nodded. It was a knee-jerk reaction, unintentionally honest. "My dad left when I was eight."

"Where'd he go?"

"The Philippines."

"Never to return again?"

"Nope." I rolled my eyes to feign indifference, feeling a trickle of sweat slowly making its way down my chest. I felt like running and hiding. Something about acknowledging that my dad had left long ago was nearly unbearable. When I had told Bradley the

same thing, about a month into dating him, he had gone silent
and then asked, without a hint of irony, "So, does that mean you
have 'daddy issues'?"

Liam stood up from his seat in the hot tub and walked over
to me, placing a warm, wet hand on my knee. The shock of his
touch sent a wave of electricity up my leg. "That's rough," he said.

"Hey, at least he didn't commit suicide." The minute it came
out, I regretted how flippant my comment sounded. "I'm sorry.
That sounded horrible—"

"Listen, I never knew her. I can't remember her. It'd probably
be just as hard if I knew she was in another country somewhere,
ignoring me."

"Who knows?" I looked into Liam's iridescent eyes just inches
from my own. He removed his hand from my knee and held it
out for me to take. When I placed my hand in his, he tenderly
kissed the top of it, the soft warmth of his lips against my skin
causing me to shudder. My breath caught. I was overwhelmed by
his touch, his proximity, my body stiffening in anticipation of
what would come next. But nothing else happened. He released
my hand and returned to his seat.

"My dad never talked about my mom growing up," he said.
"I guess he thought it was less painful that way. We didn't visit
her grave or mention her on her birthday. Her side of the family
lived eight hours away in a small town, and we never went to see
them. He even hid all the pictures of her. I think he was worried
I would ask too many questions if he left them out. Anyway, now
I can't stop thinking about sex, go figure. It's the only thing I've
cared about since I was ten. It's why I started a band. We had
groupies by the time we were fifteen, some of them in their twenties. I just had sex all the fucking time, like *all* the fucking time.
I'd try to keep a girlfriend every now and then but I cheated on

all of them. The only solution I ever came up with was to avoid sex with real people as much as possible because it always turns to shit. But when I don't do it with women, I masturbate constantly. Except for these past few months. Bobby's really been helping me get better, even though he's a bit of a wanker."

I laughed at the thought of Bobby ushering Liam away from me like a stern parent. "Yeah, how was that guy ever a sex addict? I mean, who was he doing it with?"

"Internet porn."

"Oh...right."

Liam stretched his arms behind him on the hot tub ledge and, for the first time that night, stared at me—really stared—studying my face in a way that made me feel shy. I leaned back on my hands and looked up at the sky, pretending not to care—and part of me didn't. Somehow talking candidly about my dad had made me feel strangely free, like I had nothing to hide.

"We're underdogs, Mischa. And that's a good thing. There're a lot of people walking around acting like they've got no problems, no skeletons in their closet, and maybe they don't! But that's what makes us interesting. You're a good egg, though, I can tell. Your mom probably never had to worry about you when you were younger."

"Only when I would binge-eat half a week's worth of food in one night," I said matter-of-factly. Liam looked at me in disbelief and we both laughed. I wanted to say something to prove that I wasn't as "good" as he thought—somehow that comment made me feel like he was distancing himself from me, even though he had meant it as a compliment. I lowered my voice in an attempt to sound confessional. "Hey...I had a dream about you the other night. I walked in on you with another girl, and then all three of us were having sex."

"Ooh! That's not a good girl's dream."

"Her name was Hadara. The other girl, I mean."

He raised his eyebrows. "Exotic!"

"It all seemed very real. It made me think, you probably do that a lot, huh? Have threesomes?"

"Eh. Not anymore. They're overrated."

Of course he has an opinion on threesomes. "Why?"

"You know, it's cliché but the whole attention problem. Two people start to pair off and the third gets jealous."

"Did you ever have a threesome with another man?"

Liam looked at me for a while before answering. "Yeah."

I exhaled loudly without meaning to, recalling the day in seventh-grade sex ed when the teacher talked about "high-risk" behaviors and all the terrible afflictions that came along with them. A question that should have popped into my head the minute I'd met him crossed my lips without warning. "So do you get tested regularly?"

"I'm clean," he answered, a hint of defiance in his voice. "And by the way, the time with the guy was in my early twenties."

"Of course! I'm not judging you. I'm sorry. I had a crush on a girl once. I just mentioned the testing thing because I meant to say it the other night. That was bad timing. I don't know why people take it so personally—"

"Mischa," he interrupted my rambling. "Calm down. We were safe, and I'm not taking it personally."

"Okay."

"All right." He lowered his arms back into the hot tub and watched the water as it bubbled up around him.

A long pause followed. We had hit a wall. One of my legs kicked too hard and surfaced, sending a little splash of water into his face. "Oops. Sorry," I said. I jokingly braced myself, and Liam waded over to me and grabbed my feet.

"I could do it!" he said, and gave them a tug. "You could be in here in two seconds flat!"

I wiggled my feet in his hands. "Please have mercy on me," I begged.

Liam bit his lower lip and tugged once more. "Why do you make me feel giddy?" he said.

I chuckled, my cheeks aching from smiling so big. "Ditto," I said.

Liam sat down again. He let his arms float on the surface of the water. "So what do you do? Other than run errands for that boring professor guy?"

I raised my eyebrows, surprised to hear Liam slight Julien. Obviously they hadn't hit it off when I had been hiding in the bathroom the other night. "Well, I'm working on a juice cleanse," I said, stretching out my legs in the water, "and I'm waiting to hear back from grad schools. I applied for some masters programs in nutrition."

Liam's face crumpled. He suddenly seemed distracted as he reached out for one of my toes. "Do you think I'm a slut?" he said in a gloomy tone of voice. He pinched my toe and let it free again.

"No!" I leaned forward to sit on my hands. I tried to make eye contact with him but he looked away.

"Yeah you do. How could you not? You think I'm the slut that's going to give you AIDS," he said, and flicked at the water.

"I really don't." My heart was swelling. I wanted to comfort him; he seemed so vulnerable. "Liam—"

"Never mind. It's getting hot in here." He rose from his seat, his naked torso in full view. "We should probably go."

"Okay, fine," I said. Out of nowhere, my heart had been sucked into a vat of quicksand. In the past two minutes alone, my emotions had vacillated between happy and scared and defeated so quickly I should have had whiplash. Everything felt so loaded between us now that we had opened up to each other. Yet the conversation had been so natural and fun, I had imagined us staying here on the rooftop until the sun came up, watching it rise together like a couple of wayward kids at summer camp. Now I was nearly convinced he hated me.

As Liam stood dripping by a deck chair, I realized there was nothing to dry him off. "Oh, we forgot to get towels!" I said. "I'll go down and grab one."

"That's fine. I'll just follow you." Liam's voice was hard to read. He left a watery trail as he shuffled behind me into the elevator and stood there, holding his clothes in a bundle at his waist.

"You know…I dreamt about you too," he said with a straight face as we arrived at the second floor, the doors opening before I could respond.

"Were we having a threesome?" I asked, desperate to steer things back toward flirting.

"No. Just the two of us. I don't think I'd like to have a threesome with you."

"Why not? Because I'm a 'good girl'?" I rolled my eyes for him to see.

"Because I wouldn't want to share you," he said.

Chapter 11

Inside the men's shower room, I flipped on the lights. Instantly, I was reminded how gorgeous Sasha's spa was throughout. She had modeled it, room by room, after some spa at an insanely expensive Greek resort where she'd spent her second honeymoon. This room included two massive eight-headed showers, a dry sauna, a steam room, and a large marble bench in the middle. The lighting was warm and bright, like a sunny afternoon without the sunlight.

"All right, you can take a shower if you want. We'll just have to steal the towel you use so no one notices." I was pretending to be very lax about the whole thing, but inside I felt the inevitable worry I had whenever I broke any rules. When Gracie had asked to use the showers, I had told her no way.

I started to leave Liam there, with plans to raid the second-floor mini-fridge and try to forget the last few awkward moments of conversation on the roof, but before I knew it, he was grabbing my wrist to stop me. "Wait," he said in a pleading tone, dropping his clothes so that his naked body, tanned and taut, stood before me, completely exposed.

"No, Liam. We're keeping each other out of trouble, remember?"

"But this isn't trouble. This is different," he whispered, plunging his hand into the hair that dangled at the nape of my neck, sending tingles up and down my spine as he moved in to kiss me.

I wanted to believe him, that this was different. In the moment, I actually did. Maybe it was his kiss that convinced me. His lips were extra soft after the swim. As was his skin, and the way he touched me. It was like he'd shed an outer layer of toughness in the pool and become this vulnerable person, or maybe it just seemed that way because he was naked and I wasn't. All I knew was that, somehow, he had taken me in his arms and slipped his tongue inside my mouth until all my good intentions had evaporated and I was kissing him back like my life depended on it.

My hands slinked up his arms and rested on his bare shoulders as he began rocking against me, grasping my butt, then inching his fingers around to my front and down the neckline of my dress. I raised my hands, allowing him to pull the dress over my head slowly. I was wearing a cotton pushup bra with yellow and white stripes that Liam instantly focused on. He moved his hands over my breasts, then underneath the shoulder straps.

"I like this. You could have worn it in the pool." He smiled and tugged down on the straps, pushing my boobs together as he sank his face into my cleavage. "Your tits are fucking divine," he said, kissing up the top of my chest and my neck. "Come here." He took me by the waist and walked me backward until the backs of my knees hit the marble bench in the center of the room. I sat down and Liam picked up my legs and laid them out. He held up an index finger as he walked over to the corner of the room to grab a white folded towel from the stack, then returned and placed it at the other end of the bench. He nodded a silent command, and I lay back, resting my head on the towel.

Nothing could have prepared me for this. I had believed Liam when he said he needed a friend and had accepted that his attraction to me had been a one-time thing—in his mind, I was over, used up. Barely five minutes ago, I was wondering if he would ever want to speak to me again after tonight.

He sat beside me on the bench for a moment, dragging his right hand up and down the middle of my torso. "I like you, you know that? You make me wish I was different." His voice was hushed, soothing. *You are different,* I thought as I lay there, waiting to see what he would do next, every bit of exposed skin prickly with anticipation. If he didn't believe it about himself already, I wanted to somehow show him that he was different.

Liam lowered his knees to the floor and began kissing my belly, nipping at my belly button with his tongue. He moved his mouth down to the waistband of my panties and tugged at it with his teeth, growling mischievously. Pausing for a second, he glanced up at me. "I saw up your dress when you were sitting at the hot tub."

"No, you didn't." I laughed, my belly tingling as Liam rested his chin on it.

"Yes, I did. I couldn't stop thinking about getting in it."

My stomach contracted as I laughed even harder. I felt giddy as the object of Liam's rapt attention.

He went back to work, dragging my sheer yellow underwear over my hips and down my legs, and tossing them behind him. "Thank you for wearing those, but they won't be needed," he said, his eyes on mine as he moved around to the far end of the bench. From there, he grasped my ankles and pulled me toward him, burrowing his face in between my legs. I could feel the heat of his breath on my skin as he kissed the area just above my clitoris, making me gush with wetness. He moved down, licking and nibbling at my inner thighs, the tease of his tongue driving me crazy with anticipation. I started whimpering, tensing my entire body.

"Does this feel good?" He slid his hands from the inside of my knees up to the tops of my thighs, parting my legs even wider.

"Yes," I whispered.

He ran the tip of his finger up and down my sex. "God, you're wet. Jesus Christ."

"Lick me, please," I said, surprising myself. With Bradley, I had drawn the line at cunnilingus, the very thought of which had made me shudder with embarrassment. I had been so self-conscious that I couldn't even have sex with the lights on. Yet here I was with Liam—by far the most attractive man I'd ever laid eyes on—in a lit room, dying for him to lick me, kiss me, consume every inch of my body. He had disarmed the little voice inside my head that made me hate my fluff and second-guess the way I talked, walked, dressed, smelled. His attraction was so genuinely animalistic that the only thing for me to do was give in to it.

And give in I did. The euphoria that overcame me in the next few minutes is hard to describe. It was like the happy buzz from every thrilling moment of my life had returned, this time condensed and coursing through my veins as if I'd shot up. The slick, sweet warmth of Liam's tongue poking inside me, then carrying my wetness back up to my clitoris, circling around and around, then back down, was the most maddeningly beautiful thing I'd ever felt. I held out as long as I could, savoring the electrical charge that had lit up my entire body like a light. The passage of time had become completely irrelevant—it could have been minutes or seconds that went by before I finally lost control. All I knew was that he was humming when I finally gasped for breath and felt the most incredible orgasm pulse through my body. I screamed in ecstasy, and Liam stayed, his face still buried between my legs, until I'd experienced every last thrilling twitch. I glanced down at him just as he looked up. "Your pussy tastes like cotton candy," he said.

"Mmmm…cotton candy," I repeated. My mind drifted to food, but only for a brief second before I snapped myself back into the present.

Liam crawled on top of me, kissing up my body and neck. I reached for his shoulders, hoisting him up so that I could kiss his lips and wrap my legs around his waist. His erection felt massive against my waist. I had to reach down and take it in both my hands to really believe it. "You're very big right now."

"That's how much I want you, little Mischa."

I grinned. *Little Mischa.* No one had ever called me that before, not by a long shot, and I liked it. Liam propped himself on his hands and looked past me at one of the showers.

"Hey. Let's get clean."

Still dazed from the orgasm, I allowed him to lead me by the hand to one of the showers, a large, marbled affair with eight different showerheads. I would have let him lead me anywhere. As the water came on and pulsed hot over our bodies, I took the opportunity to put my hands on his chest and drag them down his chiseled abs. He was like a statue that had come to life, every inch of him defined, deliberate. He took my head in his hands and tilted it back under a water stream to wet my hair, and I did the same to his.

We were something different now, something purer. Liam had let me behind the curtain, telling me about his mother and his own battles with depression, and I had let him in too. It hardly made sense, but when I looked at him, I felt like I was seeing a completely different person than the one who had followed me home the other night. Overwhelmed by the need to feel him inside me again, I dropped to my knees and took him in my mouth, his warm, wet skin tasting pleasant, salty. Water poured over my head and streamed down my body as I took more and more of him in, allowing the tip of his erection to penetrate the back of my throat as I moved my head back and forth. Liam rested his palm gently on the top of my head, slinking his fingers through my wet hair.

Every once in a while, he encouraged me with a little groan, or "that's it," or "keep going," as I sucked in time with the movement of his hips. I had only done this a few times. Usually I would have been self-conscious about my lack of experience, if not stifled by the fear that I was doing it wrong. But none of that even crossed my mind. We were both lost in the moment, enjoying ourselves with absolute abandon. When he warned me that he was going to come, I didn't want it to end. I kept him inside my mouth and swallowed greedily. Another first.

Sore from kneeling on the marble tile, I stood up slowly and greeted a wobbly Liam with a smile. His face was ruddy. We were both happily spent. "That was all right," he said with a wink. I poked at him playfully, and he kissed my forehead. I closed my eyes, silently wishing this would never end, as he began to lather me up with soap. We spent another five minutes in the heavenly water stream, steam enveloping us in our own little clouded atmosphere as we giggled and washed each other.

The whole thing had been so out of left field, I had no time to wonder what was happening or what any of it meant. I was simply caught up in the excitement of Liam, who was acting like a fantasy version of himself I hadn't even dared to daydream about—vulnerable, patient, adoring. Once we had dressed and made our way to the elevator, reality started to knock on the door of my consciousness, threatening to burst my bubble, but I wasn't ready for it yet.

"You know, I've never done it in an elevator," I said, glancing around mischievously as the doors closed and we began our descent.

"Really?" Liam smirked.

"Yeah, really." I leaned back against the railing and hiked my dress up to the waist, daring him to make a move. Liam, who was standing across from me, came over, but instead of taking me in his arms like I wanted him to, he leaned against the railing beside me and let out a long sigh.

"Mischa, we can't."

"Oh." Humiliated, I let my skirt drop back down and straightened up, turning to face the doors.

"Hey"—he caressed my shoulder from behind—"it's not that I don't want to."

I shook my head as the elevator arrived at the ground floor and we made our way out in silence. In seconds, I had gone from seductress to reject. I felt like running and hiding, but there was no escaping the situation—Liam needed a ride back.

In the parking lot, I led him to the Dumpster where we threw the towels we'd taken from the spa into the trash. I noticed his face had gone blank and felt a bitterness seeping into me as I remembered the scene after the first time we'd had sex when Liam had driven me back to Julien's without uttering a word.

"You know, my friend Gracie has this term for that blank look certain guys get after sex." I broke the silence as we made our way back to my car. "She calls it 'serial killer face.' You've got it now." I pointed at him, trying to sound like I was making a joke even though my heart was in the process of shattering.

"That's not true. I'm not some stupid frat boy who can't look a girl in the eye after I've fucked her."

I stopped walking. "Then look me in the eye!" I turned to face him and noticed the cloud of shame and guilt that seemed to envelop him.

Liam kicked at the ground, his hands finding the pockets of his chef's coat. He glanced at me only briefly. "I don't know what to say, Mischa. You know it's complicated with me."

"It wasn't different, was it?" I asked, my voice trembling.

"Different from what?"

"You said back there that this—you and me—was different! I don't know why I believed you. It's what I wanted to hear, I guess. I should have known better than to think somebody like you—"

"Somebody like me what? Was a good guy? Was worth more than a quick fuck?" He finally held eye contact with me for more than a second, and I could see his guilt turning to anger.

"No. That someone like you would actually want someone like me." I sounded pitiful but it couldn't be helped. The best I could do was hold in my tears.

"I do want you. But I'm fucked up." Liam groaned.

"Well so am I. I thought that's what we liked about each other." I threw my hands up as Liam kicked at the ground again. The more pitiful I became, the more angry he seemed to get.

"It's not the same. I wish I was like you. I wish my only vice was food, or booze, or drugs. But no, I have to turn myself off—shut down like a robot—so that I don't keep trying to fuck you all night, or somebody else. If I didn't control it, I'd be on the prowl constantly. I wouldn't stop. Do you know how hard that is?" He finally looked at me, his eyes squinted in exasperation.

I shook my head, no longer able to fight back the tears that traveled down my cheeks. "No. I couldn't possibly understand. I'm just a sweet chubby girl from Iowa, right?"

"Mischa, that's not fair."

"I know, but none of this is fair. I can't be mad at you, but I am," I cried. "You shouldn't have had sex with me, but you did. We were gonna keep each other out of trouble, but we didn't. Obviously this can't happen again," I said, finally voicing the thing I knew I should voice but without really meaning it. What I wanted was for him to argue the other side, to beg to be my friend or something more. But by the time Liam came up with a response, I had already opened my car door and stolen into the driver's seat, knowing he wasn't going to say anything that I wanted to hear. He couldn't.

"You're right." He shook his head, getting into the passenger seat. "I'm sorry." Liam turned to me, studying the side of my face. Now I was the one who wouldn't look at him.

"I'm sorry too," I answered, not sure to which of us I was apologizing as I started the car.

"Obviously this can't happen again." Liam's voice was warm but the message was impossibly cold as he repeated my words back to me verbatim.

"Fine," I said as icily as possible, realizing that this was a breakup, even though we'd never even been together. It felt just as painful as the only other breakup I'd ever gone through when Bradley had called me over to his dorm room early one morning after avoiding me for two weeks. In a way this was worse, because at least with Bradley I had seen it coming.

The ride back with Liam was as silent and somber as a funeral procession. We didn't even look at each other when we muttered our goodbyes and he slipped out of the car. Driving away, I let more of my pent-up tears fall and by the time I'd reached the street, they had begun to obstruct my view. I wiped at my wet cheeks furiously as I contemplated the heartbreak I'd stupidly invited into my life by involving myself with this man. *You should have known better*, I heard my know-it-all inner voice saying. It was true. I had known his story from day one: sex addict, dangerous, impulsive, in a losing battle with his recovery. That I'd decided to even fantasize about someone like Liam actually made me the crazy one, not him.

The only person who could possibly sympathize with me now was Gracie, even if she was still mad at me from our conversation that morning. I set my phone to speaker and dialed her, and to my relief, she answered on the third ring.

"Gracie?"

"What are you doing?" She sounded groggy.

"Shit, did I wake you up?"

"No... it's just two in the morning and I have work tomorrow. Why would I be sleeping?"

"I'm sorry." My voice shook. "I didn't realize how late it was."

"You sound like a mess, Mischa. What's going on?" There was a rustle of sheets on the other line. She coughed to clear her throat.

"It's Liam..." As I said his name, a fresh wave of tears hit me and I had to gasp for breath.

"You mean the sex-addict-rock-star-slash-restaurateur?"

"Slash asshole, yes."

"Oh no. What'd he do?"

I inhaled deeply in an effort to calm down. "We had sex again, but he doesn't want anything to do with me. But it was the best sex of my life."

"Not saying much. I'm sure Bradley wasn't exactly a master."

"Gracie, please don't do that right now."

"I'm sorry."

"It's okay, it's just... What do I do?"

"Sweetie, I don't know what to tell you. I'm in the same boat." She sighed into the receiver.

"Really?" My composure came back slightly as I shifted my focus onto Gracie's problems and off of my own. "With that guy? Richard?"

"Yeah. We had sex finally. In a public bathroom. At a club. I'll put it this way—it was not what I had envisioned."

"Oh no."

"He had serial killer face. Like *during* the act."

"Oh shit. Liam had it tonight. I mean, not during, but close enough. God! What was I thinking?"

"Just try not to beat yourself up, okay?"

"What are you gonna do?"

"I don't know. The thing is, I think I'm falling for this guy. I'm just hoping it was a bad first time and something will change."

"You never know," I said. "I mean, unless he tells you he can't have sex like a normal person because he's addicted to it."

"Yeah, right. In this town that's more likely than not. But seriously, you sound terrible, my dear. Do I need to put you on Taco Bell watch?"

"Too late, I've been eating Mexican pizzas on the daily. That and everything else." I heard Gracie laugh on the other end and managed a smile.

"Well, we should focus on the good stuff," she said. "Tell me about the best sex of your life!"

I thought about everything that had happened that night, but it was already tainted in my memory. "I don't think I can talk about it."

"Fair enough." Gracie was either groaning or yawning, it was a toss-up.

"You're sleepy," I said.

"Yeah, you know, two in the morning and all."

I pulled onto Julien's street and turned my headlights off as

I drove up to his curb. "I'm sorry I woke you up, friend. I just needed to hear your voice. I hope you can get back to sleep."

"Yep."

"I love you for picking up the phone…and I'm sorry about earlier," I said tentatively.

"Me too."

Her quick response made me tear up for a whole new reason. "I love you, Gracie."

"Love you back, you crazy person," she said.

We hung up just as I put the car into park and fumbled for the key to Julien's side gate that I kept in the small pocket of my purse. It was a strangely large, heavily rusted iron key that I refused to keep on my key ring, but I couldn't find it in its usual place. Then I remembered that I'd removed it to go for a walk earlier that day and must not have put it back.

"Shit!" This meant I would have to go into Julien's house and sneak through the first floor without waking anybody up, which was a long shot given my proclivity for stumbling in the dark. I'd worried that this could happen at some point, and now it was happening exactly when I least wanted to be seen, my face and eyes puffy from crying, my sanity hanging on by a thread.

Left with no other choice, I unlocked the front door and pulled it toward me gently, hoping to stifle the slight creaking noise it made. Inside the foyer, I noticed a blue flickering light coming from the living room. I figured Cecile had fallen asleep in front of the TV and headed down the hall to turn it off. As I got closer, I detected voices speaking a foreign language and thought it odd that this was her programming of choice. Just outside the living room, I accidentally kicked a doorstop and inadvertently announced my presence to the TV watcher—who happened to be Julien, not Cecile—sitting on the couch wide awake. His back to me, he turned around and looked up.

"Sorry to interrupt. I left my key to the gate," I said in a half whisper.

"That's okay." He sat up and paused the television. "Everything okay?"

I had to think for a second before I could find the words to answer. Part of me wanted to keep up the pity party I'd started with Gracie, but then I remembered what Julien had said about Liam just that morning and felt too sheepish to reveal anything about my heartbreak. Plus, he was my boss, not my confidant. "Yeah, I'm fine," I said, the timbre of my voice sounding decidedly not fine.

Julien propped his arm on the back of the couch and rested his head on his hand. "Cecile couldn't sleep. She woke me up to watch TV. Now I'm the one who can't sleep. I got sucked into this Spanish movie about a prison guard who's planning an elaborate suicide. Wanna watch? It's actually good."

I glanced at the TV, unsure how to answer. On the one hand, I was emotionally spent and should probably be facedown on a pillow right now. But on the other, Julien's presence was always comforting, and the idea of being alone with my thoughts right now definitely wasn't. "Sure, why not?" I said with an exhausted sigh. I made my way around the couch and plopped down beside him.

As he leaned forward to unpause the movie, I registered that he was wearing a T-shirt and athletic shorts. I hadn't seen him so dressed down since the day I'd moved in. "You want me to fill you in?" he whispered as the subtitles hit the screen.

"No thanks." I sank back into the soft pillow behind me, remembering how I'd coped with the Bradley breakup by watching endless hours of reality shows on the TV Gracie had smuggled into her dorm room. Just the blue glow of the screen had already coaxed me into a semi-catatonic state.

The film was dark and sad, not the kind of thing I gravitated toward on a bad day, but it was sufficiently distracting. About ten minutes in, I let my eyes close, allowing the inscrutable Spanish dialogue to mix with the steady sound of Julien's inhales and exhales to create a soothing chorus that nearly lulled me to sleep.

"Hey, wake up, he's about to do it!" Julien poked my shoulder, and I opened my eyes wide.

"I wasn't falling asleep," I said with a guilty smile.

On-screen, the lonely prison guard was rigging a rifle to a trip wire that connected to a doorknob.

"He's Christian. He thinks if someone else opens the door and triggers the gunshot, he won't go to hell."

"Oh. So he's just gonna sit there until someone opens the door?"

"Yeah, he's in his office. Another guard comes to relieve him at the end of his shift."

I glanced at Julien sideways, amused at how riveted he was. "Do you think he's gonna die?"

His eyes widened. "We'll find out."

The prison guard did die, but it wasn't from the gunshot. He was wounded when his colleague opened the door and tripped the rifle, but not fatally, and when he woke up alive in the hospital, he had a new lease on life. On the other hand, the guard who had caused the gunshot was so traumatized he went back to drinking after years of sobriety, and he eventually killed them both by running his car over a cliff.

"I didn't see that coming," Julien said as he clicked off the television.

"Really? I would think nothing surprises you. I mean you analyze stories for a living."

"I figured the alcoholic would die, not the both of them.

But that would be the Hollywood version. Foreign filmmakers don't care as much about narrative symmetry, especially the Europeans."

"Hmm, that's interesting," I said, impressed as always by Julien's authoritative certainty. He sounded this way whenever he was giving an opinion on one thing or another, and just by participating in conversation with him, I felt smarter. To be accepted by my former professor as a sounding board, someone to converse with about movies or books, his book especially, was like being promoted to a position I hadn't quite earned yet. "I remember you talking about narrative symmetry in class," I said, wishing I had more to add but too dazed from my night with Liam to think any more clearly.

Julien seemed to be on his own train of thought. "Remember the paper you wrote on Morrison?" he asked.

I nodded, even though I had already forgotten the bulk of my class work from that last blur of a semester.

"You quoted the line from *Beloved*, about working hard to forget everything. To forget the painful things."

"Oh yeah," I said. "That was a great line…"

"Obviously Sethe is not a good example of that philosophy as a coping mechanism, but sometimes I wonder if that's what it's all about. Like the guy in the movie, he wasn't a candidate for depression. He was just a guy who couldn't forget the terrible things he had seen and done. Somebody else could have lived that life and been just fine."

Again I nodded. Julien seemed to be broaching the topic of grief, maybe even his own grief, but I was at a loss for words. A brief flash of Liam kicking at the ground outside my car reminded me why.

"I put that quote on my syllabus one year, and my wife made

the comment that I was good at that...good at forgetting. 'Too good,' she said." He shook his head. "She used this shooting I had witnessed as an example. A drive-by. My whole fourth-grade class had seen it out the window of a school bus on a field trip. Two guys, standing on a corner, a couple of teenagers—dealers, probably—got shot in broad daylight while we were stopped at a light. Everybody on my side of the bus was looking."

"That's horrible," I said, noticing how Julien's face had become drawn as he recalled the painful memory.

"It was horrible. Tragic. But it didn't take me long to get over it. Other kids couldn't stop thinking about it and talking about it for weeks. I swear they had PTSD. But me? I just read my books, wrote my stories. I was doing all right. That first year after Renay's death, I was so afraid of having the same reaction, I went in the opposite direction. I thought about it too much. I wasn't conscious of it until I read the quote in your paper. I think I was supposed to read that quote again."

He had been staring off into space, but now Julien turned and looked into my eyes. His expression was an odd mixture of pain and relief. He reached out and placed his hand over mine on the seat between us. "I thought I should tell you that."

"I'm glad," I said, uncertain how to react. I looked down at my hand under Julien's, confused by the gesture. It would have been one thing for him to place his hand on mine in the daylight, at his office, in another context than this. Here we were in the dark late at night, with just enough light coming through the windows for me to see a yearning in Julien's eyes. Before this, I had interpreted whatever intimacy there was between us as pedagogical, almost familial. This was different, though. My reflexes finally kicked in and I drew my hand back, standing up from the couch like I was spring-loaded. "I'm so tired. I'd better get some sleep."

"Of course." Julien stood too. Neither of us moved for a moment. He looked sheepishly at the ground. "Mischa, I'm sorry. I—"

"What? No—" I stopped him with a chaste pat on the arm. "Please, you have nothing to be sorry about," I said, and shook my head, smiling uncomfortably as I made my way around the couch. I suddenly felt bad for making Julien feel like he'd done something wrong. He couldn't have meant anything by touching my hand, could he? "I'll see you in the morning," I said.

"I'll have to go into the office early," he blurted, awkwardly pointing to his bare wrist as if there were a watch there. "You can come as late as you want. In fact, why don't you just take the day off? One of us should get a good night's sleep, right?" His voice had switched back into authoritative mode, as if he were trying to erase the fact that we'd just watched a late-night movie together and followed it up by talking about his personal life.

"Okay?" I sounded surprised as Julien disappeared upstairs, taking two steps at a time. I stayed in the darkened foyer for a few more seconds wondering what exactly had just happened, then decided it was probably in my best interest to forget all about it.

Chapter 12

I awoke after what couldn't have been more than two hours of sleep. The only evidence I had slept at all was a wet spot on my pillow where I had drooled. A more levelheaded person would have taken a sleeping aid, but I had chosen to suffer through the night, thinking back over the past eight hours to all the magical and awful things that had transpired between me and Liam, and then the strangeness that had followed with Julien.

Fact: even after he had told me on no uncertain terms that we were done, I felt myself falling for Liam. As much as I knew I should focus on the bad and get over him, I couldn't shake the vivid memories of his tenderness when we had made love, how he'd held my hand when I had told him about my father and stared into my eyes like he really knew me. I'd never felt that close to a man before, not even Bradley. Especially not Bradley. Also, fact: Julien Maxwell had reached out for me in the dark, and I still couldn't make sense of it. In the light of day, it seemed clearer that he had been feeling something more than platonic, but how? Wouldn't I have seen signs leading up to last night? Had he just reached out for me as a source of comfort and I had misinterpreted the whole thing?

In terms of Liam, I decided in the vague clarity I had gained after my two hours of sleep that I had to face the writing on the wall. I couldn't keep giving in to moments of weakness and chasing after him. Actions speak louder than words, as Gracie would say, and Liam's actions had told me that I was only desirable in brief spurts; that just as easily as he drew me in, he could cut me loose without warning. I had ignored his ambivalence and obsessed over him to the point of ridiculousness, and it was time to stop. What I really needed was to focus on other things—my future, for one. What was to become of me after August was still a giant question mark, and all I had done in the face of that uncertainty was to eat, eat, eat, and obsess, obsess, obsess.

But what was I going to do? I hadn't even been bumped off the waiting list for the graduate program at Reid and hadn't spent any time considering the handful of programs where I had been accepted. A tiny part of me had been hoping Julien might stick his neck out and put in a good word for me with the dean of graduate studies, but had the awkwardness of last night ruined any chance of that? If I were going to be proactive and find out, I would march into his office and confront the situation, but that option was off the table since Julien had basically forbidden me from coming in by "giving me the day off."

"What do I do? What do I do? What do I do?" I said as I dragged myself out of bed, feeling heavy with defeat. All I wanted to do was eat, preferably tucked away in a dark corner somewhere where no one would find me for days. I'd never been such a mess. *Baby steps,* I heard a voice of reason speak up in the back of my head. *One thing at a time.* The first thing I needed was a shower. After that, I would change into the nicest sundress that still fit my body, put on some tinted sunscreen that made me look half alive, and with my head held high, make my way into Julien's kitchen for some breakfast. He would be at work by now anyway, so the only potential interaction would be with my number one teenage frenemy, Cecile.

Though simple, the plan took me a while to execute—the first two dresses I tried were part of my "wishful thinking" collection—but when I finally managed to clothe myself and headed into the kitchen, I looked more put together than I had all summer. A cool blast of air-conditioning greeted me upon entering, and I was relieved to find myself alone. With a deep exhale, I said, "Thank you," and dragged my juicer down from its perch on top of the refrigerator.

"You're welcome," Cecile's voice chimed in as she shuffled into the kitchen in her swim team suit and a towel. Hearing this, my stomach dropped.

"You want some juice?" I offered, opting for plan A: play it cool, act like the "Droolian Poundwell" incident never happened, try and reestablish a rapport.

"Sure." She took the bait, ambling over to the counter and placing her hands primly on the edge of it.

I grabbed a bundle of yellow-green kale that I'd let sit a little too long in the fridge and held it up for her to scrutinize. "As long as you don't mind me using this."

Cecile shrugged, and I proceeded to shove the kale into the feed chute of my juicer, not bothering to rinse it. Her silence seemed like a good omen, and I tried to tell myself that her teenage attention span had probably already moved on from Gracie's silly text.

"So, how's your crush on my dad coming along?" she said, quashing my wishful thinking.

If only I could tell her it was quite possibly the other way around after last night's developments. Of course, she would never believe me. I turned to look at Cecile, hoping to convey impenetrability. "Cecile, I told you it was my friend who had the crush."

"I don't believe you," she said. "And because I don't believe you, I'm going to ask you to do some things for me."

"Oh, c'mon, Cecile. Life doesn't work like one of your Disney sitcoms. A text from my friend isn't grounds for blackmail." I threw an apple on the cutting board and attacked it with the biggest knife I could find.

"Wanna bet?" Cecile lifted her phone from the counter and unlocked the screen. "Just dialing my dad at his office. I'll let him know what I saw on your phone."

"Stop!" I turned around, knife midair. "I'm serious."

"What are you gonna do?" She cocked her head to the side. "Kill me?"

"What do you want, Cecile?" I felt myself tearing up. It was a result of my exhaustion and heartbreak over Liam, but Cecile's taunting was the spilled milk that pushed me over the edge. "I can't fight with you right now, okay? I'm tired, and I'm sad, and I don't know what I'm doing with my life, and the last thing I want is to argue with you over some stupid text message you weren't supposed to see—"

Staring at me like I had two heads, Cecile put down her phone.

"I just want to be your friend, Cecile. I mean that." I saw her face soften and was inspired to keep going. "I can't imagine how hard it is, losing your mom, but I do know what it's like to grow up without a dad. I know what it's like to be angry and to want to take it out on somebody, but I also know that that's not worth it. And you're better than that." I detected a little tremble in Cecile's chin and determined that something I said had gotten to her. She remained uncharacteristically silent as I turned back to the cutting board, tossed the two apple halves in the juicer, and finished off our drinks.

* * *

It turned out the tough love approach was the way to go with Cecile. Over juice, she told me that since her mom had died, she sometimes found herself being mean to people for no reason and had a hard time stopping once she'd started. I gave her my best attempt at sisterly advice about thinking before speaking and counting to ten when a wave of anger came on. It was cliché stuff I guess, but Cecile seemed to absorb it thoughtfully. We even hugged before she went off to swim practice, and my heart lifted just a tiny bit. Then, an ironically timed text from my mother popped up on my phone: *Any news about grad school?*

Without answering, I shoved the phone into my purse and headed for the door, remembering that I hadn't checked in with my subletter for any mail delivered to my old apartment in the past few weeks. The day before graduation, I had provided the post office with my new address, but nothing had shown up to Julien's house yet and I was anxious about it. Especially now that I was waking up from the Liam-induced fever dream that had taken over the first part of my summer.

The old apartment building was just as I had left it—slightly depressing, a little run-down, and mostly populated with old people despite its proximity to a college campus. When she came to the door, the subletter, Anjuli, looked entirely out of place in this setting. She was glamorous and 5'9" with the exotic features of someone with a diverse ethnic background. When we had e-mailed, I had envisioned something very different—a petite, similarly fluffy girl, perhaps with an Indian accent. Instead, she sounded vaguely British and looked like a runway model. I was completely and utterly intimidated before she'd even introduced herself.

"I'm Mischa." I held out my hand and managed a pursed smile. I hated when I reacted this way to beautiful girls, but after the last twenty-four hours, I was battling a pretty bad case of self-pity. Also, I wanted to kick myself for changing out of the sundress I'd put on earlier and into my too-tight jean shorts that seemed to be shrinking even smaller under Anjuli's gaze.

"You know? I think I've only gotten junk mail for you; otherwise I would have e-mailed you about it. But I did keep it all in a pile. Please, come in."

I followed her inside and noticed immediately the cleanliness and order, not to mention the smell of fresh laundry, or a fancy candle that was made to smell like fresh laundry. I had never kept the place this nice—another strike against my already battered self-esteem.

In the kitchen, she handed me the mail and I flipped through it, seeing nothing of importance. "Shit!" I said under my breath.

"Are you waiting on something?"

"I'm waiting to hear from the grad school."

"The one here?"

"Yeah. They waitlisted me," I explained.

Anjuli placed her hands on her hips, her thin arms showcasing themselves in a perfect V. "So you're thinking of staying even longer? Wow. I don't even know if I'm gonna make it through summer term."

"Why not?" I asked, slightly defensive.

"I don't know, Oceanside's kind of a weird place, don't you think?"

"Weird how?" I had never considered it as anything other than a classic college town—albeit on the beach.

"I don't know, maybe the summer is different, but the people here just seem…bored, or boring."

"Where are you from?"

"New York."

"That's your problem, then. I'm from a small town in Iowa, so absolutely nothing is boring to me."

She let out a low laugh that made me smile despite myself. "You're probably right. I haven't given it much of a chance," she said.

Eager to leave this superior version of my apartment and its new, superior tenant, I told Anjuli I had somewhere to be, which was a complete and utter lie.

As I walked out the door, she called after me. "Hey, you should try going to the Admissions office on campus. They can tell you if the letter was mailed!"

"Yeah, that's a good idea. Thanks!" I shouted back with absolutely no intention of taking her advice. I had already filled my week's quota of face-to-face rejections—I couldn't risk another.

As I drove away, I found the car practically steering itself onto the exact route it had gone so many times before: a quick right, one left, and another right directly into the drive-thru of everybody's favorite, golden-arched fast-food haven.

"I will have two cheeseburgers, a ten-piece chicken nugget, large fry, and medium sweet tea," I barked into the speaker box. *And a straight razor.*

"Okay, two cheeseburgers and a number four."

"Whatever it is, yes."

As some sort of twisted defense mechanism, I had always refused to learn the names or numbers of super value meals wherever I went. It helped me deny the frequency with which I ate the things. Over the years, certain drive-thru cashiers had even tried to bond with me, giving me frequent flyer–type bonuses like extra sauce, or a larger drink, but I did my best to discourage them. I had a strong need to feel anonymous in these transactions, as if I could be anybody. In a way, it was the same fucked up logic that allowed me to believe that shared plates and appetizers didn't really count toward my calories for the day, because there was no telling how much I'd eaten versus the other person—denial at its finest.

Once my food had been paid for, bagged, and handed over in a sufficiently impersonal exchange, I decided to drive to the beach. Not just the beach, but the same spot where Julien had taken me for midday drinks and tacos on my first day of work. I knew I wouldn't run into him there, after observing his workaholic habit of eating lunch at his desk every day, so I felt safe going there with my bag full of trans fats. Maybe I thought that sitting in one of Julien's favorite spots would help me process what had just happened between us. Or maybe I lacked imagination when it came to favorite beach spots. Certain habits are peculiar to overeaters, and ritualistic choices about where to eat is one of them, so the odds were I had some strange subconscious impulse driving me there. But the minute I started to mull over whether or not Julien Maxwell could possibly have feelings for me, I felt myself shutting down, like there was no more room in my brain for new complications. Liam had maxed me out. *Just pretend it never happened,* I heard the voice of reason say. It sounded like a good enough plan for the moment...

Another overeater habit to which I was highly prone was the strange combining of foods. Most people don't wash down cheese puffs with a peanut butter smoothie or shove red licorice sticks into their tacos. I was currently fitting chicken nuggets inside my cheeseburgers, more of a classic taste combination, but still unusual. At least I was eating slowly and had waited to touch the stuff before I arrived at the beach. Hardly ever did I let my fries get cold, but there they were, tepid by the time I had gotten to the bottom of the container.

The meal was over within five minutes, at which point I fought the urge to crumple into a ball and weep. I had erroneously assumed that hamburgers and chicken nuggets might bring me some sort of clarity. Instead, the tidal wave of loneliness that had woken me up that morning came crashing back onto the shores of my consciousness the minute I pounded my last French fry.

With some effort, I managed to stand up and do some haphazard stretching, throwing my trash into one of the rusted metal drums that lined Oceanside's seedier beachfront sidewalks. I could hear my phone ringing inside my car but made no rush to answer it. By the time I made it back, Isabella had left me a message, begging me to save her from death by boredom. I could hear on the recording that she sounded weak, tipsy, not all there, and just knew that—unlike me—she hadn't had enough to eat.

* * *

Every once in a while, Isabella got drunk in the afternoon. It didn't take much, a couple of glasses of champagne or a particularly stiff Bloody Mary from her favorite brunch spot, and all 105 pounds of her was stumbling onto the patio and shouting at her neighbors for having "no style." When I found her that day, she was stretched out on the couch, her television set to a classical music station.

"You smell like fried chicken," she said with disdain as I sat down beside her.

"That's an accurate assessment," I responded. "What did you do to yourself?"

"Why aren't you working?"

"Hey, I asked you first."

"I don't know. I saw a charity auction on television and felt left out. So I had a champagne to make myself feel better." She sat up and lowered the volume on the Chopin concerto that was blaring a little too loudly from the television speakers. "And then I had another one. You want some? Just a little drop?"

Isabella's cheeks were sunken and pale. She clearly hadn't had a bite to eat all day, so I went directly to the kitchen to make her an omelet—one of the few dishes she never turned down. When I opened the refrigerator, I contemplated the bottle of champagne and decided to pour myself a glass, figuring I might as well add drinking in the middle of the day to my current tally of vices.

"What's wrong?" Isabella called after me weakly as she lurched into the kitchen. "I've been left to die in the middle of nowhere. What's your excuse?"

"What are you talking about?"

"Fluffy, you're not happy. Look at those lines between your eyes."

I glanced at her from behind the refrigerator door as I replaced the half-empty bottle of Moët & Chandon that she'd stuck a spoon in, handle-down. "Why the spoon?" I said, holding it up for her to see.

"Keeps it bubbly. Pour me a finger why don't you?" she said with her usual air of authority before sauntering outside to the patio.

* * *

The sun had slipped behind a series of dense clouds by the time I made it outside, lending an extra grayness to an already gray day.

I placed the omelet and a drop of champagne before Isabella and sat down with my second glass. Despite her prodding, I told her I didn't want to talk about myself and asked for a story instead.

"Happy or sad?" she asked.

"I don't care, you pick."

"Fine." Isabella held up her hands and studied her nails for a moment before launching in. "Oooookay. I pick happy!"

I smiled and took a swig of the champagne, which—surprise, surprise—was helping my emotional hangover. "Good," I said.

"Did I ever tell you about Dick Richards? The American soldier I fell in love with?"

"No."

"I called him Dickie, Dickie Richards. Private First Class Dickie Richards! He was from North Carolina, USA," she drawled, doing her best impression of a bad Southern accent. "Oh my goodness, he was the best-looking man I had ever seen. I met him at a cafe in Vienna. He bought me an Aperol Spritz. He didn't even know what the drink was, but he'd seen me having one before. He said to the waiter, 'Git her one of them orange thangs.'"

"How old were you?" I asked. Piecing together Isabella's life and all the places she had lived was like working on one of those impossible thousand-piece jigsaw puzzles.

"I was eighteen, just a baby! And he wasn't much older. He had dirty blond hair and big thick eyebrows and big blue eyes. And he had the softest skin. I fell for him like a cat falls for a dog. Is that a saying?"

I chuckled. "I don't think so."

"It was like *Lady and the Tramp*, you know? He was a scoundrel. My parents wouldn't even have him in the house. They thought he might pee on the floor or something like that. But

I was so sure he was the one for me, and we had the best sex! Anyway, one night, after a few months, we decided to run away together. He would quit the army and I would renounce my inheritance and we would start somewhere completely new. I called it our 'American Dream.'" She smiled wanly as she took the last tiny sip of her champagne. "But then when it came time, I packed a bag and slipped out in the night. He was waiting outside with his duffel bag, all ready to go. We got all the way to the train station, and then he asked how much cash I had, and I said he needed to buy the ticket because I had none. I had taken nothing of value, on principle. That way, my parents would forever regret their decision... But that's when I realized, good old Dickie hadn't imagined me poor, not really. I think he thought I would never really be cut off. He didn't understand the ways of the rich. His parents would have given him the shirts off their backs..." She trailed off, frowning at the sky. "Come back, sun! I need you today."

"So what happened?" I asked, worried that her story was taking a turn for the tragic.

Isabella looked across the table at me and shrugged, nonchalant. "We never got on the train. He said he couldn't leave his paycheck, that without it he couldn't take the risk of going with me to God knows where—we hadn't even decided where we would go."

"Did you keep seeing each other?" I asked, wanting her to say yes. I felt so embittered by my experience with Liam that I couldn't handle the thought of somebody else's heartbreak.

But Isabella shook her head. "I was so young and full of ideals when I met him. I thought love was what you saw in the movies. But then I realized how right my parents were—it was a business transaction, two people measuring up each other's worth. Sometimes it's money, sometimes beauty, sometimes youth. Whatever it is, everyone needs to feel like they're getting something out of it. It's not spiritual; it's materialistic. But the difference between me and Dickie was that I didn't care. I truly didn't. I wanted for us to be poor together, all the way up until that train station. Of course, after that, I knew better…I guess that's not a happy story after all." She forced a smile that quickly faded.

I was on the verge of tears. "No, it's not."

"Oh well," she said, and repeated her catchphrase: "Every man who comes into your life is as an opportunity for adventure. Nothing more, nothing less."

* * *

The afternoon at Isabella's ended with me putting her to bed, with a *Vanity Fair* and a peanut butter smoothie on the nightstand. She had been nothing but cheery after telling me her sad tale, while I had gone in the opposite direction. Even though I wasn't willing to talk about it, she could tell I was heartsick and kept promising I would grow out of it soon enough. She seemed to think that a natural part of growing up was accepting the ugly truth about love, like she had after her botched elopement with Dickie Richards, but I didn't want to think that way. Regardless of my recent failure, I wanted to believe in love as a spiritual thing—not as a material transaction. After her story, though, I wasn't so sure. When I drove away, I felt exhausted and sad but ravenously hungry at the same time. I detoured to the nearest grocery store to stock up on every bad thing I could think of, certain that I deserved it after all I had been through. At checkout, the cashier asked if I was hosting a party.

"Nope," I said, "it's all for me. I'll probably polish it off by tomorrow." I was incapable of smiling and certainly incapable of the usual fibs about who the food was for or why I'd bought only junk. *A friend just had a breakup,* I would normally have said. *I don't know what she likes, so I got one of everything.* Just like drive-thru cashiers, grocery store clerks were always innocently drawing attention to a food binge, but I usually knew how to handle them.

"Sounds like a party to me!" she responded—she was a heavy-set woman herself.

I nodded, my cheeks red with humiliation as I glanced at the lanky teenage boy behind me in line.

This time, when I got back to Julien's house, I didn't make any efforts to hide my contraband. Conveniently, Cecile was there to watch and judge as I shoved my bags and boxes of processed foods in the pantry and freezer, opting for a frozen pizza as my first meal. But after our unspoken truce that morning, she went easy on me.

"That looks like what I would buy if my dad let me get everything I want," she commented.

"Think of me as a cautionary tale," I joked, and shoved the oven closed a little too enthusiastically, causing the teakettle to rattle on top of the stove.

After the requisite sixteen to twenty minutes, I retreated to the guesthouse alone and ate slice after slice of pizza in a half-reclined state, my head propped on several pillows, my shorts unbuttoned to make room for my bloated belly. My thoughts bounced from Liam to Isabella and her sad story and finally to Julien, who was due home from the office any minute now. What would I say to him the next time I saw him? Could I hide out here for the rest of the night and erase my memory of the past twenty-four hours by the time we reunite at breakfast tomorrow morning? Why did the thought of him coming on to me scare me so much? Could it be that somewhere, buried underneath my industrial-sized crush on Liam, I had been harboring feelings for Julien too? Strangely enough, I had never imagined myself with someone older, despite my background; most girls like me had tried to replace their father with a boyfriend old enough to be one by the time they were out of high school. I wondered if it was possible that I had given off that vibe without even knowing it—the vibe of the girl with daddy issues. Or maybe, just maybe, Julien was the one I should be pining for, but I couldn't see how perfect he was for me through the Liam haze…

Figuring it out tonight was hopeless. I examined my last bite of pizza crust before stuffing it past my lips, already filled with regret.

Chapter 13

Friday, July 2: Ocean View Baptist Church Overeaters Anonymous Meeting
Topic of discussion: "Looking for Love in All the Wrong Places"
Calories imbibed: 4,000... at least

After forty-eight hours of the most out-of-control food binging I'd ever engaged in—which involved, most shamefully, an entire box of frozen corn dogs—I turned myself in to the Friday night meeting like a wanted criminal. In classic comic timing, the topic of discussion just so happened to be "Looking for Love in All the Wrong Places." I had to laugh, even though I felt like throwing myself off a highway overpass.

Marie, the meeting's appointed speaker, was a tall, big-boned woman who looked more "athletic" than overweight. She stood as she spoke, her hands laced together in front of her abdomen in a controlled manner. Her voice was raspy, her accent a pleasant Southern lilt. "A lot of us seek disapproval instead of love from our significant others," she started. "It's what some call a reverse codependency that keeps us stuck in our overeating patterns. As long as that other person is making us feel bad about the way we eat, we don't have to feel bad ourselves. Heck, we have a great excuse to keep doing it because that other person is being so cruel, right? But sometimes it's more subtle. Sometimes we just fall in love with people who are emotionally unavailable—maybe they don't ridicule us, but they shut us down whenever we talk about things that are important, our feelings for instance."

Bingo. Emotionally unavailable men—that was me. I hated feeling like a cliché, but there it was. The problems I'd been trying to stuff down with food the past couple of days could be summed up with those three words: emotionally unavailable men. The topic couldn't have been more relevant to my sad state of affairs. I leaned in to pay extra close attention as Marie went on to talk about her own experience. Her first husband, some human stain named "Bogey," had tormented her by rigging their refrigerator with an alarm that went off whenever the door was opened. He also wouldn't allow her to serve her own food, insisting that he doled out healthier portions, and forced her to wear pants that didn't fit to remind her what size she had been when she married him. Luckily, her story had a happy ending, but her descriptions of a long dark period of secret eating and binging and purging after her divorce gave me chills. To call it a cautionary tale would be an understatement.

When it came time for the "free share," my hand shot up, acting independently of my conscious thoughts, and by some miracle, I was called upon. By another miracle, I actually spoke.

"Hi, I'm Mischa, and I'm an overeater."

"Hi, Mischa," the room responded.

I sat up straighter, fueled by adrenaline just from saying my own name. "I've never shared before—" My voice immediately began to shake and I fought the urge to go silent. "I've been coming since I was fifteen, when I first decided I had a problem because I had stopped hanging out with certain friends just to eat more and not feel so bad about it. Pretty much all the skinny girls I knew, I had to stop being friends with. Just seeing them made me hate myself. And I was never *that* overweight, but it's all relative, I guess. Ever since I can remember, I've needed two sets of clothes for my weight fluctuations. Right now, I'm so bloated I can't fit into any of my pants. I've been eating pretty much non-stop for the past two days…"

Some knowing hums greeted me as I glanced around the room. "But today," I continued, "I really want to give it up. For good. I didn't know I was going to say that just now, but I think I mean it." I laughed and felt comforted by the scattered laughs from others in the group. "This last binge ended an hour ago, and it was pretty bad." More knowing hums all around. "What started it was…well, I got involved with a sex addict. I mean, I was fucking him I guess. I'm sorry, excuse the harsh language. I just don't know how else to say it. I thought we were making love, but now that I know better, I think it was just fucking." The words that flowed out of my mouth felt somehow out of my control. It was as if someone had pushed me onstage at an amateur comedy night and I had unexpectedly taken to the microphone.

"We only got together twice, really, but in my pathetic excuse for a love life that is like an epic romance. And ever since he told me he can't be with me because of his sex addiction, I've been driving myself crazy with thoughts about how *I'm* inadequate… how, if he really liked me, he would find a way to be different. Which is really backwards, and I know love doesn't work that way, and the fact that I'm even calling it love shows how messed up I am. But I don't know." I shook my head and noticed my commiserators doing the same. "The last time, it felt different. For me at least. So for a second I was the idiot thinking, 'Maybe this *is* good.' But why would I think that? And then, this other thing happened with my boss, who I also live with. We sort of held hands the other night, but he's hardly spoken to me since. He's way older, and he has a fourteen-year-old daughter who thinks I have a crush on him, even though I really don't. Although, now I've been thinking about it and wondering if maybe I do. He has this aura about him and he's so sophisticated, I feel like if he were to choose me, that would mean I was special. But I don't know, I thought I just looked up to him... How food is supposed to solve any of this I have no idea, but I've been eating enough for a goddamn army."

I paused for a breath. A couple of the women around me seemed to be in minor states of shock. I had forgotten this was technically a Baptist church, and some of the words I had been throwing around certainly did not qualify as reverent. What a jump I had made from nonparticipating wallflower. "I'm sorry for my language. But that felt really good. Thanks for listening." I sank back into the pew, exhausted from my mini-catharsis.

To my surprise, the next person who spoke thanked me and offered her own similar story of unrequited love, sans the salty language. The things she said struck a chord, and I found myself really listening and caring about another person's experiences in a way that I hadn't before. Despite all the hours I'd spent in meetings just like this one, I had never fully grasped the sense of community and support OA had to offer. Before it had been a one-sided experience in which I listened without participating, observed without exposing my own flaws. But today I felt like I'd been split open, and some strange version of happy was starting to replace all my sad.

When the meeting came to a close, we all said what we were

grateful for, and I gave an answer that, again, surprised me as it came out of my mouth. "Everything," I said. And even though it drew some suspicious looks, I really, really meant it. I was inexplicably thankful for every single great and terrible thing that had led me to this point. Maybe it's why I'd said I was thankful for my dad those weeks ago when I'd been caught off guard by the first "gratitude share." If it hadn't been for him, after all, I wouldn't be here. And if it hadn't been for Liam and Julien and Cecile, and my unclear future, and my problematic eating, and my extra fifty pounds, I wouldn't have reached my breaking point today. All of it was what made me "me" at this very moment, and if I didn't choose to like myself now, I may as well tie a trip wire to a doorknob and wait for the next prison guard to relieve me of my shift.

Epiphanies are a wonderful thing. Like a recently awakened, slap-happy coma survivor, I decided to think of everything I was legitimately grateful for: the sunshine, the beach, this meeting, OA, all the healthy foods I'd ever eaten and all the ones I planned to eat in the future—including but not limited to the Mischa Jones Patented Juice Cleanse!—my job, good old flaky Sasha Myers, Julien's guesthouse that I got to live in rent-free, Julien's tortured and complicated daughter, Isabella (!!), Gracie (!!), and Liam's tight pants (even if I never got to see them again), my childhood dog Jolene (named after the Dolly Parton song), my mother…

I could have gone on like that for hours, throwing my arms around everything in my life as if I'd just unwrapped it on Christmas morning and discovered that it was exactly what I wanted. Walking out to the parking lot, I was stepping on softer ground, breathing better air. I felt like someone had saved me from a burning building and now it was time for me to pay it forward. I decided to call my mother right there from the parking lot and left a mushy voice mail about how much I loved her. After that I left another for Gracie, a long rambling speech about friendship and fate and how I'd die without her, then repeated the sentiment in a message to Isabella. Hanging up, I decided to make some plans: First, I would throw away all the junk food I had left in Julien's pantry, burn it if possible; second, I would eat a healthy snack, maybe talk to Cecile if she was around, see if I was on her good side today; third, I would take a walk; fourth, do some sit-ups; fifth, make a to-do list for tomorrow and get to bed early…

I was whispering this laundry list to myself, walking faster than normal with an (inevitably) insane-looking grin on my face, when a frantic male voice called out from behind.

"Milla! Hey! Hey there! Meena, Milla? Hello?"

Answering reluctantly to these approximations of my name, I turned around to find Bobby, Liam's sponsor, speed-walking toward me, pumping fists and all. He was downright winded by the time he reached me, as if he had just run a mile. "I need your help," he said between gasps. "I'm looking for Liam. He didn't show tonight."

"I'm sorry, I don't know where he is," I said, adding, "I'm turning over a new leaf!" as if someone like Bobby cared.

He looked at me quizzically.

"Have you tried the restaurant?" I stated the obvious with a polite little shrug.

"They haven't seen or heard from him in three days. Milla, this is important. Have you talked to him at all?"

"I'm actually Mischa," I clarified, "not Milla."

Bobby jerked his necked impatiently. "I'm sorry, *Mee-shah*, can you remember the last time you saw or heard from him?"

"I saw him Tuesday."

"And where was that?"

"At his restaurant. He was working," I said, leaving it at that.

"Okay, listen. We've gotta find him." Bobby continued to sound very desperate. One side of the chain that held his drugstore reading glasses had come undone and was dangling around his neck. Personally I didn't see how someone like Liam falling off the map for three days could warrant this much hysteria—a grown man with a sex addiction was liable to go missing sometimes, no?

"Bobby, he doesn't want to talk to me," I said. "And frankly, I don't want to talk to him. Why don't you just wait till he comes down from his latest binge, or whatever you call it. I'm sure he'll be fine."

"The last time Liam missed a meeting, he was considering suicide, okay? Does that sound serious enough to you?" Bobby jerked his head again and placed his hands on his hips, his spindly arms looking like they belonged to a skinny teenager.

I froze upon hearing the word *suicide*, officially shocked out of my good mood. If Liam hadn't told me about his attempt to jump off a bridge at eighteen, I would have thought Bobby was exaggerating. Unfortunately, I knew he wasn't. "Of course it does."

"Well, I don't know what your 'new leaf' entails, but I would hope that helping friends in need is part of it, instead of just standing there bug-eyed."

Hearing this, I tried to make my eyes less big but couldn't. And then came the inevitable realization that it was my duty to help. If I was really turning over a new leaf—like he said, like *I* had said—then I had no other choice. "Fine," I answered after another moment of mulling it over. "What can I do?"

* * *

Bobby didn't really explain where we were going. He just instructed me to follow his car, and I did so blindly, trusting that he hadn't been secretly plotting my death and using Liam as a way to get me alone on the edge of a cliff somewhere. He drove slowly through the main drag of Oceanside—so slowly that I had to stop at two red lights because he'd inched through the yellow like a slug. Fifteen minutes into the drive, I followed him up a hilly street that I'd never seen before, lined with nice houses. At the top of the hill, we stopped outside a gated lot, the house obscured by lush palms all around the periphery. Bobby pulled to the curb, parked, and put on his hazard lights. As he walked to my car, his puny chest puffed out as far as it would go. I rolled down my window, bracing myself for whatever was next.

"So I need you to call up, just press the button on that box at the gate," he said, pointing authoritatively.

"Where are we?" I must have been completely disoriented, or the obvious answer wouldn't have evaded me so easily.

"Liam's house," Bobby answered like I was crazy. "You've never been here?"

I shook my head. I chose not to explain that Liam's and my relationship had only involved sex in public places.

"Well, I think he will buzz you in, hopefully. That's the plan anyway. Then I'm gonna sneak my car in behind yours, and you'll be free to go."

"Isn't that kind of misleading?"

"I'm not worried about misleading. I'm worried about saving a life."

Bobby's plan wasn't what I had been expecting—although what I had been expecting was anybody's guess. I started to question his level of intensity and whether or not his claims about Liam's mental state might be a little overblown. However, I had agreed to help, and if this is what helping entailed, I figured I should take a shot.

"All right," I said after a few seconds of hesitation.

"Make it sound like you're here for a rendezvous, okay? Make it suggestive."

"What?" I took offense to Bobby's command, but he didn't seem to care. He gave me a thumbs-up and ran back to his idling car.

Despite my misgivings about the covert-ops-style mission Liam's sponsor had concocted, I pulled forward, waiting to approach the gate until Bobby had maneuvered his car behind mine. At the bottom of the driveway, the call box was positioned just as it would be at a drive-thru. In other words, I drove up to it expertly and rolled my window down out of sheer muscle memory.

The ringing seemed to go on forever after I'd pressed the red button that loomed below the speaker. I hung up once and redialed, as if that would make some sort of difference—which it did, I found out, after four more rings. Liam answered without saying anything. I knew he was there because I could hear him clearing his throat.

"Liam? It's Mischa." To the best of my abilities, I tried to sound flirtatious, or at least hide the fact that I was still mending from the massive heartbreak he'd caused.

"What're you doing here?" Liam was slurring, but somehow his Australian accent helped instead of hindered.

"Are you okay? I went to the restaurant looking for you." For a bad liar, I sounded pretty convincing.

"Ya wanna come up?" he asked.

"Sure." I tried not to sound overeager. "I need to see you."

"Then tell that fucker to get off your tail," he snarled through the call box.

I tensed in my seat. *He knew.* Trying my best to sound clueless, I asked what he was talking about.

"You know what I'm talking about. Tell Bobby to leave me... hell alone. He doesn't get it, got it? He doesn't get *me*. But if you wanna see me? Be my guest. Can't turn down a pretty face."

"But, Liam—"

"I'm not talking to him. That's the deal. Take it, leave it."

"Fine. Hold on." I took my finger off the red button. Somewhat reluctantly, I got out of my car and made my way back to Bobby's station wagon. I was afraid of him the way I had been afraid of my high school gym teacher, another stern nerd with an undercurrent of mania.

"Liam knows you're here. I think he's drunk. He says he'll let me in if you leave."

Bobby banged his steering wheel and let out an irritated exhale followed by a couple of deep breaths. This was a man in desperate need of anger management training. "Your presence will do him no good. I'm the one he needs to see," he said.

"I'm sure you're right, but I don't know what to do." I looked back toward the house, wondering how I could possibly handle the situation if Liam was in fact on the brink of suicide. "This was your idea," I reminded him.

"Fine," said Bobby, exhaling through flared nostrils. "Listen... Dammit..."

"Just tell me what you want me to do when I get up there." I was becoming impatient, worried my invite would be rescinded if I waited too long.

"You need to get him to call me."

I shook my head. "What if he refuses? I can't force him to do something he doesn't want to do."

"Someone's gotta stay with him through the night, okay? And

it looks like it has to be you." In his voice was resignation, defeat. I actually felt bad for him. Did this man have a life outside of Liam? Was there a Mrs. (or Mr.) Bobby to go home to?

"Are you married?" I asked. I couldn't help myself.

Bobby held up his left hand indignantly. "Happily," he answered. "Why?"

"No reason. Listen, I'll try to get him to call you." As I started to back away from his car, Bobby reached out to grab my right hand like he was trying to yank me inside.

"Do not have sex with him! Do you understand?"

"Are you kidding me?" I said, ripping my hand away. "Who do you think is the sex addict here?"

Bobby scowled and shifted his car into drive. "Liam could do a lot better than you, you know."

"Ha." I couldn't believe the same person who had begged for my help was actually insulting me. "Actually, I think it's you he could do better than." Although I tried to hide it with anger, I felt Bobby's put-down killing the good mood I'd just been enjoying. Of course I knew Liam was out of my league, but to hear someone else say it brought me right back to high school, to all the times I'd been teased for being too short and too curvy, for having big breasts, or for buying an extra slice of pizza at school lunch.

I turned and marched back to my car, willing the newly enlightened Mischa to make a reappearance. *I am here for Liam's sake,* I coached myself. *This is not about me, or my insecurities, or Bobby's stupid insults.*

"Good work." Liam's voice piped in over the speaker box as Bobby's car disappeared over the hill.

"Thanks," I said, not quite sure what I was in for as the solid wood gate that stood before me disappeared into the stucco wall that lined the property.

Chapter 14

I hadn't imagined Liam as a homeowner. In my mind, he lived in an apartment—on the nice side, but certainly not a penthouse or anything so lavish. Yet here he was, in a neighborhood so nice I had never even heard of it before. I advanced slowly up the windy driveway to his house—a white, modern-looking affair surrounded by lush green palms lit by spotlights. The place was intimidating to say the least, the kind of swanky retreat that would be profiled in an interior design magazine. Had he really made that much money being in a band? I had mistakenly assumed that Liam's story was just like the ones I had seen on TV about musicians who had made money too young and lost it all on drugs or gambling or multiple divorces, or all of the above. But clearly he had done all right for himself.

Before getting out of the car, I glanced in the rearview mirror and cursed my flat hair that desperately needed a trim. I adjusted my bra underneath my shirt, a little boost to the cleavage, and checked my teeth. Then I remembered the state that Liam was supposedly in and cursed myself for being vain. The truth was, I had jitters about what I was walking into and worried that I wouldn't be able to do or say the right thing to help him if he was in dire straits. I had spent the past few days trying my best to forget how much I cared about Liam, to write him off as an ill-advised fling, but now I was being asked to care about him again and my feelings had come back all too easily. I desperately wanted to be the one who could help him and worried it might send me into a deep depression if I failed.

Nervously, I made my way down a dimly lit stone path to the front door, which opened just as I walked up. Loud rock music blasted from somewhere, seemingly everywhere, probably through speakers set inside the walls or something fancy like that. Liam was already walking away from the door, his back to me as he patted his right hip to the music.

Oh no. I am officially entering the void. I wandered inside and shut the heavy wooden door behind me. There was silence—no pleasantries exchanged, no faux-polite greetings—as he led me past the dark wood staircase in the foyer and into the kitchen where a sea of liquor bottles littered the counter. For the first time that I'd ever seen him outside work, Liam wasn't dressed like he'd been styled for some edgy rocker photo shoot; instead, he was wearing loose, navy blue athletic pants and a faded, tight gray T-shirt. Grabbing one of the bottles, an expensive-looking Scotch, he unscrewed the cap with his teeth and took a swig before turning to face me. Liam's face was a wreck—as much as it could be at least. Dark circles loomed under his eyes. The stubble on his cheeks was patchy, as if he had started to shave but given up out of exhaustion.

"So what? Are you here to save me? Bobby's worried about me so he sent a little Trojan horse?" Liam finally made eye contact with me. There was sadness in his glassy eyes.

I shrugged, fighting the urge to run to him, throw my arms around him. "He said you've been MIA for three days."

"And the last time that happened I got all sad, right? Did he tell you that?"

"Yes."

"Drink?" He held out his bottle of Scotch.

"No thanks."

"I'm sorry, I formed that as a question. What I meant was: drink." He walked around to the side of the counter where I was standing and placed the bottle in my hands, manipulating my fingers so that they grasped its neck. "Please, join me in my misery, Mischa."

Before I could think to protest, I took a small swig. The Scotch burned my throat.

Liam snapped his bottle back with a fake look of disgust. "Lightweight," he teased. He shuffled over to the fridge, retrieved a bottle of water, and walked it over to me. "Wait," he said, and fumbled for a glass in one of the cupboards. "Only the finest for my finest guest." He twisted the cap off the bottle and poured the water.

"You're scaring me, Liam," I said as I accepted the glass. "You're not acting like yourself."

"As if you know who *myself* is! As if Bobby knows who myself is! You know who I am? You see this house? Look..." He took my wrist in his free hand and led me clumsily out a sliding glass door to the backyard. On a flat stretch of lawn, there was a bizarre-looking mountain of guitars and amplifiers, most of them bashed in and torn up. I saw an ax, a shovel, and a shiny aluminum baseball bat lying on the ground by the detritus.

"Whoa," I muttered.

"Yeah, whoa." Liam picked up the bat and began swinging away at a semi-intact electric guitar. "You should try it! It's very cathartic."

"What are you doing? Why are you destroying your instruments?"

"My instruments? Ha-ha. I've got the only instrument you need right here, baby." He dropped the bat and walked deliberately toward me with his lips puckered, taking my face in his hands as if he were about to kiss me. "C'mon, can't you just give me a smile?"

"Liam, please." I grabbed his shoulders and held him at arm's length. "Talk to me. I know I don't know you that well, but I'm the only person you've got right now. Tell me what's going on."

Ignoring me, he leaned in, his mouth agape. I felt his breath, hot and sour-smelling, against my lips. I hadn't realized it was possible that a kiss from Liam could ever be unappealing, but this time it was.

"No." I backed away, stumbling a little over my own feet and feeling my legs go weak. Deciding to sit before I fell, I allowed myself to crumple to the ground. I had no idea what I was doing; I was in over my head. Bobby was probably right—I wasn't the person Liam needed to see right now. But here I was.

Liam went back to destroying his electric guitar with a bat, and it went on like that for several minutes. I sat and watched while he hacked away, neither of us speaking. I searched my brain for what to say but kept coming up empty. *What would Bobby do?* I thought to myself, only half kidding. And then it dawned on me: The minute he arrived, Bobby would have gone straight to pouring all of Liam's alcohol down the drain, devoted twelve-stepper that he was. I shook my head, ruling it out as an option. Being much smaller and weaker than the loose cannon who was presently bashing expensive musical equipment in front of me, I had no business agitating him any further.

When Liam determined his latest victim was sufficiently

wrecked, he dropped the bat and walked over to where I was sitting. I patted the ground beside me in the hope that he would sit, but he shook his head, hovering at my feet in a menacing stance, a demented twinkle in his eye.

"Wanna go to bed, little Mischa? Misch-Misch? Mishmash?"

"That's not why I'm here," I said, hiding my amusement at his silly riffing.

"Oh, screw that!" Liam's face twisted into a grimace. He kicked at an invisible object like a child who hadn't gotten his way. "Yes, it is," he said. "You're just like all the others."

"Oh, really? Thanks a lot!" I scrambled to my feet, briefly contemplating whether or not to storm out.

"What do you want me to say, Mischa? You're a groupie. You're a groupie and you don't even know it. That's the saddest kind of groupie, don't ya think?"

I knew he was just lashing out, but I couldn't help taking it personally. "Why don't you get off your high horse? You're not a rock star anymore—"

Liam scoffed, continuing on his tangent. "There's lots of different kinds of groupies, actually. There's the party girls, who forget what band you're in after they've sucked you off for a bump of coke. There's the fucking gorgeous, delusional ones who think you're gonna want them as your girlfriend just because they let you put it in their backsides. Then there's the ones with their prized fake breasts, always wearing those tiny string bikini tops under their shirts, just begging you to ask them for a lap dance. And there's the ones who like to do it all together, groups of four or five girls who want you to do them all together. But you gotta watch out for those ones! There's always some junkie in the mix—everyone's having a good time except for the one quiet girl who ends up OD'ing in the bathroom at four a.m.—"

"I get it," I interrupted, wanting to plug my ears at the mention of Liam's sordid sexual history. "You've slept with a lot of people."

Liam ran a hand through his hair, avoiding my irritated gaze. "I need a drink."

He stumbled back into the house and I followed, hating him but at the same time feeling sorry for how severely messed up he was. Part of me wondered how much that night at Sasha's spa had played into this meltdown. Maybe it was a self-centered thought, but it seemed plausible. I also wondered what the hell I could say to make any of it better.

Inside, I slid the glass door closed behind me, and something small and hard nudged my lower back. "Drink," I heard Liam say as he poked me with the open end of his Scotch bottle.

Feeling emboldened, I took the bottle, reopened the sliding glass door, and hurled it at the mountain of destroyed guitars and amps.

"Ha! Now you've got it!" he cried. "Don't worry, doll, there's more where that came from." Seconds later he had located a half-full bottle of tequila.

"What are you doing to yourself?" I said.

With one eye closed and the other trained on me suspiciously, he leaned back against the counter. His head wobbled as he slurred his words. "Well! The drink is the only way to stop the sex, right? Gotta exchange one vice for the other, or else"—he made a blow-up motion with his hands—"boom. Explosion. Life over. May as well die in a fiery car crash—which the drink also helps facilitate."

I pointed to the mountain of guitars outside. "What about that? I bet those are worth a lot of money. Why would you destroy them like that?"

"Because, princess, symbolism! The music is what made me bad—get it? It's why I had the groupies, and why I cared so much about fucking the groupies, and why the groupies took over my life and made me hate myself."

"Groupies didn't do anything to you."

"Just like food never made you fat, did it?"

"Go to hell!" I shouted, finally losing the shred of cool I had been holding on to. Liam's words had run me through like a sword. Tears welled up in my eyes but I fought them back.

"Hey, don't be mad. You know I like a girl with a little extra. You've got it in all the right places, baby. And now you're trying to throw it in my face." Liam raised his voice and advanced toward me. "*You* remind me why I can't have sex anymore without hating myself!"

"Yeah, well you remind me that I don't love myself enough to be with a normal person! You remind me why I've wasted years pining over assholes! But you know what? I wanna get better, and I *am* going to get better."

"Oh, are you?" Liam said. He was only inches from me now. I could see his chest heaving. "Good luck with that."

"Thanks, I appreciate it." I rolled my eyes, feeling certain now that my presence was doing more harm than good. Accepting defeat, I grabbed my keys from the counter and started out of the room.

"Nobody changes, Mischa," Liam called after me. "You're screwed, and I'm screwed. We may as well screw each other, no?"

I grunted loud enough for him to hear. I was angrier than I'd ever been, even angrier than the first time Bradley had ignored me on campus after our breakup. Turning as I reached the hallway, I flipped Liam off with both middle fingers before charging out and straight out that stupid, heavy front door. I doubted he'd follow, but when I got to my car, Liam was right behind me, panting for breath.

"Wait! Mischa! I was kidding. Don't leave." He sounded frantic, but I had lost all sympathy.

"Please, just stay out of my life," I said. Unlocking the car, I remembered the one thing I was supposed to accomplish. "Oh, and call Bobby. He's convinced you're going to kill yourself, but I know now you're too narcissistic for that."

I tried to slide into the car through the narrow opening I'd made with the door, but Liam stopped me, placing his hand proprietarily on my waist and whipping me around to face him. Up close, he smelled of pure alcohol.

"I didn't mean it," he slurred gently.

"Which part?" A better person would have wrestled her way out of his grasp, but I still found his touch hard to resist.

"I'm a fucking mess, Mischa." Liam's face crumpled and he started to weep, at first silently, then in a sad, high pitch that made him sound almost childlike, like a helpless animal. There was nothing for me to do, it seemed, other than commiserate. I gave up feeling angry, reaching around him to pat his back. Hunched over me, Liam laid his forehead on my shoulder and continued to cry. The other times I had had Liam within my grasp, he had been powerful, voracious, predatory. Now he was vulnerable, even weak.

"I'm sorry. It's gonna be okay," I said, even though I had no idea how anything was going to be okay. I didn't know Liam well enough to know whether he would succeed or fail in this life. In a way, he had been right about me being just another groupie. I had viewed him as an exotic object of desire, untouchable except in moments of reckless abandon. Of course, he had presented himself that way, at first. But even after he had revealed his weaknesses to me, I hadn't really tried seeing him as anything other than the dark and dangerous sex addict who was using and abusing me.

His hands eventually found their way to my waistline, his lips gently kissing the nape of my neck. I stopped him, knowing I had to.

"I wanna be your friend, okay? Not your groupie. I wanna help you." I pushed him away, but he came back at me with greater intensity.

"This is how you help me." He ran his hands up my abdomen and planted them on my breasts.

"Stop it!" I wrestled myself away from him a second time and forced my way inside the car. He placed a hand on the frame so that I couldn't shut the door. "Liam, I'm gonna close it," I warned.

"You'll break my hand."

"Seriously, move away from the car. I will break your hand."

"No, you won't, you sweet girl."

"Ugh! You're making me so mad right now!" I stomped my feet and pounded the dashboard, reverting to my own form of childishness. I looked back up at him and noticed his face wet with tears. He smiled a weak smile that betrayed the opposite of happiness.

"Don't you see? You wrecked me the other night. I don't know what I'm doing anymore." Liam shook his head, swaying a little in his stance.

I slumped forward, letting my head rest momentarily on the steering wheel, thinking, *Thank God. It meant something to him too.* It was validation—maybe not in the form I would have preferred but reassuring nonetheless. In a way, I felt like we were back on the same page again, like we had been the other night at Sasha's spa before he had told me it was over. Liam had that magical ability to draw me back in just when I was ready to give up on him. "Fine," I said. "Let's get you to bed."

"That's more like it," he laughed.

"You know what I mean." I smirked. "Don't get any ideas…"

"Oh, I've got some ideas," Liam said, "and they don't involve bed."

* * *

I had never watched a gourmet chef cook this up close before. It was a thing of beauty—him whipping up a simple frittata with tomato, asparagus, and goat cheese, even if he was half drunk and stumbling between the cutting board and his skillet. Liam chopped like he had been the top of his class at culinary school, and he did this thing with fresh tarragon and chervil like he was weighing little heaps of the herbs in his palm. It was probably for show, but it made him look like a food wizard. While the frittata finished cooking in the oven, Liam arranged beautiful place settings on his formal dining room table, then lumbered into the backyard to cut some fresh flowers for a centerpiece. It was the most adorable drunken display of hospitality I had ever witnessed.

"Dear Lord"—he took my hand when we finally sat down to eat, our steaming slices of frittata giving off tantalizing eat-me-now aromas—"thank you for sending Mischa, goddess of love, to take care of me on this dark night of the soul—"

I laughed through my nose the way kids do in church.

"And may you keep her warm and safe from my inevitable advances"—Liam glanced over at me with a mischievous smile—"forever and ever, amen."

"Amen," I echoed, and dug in. "Oh my God," I said, tasting the eggy, cheesy perfection.

"Good?" Liam asked, his mouth half full.

"Beyond," I replied.

At the same ravenous pace, we ate our way through firsts and seconds and thirds in a comfortable silence that reminded me of the times Gracie and I had gone for greasy diner food after nights of drinking. Every once in a while, I studied Liam's face when he wasn't paying attention, noticing how his mood had magically changed from dark to light. It had happened, actually, the minute he'd started cooking, and I realized what he had told me the other night must be true—that he forgot his problems at work, that cooking really was his salvation. It was something to aspire to, I thought, to find the thing that would make me forget my problems.

After we'd finished, I walked him upstairs to his massive bedroom and helped him into his bed, which sat low to the ground on a minimalist frame. Knowing how drunk he was, I had no fear that Liam's sex addiction was much of a threat at this point, so being in his bedroom felt like no big deal other than that it was intimidatingly grand like the rest of the house. On the wall behind his bed, there was a giant, modernist painting, and several other pieces of seemingly expensive art hung on the opposite wall.

"It's hot in here," he said, throwing off the sheet that I had placed on top of him.

"Come here." I took Liam's hands and tugged until he sat up. "Put your arms over your head," I instructed, then pulled off his T-shirt. Glancing behind me, I saw the bathroom door ajar and went to deposit the sweaty shirt in his laundry basket. Behind another door beside the massive glassed-in shower, I found the linens and grabbed a washcloth that I ran under cool water. Returning to Liam's bed, I placed the compress on his forehead.

"Oh my God," he groaned. "That's the best thing I've ever felt."

"How are you so friggin' rich?" I asked, giving voice to the thing I had been thinking ever since I'd arrived. Even though it was a rude question, I felt like Liam could use a little frivolous conversation.

"My dad had money." He patted the small sliver of bed between him and the edge of the mattress. I shook my head, choosing to lie on the other side of him, on top of the covers. Liam glanced at me sideways with a pained look in his eyes. "But I wanna *lay* with you, like in the biblical sense," he whined.

"How about this?" I reached out for his hand, and he let me take it. "Turn on your side," I instructed, and used my free hand to adjust the washcloth as Liam turned to face me. "So, your dad *had* money. Does that mean he died?"

"Yeah."

"Recently?"

"Two years ago."

"I'm sorry," I said.

"Stop telling me you're sorry…" He squeezed my hand a couple of times. "I know you care," he said, then took a deep breath. I waited for him to say something else, but the minute he had hit the bed, I could tell it was going to be a matter of seconds before he passed out. His eyelids started to flutter, and he tried to make a joke but I could barely hear it.

"You're gonna be okay," I said. I knew he was probably sleeping already, but I uttered the words anyway, because in that moment I wanted to believe them—for him and for me. Maybe it was left-over from my revelations at that night's OA meeting, but I sensed that change was on the horizon. I couldn't put my finger on why or how, but it was the closest thing to a psychic intuition I'd ever experienced. "We're both gonna be okay," I whispered moments later as I let go of his limp hand and kissed his forehead, hot from the alcohol.

I stayed on the bed a little while longer to make sure he was fully asleep. I wanted to stay all night, cozy up to him and lay my head on his warm bare chest, let the sound of his breathing coax me to sleep. It took all the self-discipline in the world not to burrow under the sheets and do exactly that. At the end of the day, I knew it wouldn't be right; in the morning, we'd be facing the same problems we'd come up against before: Liam was an addict and I was his drug. I cared for him too much now to ignore that.

Even though it ripped me apart, I slowly rose from the bed and went down to the kitchen where I found a bottle of aspirin and filled a large glass with ice water, then tiptoed back upstairs to place the items on his nightstand. I fought the urge to leave a note. Mostly I just wanted to kiss him once more, somehow sensing this was a final goodbye. He was even more beautiful asleep. I could see the way he would be when he was mended, peaceful, no longer tortured by his compulsions, and longed for the parallel universe where Liam and I could be together.

Outside it was foggy and dark; not even the stars or the moon could offer me company as I parted ways with Liam, seemingly for good. I drove up to the gate and it opened automatically from the inside, giving me no last-minute excuse to stay. If someone had asked me three days ago whether or not my heartache could have gotten any worse, I would have told them no. And I would have been wrong.

* * *

I didn't realize how exhausted I was until the minute I crawled into bed at two a.m. But before I let myself fall asleep, I tried to get back to that ecstatic peace of mind I had had in the parking lot, just before Bobby had accosted me, by taking deep breaths and naming all the things I was thankful for again. Just when I got to Gracie, I heard my phone ring and was shocked to see her name on the screen.

"What's up? Is everything okay?" I said as I picked up.

"Yeah, yeah, yeah, I'm fine. I just can't sleep."

"Phew. Also, are your ears burning? I literally was just saying your name in my head."

"Ha-ha, why? Are you obsessed with me now too?"

"Basically." I laughed. "You sound good for someone who's up at two a.m."

"Oh you know, just livin' the life. I miss you!"

"I miss you too. We gotta hang sometime. What are you doing tomorrow?"

"I don't know, I think I'm free. Ha-ha. Wouldn't that be great, if I could just come over and hang?"

"Maybe you should visit."

"But I just left! I don't know if I can handle the instant nostalgia thing. So...how are you?"

I turned on my side and propped myself up. "I'm actually good, all things considered. I mean, I had to talk Liam off the ledge tonight—"

"Really, what was that about?"

"Oh, where to start?" I took a deep breath and searched my mind for the relevant details. "You know what?" I said, after a substantial pause. "It's not important. What about you?"

Gracie sighed. "Meh. Same here, I guess. Haven't seen the guy. It's probably a good thing...It's all much ado about nothing, right?"

I smiled, allowing my eyes to close. "Right on, sistah."

* * *

The rest of the weekend went by quietly. On Saturday, I took Cecile to a matinee showing of the R-rated movie she'd been dying to see, but said no when she begged me to get her nose pierced afterward. On Sunday, still artfully avoiding me, Julien took Cecile to his mother's house to celebrate the Fourth of July, and I went to Isabella's, where I made virgin daiquiris and she and I watched the neighborhood association's fireworks show from the perch of her golf cart. When it came time for the grand finale, I squeezed my eyes shut and made a wish that I would be accepted into Reid's graduate program, even though it seemed more and more like a long shot as time had ticked by.

"What are you doing, Fluffy?" said Isabella, poking furiously at my side. "Open your eyes—you're going to miss it!"

The next day was Monday, and back to work. By that time, Julien and I had eased back into talking as if our late-night run-in had never happened and I was grateful for the awkwardness to subside. It seemed clear now that in my heightened emotional state after seeing Liam, I had misinterpreted the hand-holding with Julien, which was in actuality nothing more than a fluke, not even significant enough to warrant a conversation. It was a great relief, and I was happy to return to our easy mentor-mentee dynamic. I even mustered the courage to ask him to put a good word in with the graduate studies dean, and he eagerly agreed, throwing out a quote from a Maya Angelou poem about new beginnings, which I was miraculously able to counter-quote.

That night, Cecile reminded me of a promise I'd made to cook her dinner, and I obliged. It helped that Julien was out for the night. It also helped that she had stopped bullying me ever since my meltdown the other morning. The only nasty comment came at the end of dinner when she requested fruit for dessert but suggested I skip it. "I mean, you're gonna need to lose at least twenty pounds if you want Droolian Poundwell to look twice, don't ya think?"

"You're funny," I said, convincingly unfazed. "We never negotiated dessert. I'm gonna go shower." With that, I walked to the back door, swaying my fluffy hips back and forth so that she could tease me if she felt so inclined. She didn't. I silently congratulated myself, having finally come up with a strategy for Cecile that semi-worked.

I had left the air-conditioning off in the guesthouse all day. Thus, my small but powerful window unit was still trying to catch up to the sweltering heat after the lukewarm shower I had taken to cool off. It was the kind of heat that dried you instantly once you stepped out of the shower, rendering towels completely unnecessary. Usually I swaddled myself before I even emerged, to negate the risk of catching my naked reflection in the mirror. But this night I found myself staring down my mirror image in the buff, and for once, I didn't want to recoil in horror. My body hadn't changed, despite being on the wagon all weekend, yet I found myself looking in a different way. Of course, the flaws were all still there—the fat and stretch marks, the big oval birthmark on the right side of my rib cage that I had always hated, the red creases where my belly folds—but the voice inside my head, which sounded a lot like Cecile on one of her snarky days, was strangely absent. It probably helped that I had taken my mind off Liam and how I might win his love and had gotten back to worrying about my own life and what to do with it. I put my hands on my hips and allowed myself to stare, really stare. This was my body today, and nothing was going to change that. There were some good things about it too. I liked my breasts, and my feminine, rounded shoulders, my peachy skin tone. I liked my hands, one of the few places my weight never showed. I liked my smile, my eyebrows, my ears. Most important, I liked that I was still standing in front of the mirror and hadn't run away in shame.

Chapter 15

For the rest of the week, I ate healthily and stuck to three meals a day without snacks. My skin looked better, and my mood improved dramatically. The stack of acceptance letters from grad schools that I had been ignoring finally made its way to the top of my priority list as I sorted through it, discarding the envelopes from schools whose registration deadlines I had already missed and poring over the remaining three as if they contained secret messages that would help me choose. And as hard as it was for me to imagine moving so far away, I finally decided on a plan B—a small program at a big state school in New Mexico. The decision was based on the academics alone, but it also helped that classes didn't start until January and I could still wait to respond, just in case Reid decided to accept me at the last minute.

By Friday, I had dropped five pounds with what seemed like hardly any effort. I decided to celebrate by wearing a pair of plaid shorts that had long ago stopped fitting and surprising Cecile at her swim meet.

"Hey!" Cecile ran up to me at the side of the pool where the spectators were gathered, dripping wet after placing second in a relay race.

"Cecile! You did great!" I held my hand up for a high five that she reluctantly obliged.

"Thanks," she said, still catching her breath.

"Did you see this?" I held up the crude sign I had drawn with a Sharpie sketch of a big, blue shark and Cecile's name in gold.

Not surprisingly, she rolled her eyes. "Yes," she groaned.

"I figured it would embarrass you."

"Thanks a lot."

"Anytime!" I held out my hand for another high five—this one she denied.

"Hey, I'm gonna go out with the team after, and Stacey's parents are giving me a ride."

At the mention of her name, Cecile's friend Stacey ran up behind her and nodded at me from over Cecile's shoulder. Stacey was a hyper-seeming girl who was very tall for her age, a good four inches taller than me.

"Does your dad know?" I asked. Julien hadn't been able to make it to the swim meet that night. Just before I had left his office, he had mumbled something about a work dinner.

Cecile shook her head while Stacey nodded at the same time, sending them both into fits of laughter. I smiled at the two, remembering that frantic rush of middle school camaraderie—here today, gone tomorrow friendships that bloomed and withered as quickly as actual flowers—and told them to have a good time. "It's not really my place to say yes, but I'll take the heat if your dad gets mad," I said, choosing to play good cop.

"Thanks a mil!" Stacey piped in, and the two were off and running.

* * *

I had walked to the pool. On the way home I took the long route, following a street that looped around the periphery of Julien's neighborhood. It was almost summer solstice, and the sun was barely setting at eight p.m. I could see the fireflies flitting about people's yards and could smell the dinners being cooked on outdoor grills; the whole effect made me long for a trip home. This was the first summer I hadn't spent in Iowa, and I missed it. The summers had a certain balmy charm there, and whenever my mother had days off, she and I would fish, or sunbathe at her boyfriend's neighborhood pool, or just sit around on her tiny porch and play cards. Wherever I ended up this year, I'd have to find a way to make it home next summer if only for a short trip. I made a mental note, tacking it onto my list of a gazillion to-dos.

When I got back to the guesthouse, I passed out unexpectedly, facedown on the bed. My sleep patterns had become erratic now that my sugar and caffeine intake had gone down drastically, and these oddly timed naps were becoming a too-frequent occurrence. The next time I opened my eyes, it was three in the morning and I was starving for the dinner I never ate. Knowing I wouldn't be able to fall back asleep without something in my stomach, I got up and snuck into Julien's kitchen as quietly as possible. The light from the refrigerator guided my way as I threw together a salad with some roasted chicken I'd bought at the grocery store. It was simple, yet delicious and left me with no desire for dessert or any other sort of junk. Who was this stranger I had become?

After that, I felt like another walk, so I crept back out of the kitchen and left the house through the side gate. It was cool and breezy outside, and the sound of the wind rustling through the magnolia trees was soothing, albeit a little eerie at this hour. I wandered for nearly half an hour, taking streets I'd never gone down before, discovering cul-de-sacs littered with abandoned toys and strange, New England–style gingerbread houses that looked terribly out of place among the scattered palm trees.

I tried to put my mind on future plans, but thoughts of Liam kept popping into my head. I wondered if he was okay after the other night or if he'd woken up even more depressed, as I inevitably did on the rare occasion that I drank too much. I wished I could call and check in on him, to hear his voice and gauge whether he was in need of more emergency intervention. Unlike the way I'd felt after our night at the spa, I had no resentment toward Liam after seeing him at his lowest. I just knew that I cared about him deeply and wanted him to be okay. At the same time, I knew the best thing for him was for me to stay away. He was never going to get better with me around—the harshest pill I'd ever had to swallow. And where did that leave me? If I was so intent on moving forward, I also had to realize that thinking about Liam wasn't going to help me either. But how could I stop? So much had happened over the past few weeks, I felt like I'd had a year's worth of experiences condensed into that short amount of time, and I was still trying to process all of it. Strange how a life can creep along at a snail's pace, like mine had all senior year, and suddenly kick into high gear like a bullet train racing through time.

I was glad to be up at this hour, to have space to think about everything without distractions. I used to take late-night walks like this back in Iowa. For some reason, it had never scared me to be out alone; in fact, it had a calming effect. I embraced the way the world felt empty, like everyone had cleared out just so I could enjoy some peace and quiet. But wild animals were not something to be messed with—this much I knew—and as I neared the end of a particularly dark dead-end street around the corner from Julien's, I got spooked by a stray dog that looked hungry and wild-eyed, its dirty white hair matted into dreadlocks. Switching into flight mode, I did an about-face and walked in the opposite direction, careful not to provoke the animal by breaking into a run.

When I rounded the corner onto Julien's street, stepping quickly and quietly with fists pumping the way Bobby had pursued me in the church parking lot, I glanced over my shoulder for the dog but it wasn't there. Then, just as one threat was gone, another materialized as I turned my gaze back toward home and saw a figure running at me in the distance. I stopped in my tracks and looked again for the dog, hoping that it might morph into my sidekick and team up with me to scare this new menace away, but the animal was nowhere to be found. Meanwhile, I noticed the runner had stopped, too, right around Julien's driveway.

Squinting as hard as I could, I registered the green reflective stripes on the person's shoes and realized the shadowy figure was Julien as he made his way to the front door.

"Julien!" I called out from several feet away just before he walked inside.

"Mischa? Is that you?" He moved off the front steps, tentatively making his way toward me as I headed up the driveway. "What are you doing?"

Relieved that it was him, I beamed as we came face-to-face in the driveway. "Taking a walk. I couldn't sleep," I said.

"Oh, wow. Me too. Huh."

"Did you get my text? Cecile went out with Stacey after the meet."

"Yeah, did I not text you back? Shoot. I meant to say it was fine."

"That's okay. How was your dinner?"

He raised his eyebrows. "Umm...fine. It was fine."

Fine, fine, fine. Julien and I might have moved on from our awkwardness, but a bit of it obviously still remained. It didn't help that we were standing alone together in the middle of the night.

"Funny running into you," I said. "It's rare to see someone at this hour, but we seem to have a knack for that." I shifted in place, hoping that my comment hadn't come across as flirtation.

"Yeah, I guess we do." He rubbed at his forehead like he was annoyed or had a headache. I noticed his chest heaving underneath his shirt and wondered if it was leftover from his run or if there was something else quickening his breath. Julien seemed to notice me looking at his chest and tilted his head, as if he was assessing what to do next. The same confusion I'd felt that night he'd touched my hand came over me, but this time I felt drawn to him. He was standing close enough for me to smell his sweat, clean like he'd taken a shower just before his run. "You look different," he finally said.

"I lost a few pounds," I said, both flattered and embarrassed.

"I don't think it's that. You look...happier."

"I am, I think." I laced my hands in front of my chest, rocking back onto my heels. The other night, I had been so quick to leave the minute things had gotten weird between us. Now I wanted to stay put and see what came next. Maybe I just needed the attention, but it didn't feel as superficial as that.

"Is it because of that guy?" Julien asked. "The one from the restaurant?"

I shook my head, taken aback. Was that a hint of jealousy in his voice?

"No. We're not really seeing each other anymore," I said, preemptively arching my back as Julien inched closer to me, and my chest spontaneously began to heave in time with his. With almost no space left between us, I could see his big brown eyes above me, just visible in the moonlight.

"I've been thinking about the other night," he confessed.

I leaned in, closing the gap between our bodies. I had no idea what I was doing—acting on instinct, apparently. It felt reassuring to be this close to someone again, as if I had feared it would never happen after Liam. I closed my eyes and sensed Julien's large, powerful hands gently landing on my shoulders, lightly massaging them. Under his touch, I felt dainty and small. I hadn't thought much about the comparison, but he was a few inches taller than Liam, his build a little more muscular and wide. I let my forehead fall against his chest.

"It was nice, holding your hand, talking to you. You're easy to talk to, Mischa." Julien's hips pressed into my stomach. I turned my head to the side and heard his heart pounding. His chest was warm and a little damp from sweat. *What are we doing?* I thought as I breathed in the smell of his deodorant, a lovely scent like cut grass. Every breath, every slight movement from either of us, was emotionally charged as we stood there, our bodies refusing to part. The moment felt clandestine. My fingers found Julien's, hanging at his sides, and we joined hands. I tilted my head back to look at him just as he leaned down to kiss me. The minute our lips collided, a well of passion seemed to pour out from both of us. Julien's tongue was warm and electric as it touched mine, causing my entire body to melt.

"I want you," he whispered as he crouched down to kiss my neck and my collarbone. "I'm sorry."

"Don't be sorry," I whispered back, unlacing my fingers from Julien's and running them up the front of his body. Grasping his shoulders, I stood on tiptoe to kiss the base of his neck, then closed my eyes and hung my head back, dying for him to kiss me again. I finally understood what it was about an older man that Gracie found so appealing. I felt young and innocent in Julien's arms, eager to be taught.

But seconds went by as I anticipated another kiss, and nothing happened. When I opened my eyes again, I saw the same low-angle view of the stars I'd had the night Liam and I had made love on the street and felt Julien's hands slip away from my waist.

"Good night, Mischa," he said, awkward and abrupt.

"Wait! No!" My voice trembled from the electric current that was still coursing through my body as I stood there on the driveway, suddenly abandoned.

Julien only made it a few steps toward the house before approaching me again, this time to push a few strands of hair away from my face as he gave me a long, sweet peck on the cheek and told me "Good night" for the second time.

"Okay," was all I could think to say as he drew back again.

"I'll see you tomorrow," he said, his eyes darting back to the house.

I nodded, trying to make sense of what had just happened as Julien drifted away in slow motion.

Before he strayed too far, his big brown eyes met mine once more. After that, he turned around and disappeared inside, back to his house and daughter, back to his widower's bed.

* * *

When I awoke the next morning, it was to the sound of birds singing outside, something I hadn't noticed once since I had been staying here. Instinctively, I turned to look out at Julien's bedroom window but saw no trace of him there.

The kiss last night had been wildly confusing, our goodbye premature. Yet it also seemed like the precursor to something potentially great. Part of me wondered if Julien was the answer, after all my tribulations with Liam, like everything I had gone through had been a trial run for my first real, adult relationship with a stable, reliable, older man. An unexpected knock on the door shook me out of it. Feeling certain it must be Julien, I rushed out of bed to answer in my tank top and boxer shorts.

"Hiiiiiiiii," Gracie greeted me—a zombie behind large sunglasses—as I opened the door. I couldn't believe my eyes. It was the closest thing to a mirage I had ever encountered. "I know I didn't call," she said, her low voice dry and gravelly like she hadn't slept.

"What?! This is amazing. What are you doing here?" I exclaimed. I hadn't known how much I had missed my friend until the moment she showed up on my doorstep. I embraced her excitedly, but her side of the hug was weak, like the life had been drained out of her. "Oh no. What's wrong?"

"Can you smell the despair?" She lowered her sunglasses to reveal the puffy eyes behind them.

"Come in." I ushered her inside, where she dropped her stuffed-to-the-gills carry-on bag and hobbled to the bed.

"I think your host family thinks I'm a nutjob," she said.

"Did Cecile say something rude? She's very fourteen."

"No, Droolian looked at me like I had two heads when he opened the door."

I couldn't help but smile at the thought of Julien doing anything. "Well, I've never had a friend over. And didn't you tell him you were going to D.C.? He probably thought you were a mirage, just like I did."

I plopped down beside Gracie, and she immediately fell back

onto the mattress, bringing her hands to her face in anguish. "So, that guy's a real asshole I found out. One of the great assholes, in fact."

"The junior senator?" I said.

"Yes. Richard." She sounded utterly heartbroken upon saying his name. "Richard Jackson Wellington Stipe the fourth."

"Stipe?"

"Yes, like Michael Stipe of the ancient rock band R.E.M. He claims no relation, but who else has that name?"

"I mean, that's some name he's got on him, with 'the fourth' and everything."

"I was listening to bad airplane radio on the way here—because my phone is broken, because *everything* in my life is broken—and there was some song about how all that matters is being born with a good name. And I'm telling you, this guy is like the walking example of that theory. He's had everything handed to him. How I didn't suspect he would be an asshole is unfathomable."

I looked back at Gracie, who was staring into the middle distance like she'd just received electroshock treatment. "Do you want something to eat?" I asked.

She shook her head fervently. I was secretly dying for an excuse to go into the kitchen, to feel out what Julien was thinking after last night. "I'll get us waters!" I said. "And maybe aspirin? Do you want aspirin?" Gracie had been massaging her temples like a madwoman.

"Yes. For God's sake, get me twenty," she groaned.

I smiled and popped up from the bed, my heart speeding up as I changed out of my pajamas in the bathroom and threw on a little sundress that showed just enough cleavage to make me second-guess it. I brushed my teeth in record time and threw my hair back in a ponytail and waved at Gracie as I sped out the door.

"Knock, knock," I called out as I opened the back door to the kitchen. When no one answered, I wandered inside and found it empty—no Cecile, no Julien, no dishes in the sink to suggest that they had been there at all that morning. I thought it odd, particularly because Cecile usually left her cereal bowl for someone else to clean, but today there was no trace of them.

I filled a couple of glasses with water from the refrigerator dispenser and poked my head into the hallway. "Hello?" I called upstairs, to no response. They must have gone out for breakfast, I decided, a little let down. In the guest bathroom, I grabbed a couple of aspirin from the medicine cabinet before making my way back to my pale, exhausted friend.

"Tell me everything," I said, delivering the water and pills, which she gulped down immediately. With a big sigh, Gracie deposited her glass on the nightstand and fell back on the bed. I did the same so that we were lying face-to-face.

"Okay, so you know how I told you we had sex in a public bathroom and it wasn't great?"

"Yeah?"

"So after that things were obviously weird. He was texting me kind of impersonal, jokey things and I wasn't responding because I didn't know what to say and I didn't want to be all chummy."

"Good for you," I said in solidarity, reminded of my similar resolve with Liam. It was always easy for me to relate to Grace's stories about guys. I had a long history of going after the bad ones just like she did, so I felt her pain as if it were my own. The only difference between us had always been that Gracie consummated her affairs and I didn't. Until this summer, that is.

"And then," she continued, "about a week after, we ran into each other at a fund-raiser."

"You guys go to a lot of fund-raisers."

"That's all D.C. is. Fund-raisers."

"Sounds good to me," I said.

"It's great for free appetizers and booze, I'm not gonna lie. Anyway, so he makes this big deal about me ignoring him, and I was like 'I haven't been ignoring you. I've just been incredibly overworked.' And he was like, 'Oh, well you should come to the lake with me this weekend,' and I was like, 'Wha?' But I did it! I went to his family's lake house in Virginia and the first night we got there, it was like this glorious sex fest, like nothing I've ever experienced before." Getting fired up by her own story, Gracie propped up on one elbow. "Mischa, I'm not kidding you, we did it eight times in one night."

"That's impossible!" I poked her side, teasing.

"I'm not lying. Every available surface: kitchen, bathroom, two bedrooms, living room in front of the fire."

"Wait, why did you have a fire going in July? In Virginia?"

"Oh shut up, it was romantic."

"I'm just saying. Hot! Like *hot* hot."

"Exactly. So anyway, cut to his parents and brother arriving unexpectedly the next day. And it's super awkward, because he thought they were going to New York, so obviously unannounced change of plans, boom, suddenly it's a family affair. And this is not your typical family scene. He has a super old, rich dad, and way younger stepmother. And the half brother's like fifteen years younger than him, still in college. So anyway, we've got about seven generations represented."

"What did you do?"

"Well first of all, Richard introduced me as his 'work friend.' Which was pretty offensive to me after the sex we'd had. Honestly, I would have been flattered if he had just said friend, but somehow 'work friend' sounded like he was making a point... drawing a line, so to speak."

"Well, it was an awkward run-in. I mean, people say things off the top of their heads."

"No, it gets worse. So we all sort of do our own things that day. I read a book and laid out on the dock. The men went fishing. Richard's mother did God knows what in the house all day. I'm pretty sure she's a pill popper. But everybody came together for dinner that night, and it was surprisingly fine. A little awkward, but fine. However, I was drinking...a lot...because I felt uncomfortable and that's what I do."

"Right." I immediately pictured drunk Gracie with her red, red cheeks and felt a sense of dread about what was coming next.

"So later, after the parents go to bed, it's just me and Richard and the half brother, Bryan, who's twenty-one maybe but looks twelve—he's like a skinny, mop-headed, bizarro Justin Bieber—and Richard suggests we go in the hot tub on the deck. And I kind of rolled my eyes, but I'm like, 'Fine.' What I really want is to have sex in front of the fireplace again, but I figured there was no way for that to happen with his parents around, even if moms is catatonic after nine p.m. But then we go into the hot tub, and we're passing around a bottle of champagne, and Bryan starts talking about how he can't get laid at his school because all the girls are fucking older guys these days. And then...oh my God, Mischa..." Gracie's voice filled with dread. She flopped onto her back and stared at the ceiling. "Richard suggests that Bryan sleep with me!"

"No. No, no, no." My stomach sank. "Oh, Gracie," I said, reaching out and touching the side of her arm, not sure what else to say. Bringing her hands to her face again, she started to cry.

"He highly recommended me. He said I was a very good lay, and they both just laughed like it was the funniest thing ever."

"What did you say?"

She shook her head, wiping at her tears and turning back toward me as she regained her composure. "I said nothing. I stormed out of the fucking hot tub, and I got dressed and got my stuff and called a cab to the nearest train station. And then I waited for five insanely long hours to get a train home."

"Did he try to apologize?"

"That's the worst part. He didn't follow me inside, so he didn't even know I'd left the house. Then he was texting me all these stupid fake apologies, telling me he was just kidding and all that."

"Did you respond?"

"No!"

"Good." I held my hand up for a high five and she slapped it with gusto. "What a jerk. I can't believe it."

"I know, right?"

I felt so bad for her and wanted to do something to cheer her up. I searched my brain, trying to come up with inexpensive alternatives since I'd already spent last week's paycheck on expensive organic groceries. And then it dawned on me. "Hey—guess what? I'm taking you to the spa!"

Her eyes widened with excitement, but at the same time, she shook her head. "No. You can't afford it."

"No, really, it's free! Listen! When I left back in the fall, Sasha gave me a couples' massage as a parting gift. She probably knew I would never use it because I'm perpetually single."

Gracie beamed. "Why didn't you tell me about this before?"

"Because I thought it might be a little weird, getting a couples massage with a friend."

"Oh forget weird, we're doing it!" Gracie flipped onto her back and sat up, suddenly alert. Something I'd known about my friend ever since I had started the receptionist job at Sasha's spa was that she loved a good massage. In fact, she had regularly booked

appointments under my name so she could get the employee dis-
count. "You know what, Mischa? You're all right." She winked at
me from her perch on the bed. "That guy doesn't know what he's
missing," she said, referring to Liam.

For a split second, as I picked up the phone to call the spa,
I thought about telling Gracie what had happened between me
and Julien, but it didn't seem right. She once had a major crush
on him, after all, and she was now nursing a broken heart. Even
though I desperately wanted to talk about it with someone, I'd
have to wait to spill the news to Isabella.

Chapter 16

So what's the deal with your perma-grin?" Gracie's voice wobbled along with the movements of the large Russian woman who was kneading her back with hot stones.

"My what?" I turned to look at her quizzically before returning my face to the towel-covered hole below it.

"Your perma-grin—the shit-eating Joker smile that spreads across your face whenever you're not pretending to feel sorry for me."

"Gracie! I'm not pretending. I feel very sorry for you!"

"Of course you do, now spill the beans."

Gracie made a clicking noise with her tongue, urging me to obey. I didn't know what to say. I hadn't realized how much I had been smiling. I'd have to tone it down and think of another reason for my good mood, other than "Droolian Poundwell told me he wanted me last night." "Hey, Gracie," I said, "let's have our couples massage in peace, okay?"

"If we don't talk through the entire thing, then what's the point?"

"It's free! That's 'what's the point.'"

"Here, hold my hand. Let's embrace the moment here."

"Are you kidding?"

"Nope." She was clearly amused with herself as she reached over from her massage table five feet away. Humoring her, I looked over and took her hand as my masseuse pressed my head not so gently back into its towel hole.

After we'd been rubbed down, we sat in the steam room together in delirious silence. I had stayed up late, going over and over the kiss with Julien in my head, and who knows when Gracie's last full night of sleep had been, so we were both on the verge of collapse. Still, my head wasn't devoid of thoughts. As we wandered into our separate shower stalls to rinse off, I found it impossible not to think of Liam—the girl's shower room being practically identical to the men's. However, now that I had kissed Julien, the memory was less painful than wistful—I could look back on it fondly and not beat myself up for falling under Liam's spell. A good thing, as more flashbacks awaited me on the sundeck, where Gracie and I tottered in our bathrobes after the showers. Luckily, I wasn't so overwhelmed by them that I couldn't nap on one of the deck chairs.

In fact, we both felt quite refreshed after an hour of drifting up there, our hair naturally air-dried, our rumbling stomachs telling us it was time for lunch. Downstairs, at the checkout counter, we saw Sasha, who hadn't been around when we checked in.

"Mischa, darling! You look fabulous. What have you done?" My old boss—a mess of blond frizzy hair and too much bronzer— placed her hands on her hips, rocked them side to side, and shook her shoulders in some sort of congratulatory hula dance. She was wearing a sequined beach cover-up that looked cheap but probably cost five hundred dollars.

I smiled, flattered. If she only knew that I'd broken into this place for a sex romp, she might not be singing my praises.

Gracie piped in to answer Sasha. "I don't know what it is, but she's high on something."

"Well! Let's hope it's not coke! Or if it is, tell me where you're getting the good stuff." She winked at me, then Gracie, closing one eye and then the other.

* * *

"Wow, that is one crazy broad," Gracie said as we walked outside with the gift bags Sasha had personally prepared for us. "Sweet, but crazy."

"I know. Hey, you want some tacos?"

"Funny you should ask. I want my weight's worth in tacos."

Ravenously hungry, Gracie and I practically sprinted to my sweltering car, where we both burned our fingertips trying to buckle our seat belts.

"Where are we going? Taco Hell?" she asked.

"No. I'm gonna take you to this food truck run by these two Mexican women. Their tacos are out of this world. Julien showed it to me."

"Oooooh, Julien," Gracie cooed.

I smiled but didn't take the bait. However, minutes later, tacos in hand and sitting on the bench by the beach where Julien and I had sat before, Gracie pressed the issue once again. "Listen, you've been holding back on telling me whatever good news you have and that's very sweet. But seriously, I wanna know. It will be life affirming to hear about my friend having something fabulous happen to her for once. Guys are not all debauched rich assholes from Rhode Island with four names and sociopathic tendencies. I need to remember that…So, is something happening with you and Julien because I'm seriously getting a vibe."

"All right, all right," I said, another perma-grin creasing my cheeks. "We kissed."

"Omigod!" Gracie shot off the bench and walked in a quick circle before sitting back down. "What? When? Where? *How*?"

"It was last night—"

"Omigod!" Gracie's squeals made the taco ladies crane their heads out of the truck, perhaps concerned she'd found a palmetto bug in her carnitas.

"It was"—I shook my head, searching for words to describe the experience—"surprising. I hadn't even thought of him that way. I know that must sound implausible to you—"

"Right, because he's a god."

I laughed. "I know you think that, but until last night, I had viewed him as untouchable. I never imagined he would go for someone like me anyway. And then we ran into each other in the driveway in the middle of the night, and it was different. When we kissed, it was strange but exciting. Now I have this weird feeling, like maybe he should have been the one I was obsessing over all along. He's so smart and inspiring…"

"What's Cecile going to say? Ooh, she's gonna hate you!" Gracie hissed, diabolically amused.

"Oh God, I didn't even think about that. And we were just starting to get along."

"You know you're closer to her age than his."

"Barely. I'm like exactly in between."

"He's thirty-five, right?"

"Something like that."

"And she's fourteen?"

I nodded.

"So you're about two times closer to her age." She smiled with her mouth closed. "I'm a wizard at basic math."

"Gracie! Why are you making me feel bad now? You're the one who encouraged this in the first place!"

"Hey, I'm just teasing you. Age ain't nothing but a number. So tell me what happened. How did you leave it?"

I shook my head and took a bite of my taco. "That's the thing. He kind of ran away."

"Okay, start from the beginning," she said, and crumpled one of her taco wrappers into a ball.

Gracie listened attentively as I gave her the play-by-play. When I got to the kissing part, she demanded every detail—where had he put his hands? How long was his tongue? Were his kisses hard or soft?—and nodded enthusiastically enough to give herself whiplash. I was embarrassed talking about the specifics, but I obliged her because she was like a sister, and spilling the details allowed me to relive everything in my mind. After I'd told all there was to tell, Gracie dropped into a brief melancholy, apparently remembering the heartache she'd briefly escaped while listening to my story.

"Listen, I know I'm in a happy mood today, but who knows what's going through Julien's mind. If I've learned anything these past few weeks, it's that the only person I should count on for my own happiness is myself."

"Preach," said Gracie with a solemn nod.

"Easier said than done. But I've been trying to make some positive changes lately, and I think it's working. I started actually participating in OA instead of just lurking in the back and not saying anything, and I've been eating healthy, and started praying—"

"Wait—you found Jesus?" She slapped a hand down on my knee, her eyes as big as saucers, and not in a good way.

"No, nothing like that. I just started praying to some unspecified god."

"Well, I'll try anything once." She rolled her eyes up to the sky and pretended to whisper something rapidly, then clicked her tongue and winked. "Got it, God?"

"Got it," I answered in my best all-knowing God voice, then hopped up from the bench and held a hand out for my friend.

* * *

On our way back home, we formulated the following grand plan: Greek yogurt face masks and a movie marathon on my temperamental laptop. The first stop, however, would be at the main house—Gracie was hell bent on reuniting me and Julien after last night. "I want to see the sparks!" she insisted.

But despite her purported enthusiasm, I could tell Gracie was struggling. She had put this Richard person on a pedestal only to find out he was a world-class jerk like so many of the other guys she had fallen for. It was a feeling I knew too well, but there was nothing I could say to make it any easier, so I focused on driving us home. Meanwhile, Gracie stared out the window, occasionally pointing to her old Oceanside haunts and proclaiming how little she missed them.

As we pulled up to the house, I saw Julien's car in the driveway and felt my body tense. At least I would have Gracie with me to break the tension with her witty one-liners. At the front door, I knocked gently before letting us in. Just like this morning, the house seemed empty. I led Gracie on a "tour" of the downstairs in hopes of running into Julien, to no avail.

"So here's where I keep all my food and make my meals, et cetera," I said as we entered the kitchen, noticing Cecile out of the corner of my eye as she came bopping in behind us.

"Hi. Who are you again?" she demanded, giving Gracie a once-over.

"Cecile! I believe you met Gracie this morning," I said politely, hoping to encourage some hospitality on her part. "Gracie, Cecile. Cecile, Gracie."

"Hi again!" Gracie extended her hand, but Cecile only grasped the tips of her fingers, purposely making the handshake as awkward as possible.

"Please be kind, Cecile." I was pulling vegetables out of the refrigerator, buying more time in the kitchen by making a salad that neither Gracie nor I were hungry for.

"Yes, Cecile, I'm very fragile right now," Gracie added.

Ignoring Gracie's comment, she sidled up to me at the counter. "Whatcha making?"

"Salad. You want some?"

"Yeah. I'm gonna copy everything you eat from now on because you're losing weight and I'm not."

I glanced at her sideways. "I disagree. I think you look great. Probably from all that swimming you're doing."

Gracie plopped down on a stool and stole a carrot from my cutting board. "Cecile, don't worry about it. I was my chubbiest when I was your age, lost a bunch in high school. No diet, no nothing."

Hearing this, Cecile looked happier than I'd ever seen her. "Really?"

"Oh yeah. Plus, guys like a little meat on the bones, believe me."

"People say that, but I don't believe it." Cecile moved around the counter to sit by Gracie, who was quickly becoming her new favorite person.

"No, it's true, but don't worry about what guys want anyway. They're all asswipes. Except for your dad, of course." Gracie glanced over at me with an impish smile. My cheeks flushed, and I shook my head to discourage her.

"Why would you say my dad? You don't even know him."
Cecile eyed her suspiciously. "Wait, are you the one who sent that
text? Droolian Poundwell?"

"Huh? Is that another language? I don't know what you're
talking about." Gracie shot me another impish glance. I glowered
at Cecile, unwilling to reopen the can of worms that I had hoped
was closed by now. "I was just saying," Gracie went on, "I'm sure
your dad's not an asswipe because dads are kind of exempt."

"Exempt from what?" Julien's voice carried in from the hallway as he made his way into the kitchen.

Stricken with fear that he had overheard the entire exchange, I
looked up mid-chop and let my knife slide, accidentally scraping a
layer of skin off the tip of my left thumb. "Hello!" I said nervously.
"You saw Gracie earlier, right?" I was speaking entirely too loudly,
and my thumb had started dripping blood onto the cutting board.

"Ew. You're bleeding." Cecile pointed to my hand, which I
tried to conceal as I went to run it under the sink.

"Hi again, Gracie." Julien waved, polite and formal. "Cecile,
go get a Band-Aid for Mischa." He nodded toward the guest
bathroom, and Cecile grudgingly obeyed. Making his way over
to the sink, Julien patted my shoulder. I blinked my eyes closed,
enjoying the rush of being near him again as his hand gripped
the base of my neck and massaged it for a few blissful seconds
that told me, *Yes, I wanted you last night and still do.*

"You have a beautiful home!" Gracie's voice piped in from
behind us, bringing me back to reality. "And although I wasn't
technically invited here, I appreciate the hospitality."

Julien's hand dropped away from me as he turned to face her.
"You're very welcome. So how's D.C.?"

"You mean the land of sleazy politicians and all things foul
and soulless?"

"Hey, that's my hometown you're talking about," he chided.

"Oh really? Did you tell me that before? Mischa, did you know Julien was from D.C.?" Gracie had always been a very generous, if obvious, wingman. She liked to draw me into conversations with pointless, rhetorical questions.

"I don't know," I answered, turning off the faucet and sticking my still-bleeding thumb in my mouth.

"She probably didn't know," Julien said.

"No." I took my thumb out of my mouth. "You told me." I couldn't help but grin at the memory of our stolen afternoon together at Salty Sal's. In hindsight, it seemed so romantic—how could I have seen it any other way? Julien, on the other hand, was poker-faced as he accepted the Band-Aid from Cecile. Part of me (well, all of me) wished he had less self-restraint in front of his daughter and my friend. I wanted his arm around my shoulders, the heat of his body against mine. "Remember?" I said, daring to nudge him with my elbow. "My first day at work?"

Julien unwrapped the Band-Aid and gently took my hand, looking into my eyes with an intensity that made me quiver. The look seemed to have meaning behind it, but I couldn't tell if it was good or bad. "Strangely, I don't," he said, lowering his eyes to the task at hand as he placed the Band-Aid on my cut. "Anyway!" He glanced up at the clock above the pantry, and the Band-Aid wrapper drifted from his palm to the floor. "I gotta get to campus. I know it's bad form to work on a Saturday but I'm behind on the writing."

"But, Dad! You said we would go to the mall!" Cecile whined.

"Tomorrow, sweetie. I'm all yours then." Julien glanced back at me as he walked out of the room, and my heart swelled. "Oh, Mischa?"

"Yes?" I answered expectantly, hoping for an inside joke or a coded reference to last night.

"Will you girls be around tonight? I have another dinner and I don't want Cecile to be on her own here."

"Umm…" Trying to hide my disappointment, I looked at Gracie, whose own face bore a sympathetic frown. "Were you wanting to go out tonight?"

"And get a taste of the thriving Oceanside social scene that I've been missing so dearly in D.C.?"

Julien chuckled as Gracie shook her head slowly.

"We'll be here," I said.

"Okay, great!" He smiled and shot me a thumbs-up before disappearing down the hall.

With Julien out of sight, I let out a long sigh, pretending that my thumb was the cause of my consternation as I held it up for examination. "I might need a second Band-Aid. Cecile, would you get me another one?"

"What's in it for me?" She cocked her head, arms crossed, like she was auditioning for the role of Bratty Teenager #1.

Gracie rolled her eyes. "Just get her the Band-Aid," she said authoritatively.

Later, when we had retreated back to the guesthouse, I finally allowed my face to match my emotions: a mix of lovesickness, confusion, and fear.

"You don't look too good," Gracie remarked.

I shook my head. "I think that cut was deeper than it looked…"

Chapter 17

Friday, mid-July: emergency meeting held in Julien Maxwell's guesthouse
Topic of discussion: Julien Maxwell
Calories imbibed: Not enough

I don't know what I expected him to say or do. I mean, his daughter was right there." Like a lost puppy I followed Gracie, who had just emerged from the shower, as she wandered around the room trying to get dressed.

"Well, you know what my opinion of men is right now. So all I have to say is, expect the least." Gracie's mood had turned somewhere between our afternoon salad course and now. I couldn't blame her, but her bummed-out vibe wasn't helping me.

"You're right," I said. "I don't think he's in a place for a relationship right now. Or he's not sure yet. And I understand it's nothing personal. I mean, the man's wife *died* tragically. Who knows how long that takes to get over?"

She pulled a T-shirt over her head and shook out her wet hair.

"Well, as long as you're fine with that. I just don't know where that gets you."

"I think Julien and I might have a future, I really do. I'll just have to be patient!"

Gracie glanced at me incredulously through wet bangs. "I thought you weren't even sure how you felt about him."

"No. I think the problem is just timing," I said, continuing to pace. "This may not be the best time for him, and I may not get accepted into Reid. Meaning, I'll have to move somewhere else, and *then* it becomes a long-distance thing—"

"Where would you go?" she interrupted my rant.

"New Mexico. But I haven't responded yet. I'm still waiting on Reid."

"Well, no offense, but don't you think figuring that out should be your biggest priority right now? Not whether some old dude can get over his dead wife in time for you to have a slightly inappropriate student-teacher romance?"

To this, my eyes widened in disbelief. I shook my head in slow motion. "Wow, Gracie, 'some old dude'? You referred to him as a god earlier, did you not? Also, since when are you the voice of reason on inappropriate romances? I'm pretty sure slutting around in public bathrooms with spoiled brat senators like Richard could be considered slightly inappropriate too."

Gracie stopped in her tracks, as if someone had just body-blocked her. "Are you kidding me?"

"Shit, I'm sorry," I said, instantly regretting my choice of words.

She turned toward me, her eyebrows knitted. "Slutting around? *Slutting around*? Thank you very much for that unwarranted judgment."

"I didn't mean it that way."

"No, really, that means a lot coming from someone who's been having sex with a nymphomaniac who fell off the wagon—"

"Like you wouldn't have."

"Oh, stop acting like you know me so well."

"Well stop acting like you know everything about everything!" I was shouting now, my voice high-pitched and irritated.

"Maybe I would if you'd stop begging me for advice. I should have known better than to come here when I needed something. Of course all we end up talking about is you!" She ripped a hairbrush through her hair and threw it back down in her bag.

We went on like that, lobbing back-and-forth insults for another minute before Gracie finished dressing herself and stormed out. I allowed her to go, too emotionally exhausted to follow and knowing she'd be back because she had nowhere else to stay. But hours later, when she hadn't returned by sunset, I started to worry. And by the time I'd joined Cecile in the living room, where she was watching some contrived reality show about two teenage girls on a blind date with the same guy, I felt absolutely horrible.

"Is there anything else on?" I asked, plopping down on the rigid love seat that sat farthest away from the TV.

Surprisingly compliant, Cecile switched the channel to an action movie featuring some lesser-known comic book character.

"That's better."

"What's wrong with you?"

"Nothing."

"You sound like someone killed your goldfish." Cecile smirked.

"I don't have a goldfish. And if I did, I probably would have eaten it in a moment of food mania." I threw my legs over the armrest. "Gracie and I had a fight."

My teenage companion chuckled and made a joke insinuating that Gracie and I were secret lovers. Other than that, she took it easy on me, which I greatly appreciated. My day had been hard enough already.

The movie didn't do much to distract me, but I needed the company, so I stayed until the end, pretending to care what happened to the shape-shifting hero. Then I realized I hadn't eaten dinner and offered to cook something for the both of us.

"Yes! I'm starving!" Cecile answered. She hopped up from the couch and ran into the kitchen before me. When I rounded the corner, she was holding up a box of mac and cheese and saying *please* over and over again, like a four-year-old.

"Nope. Broiled salmon and veggies," I said as if I were talking to a four-year-old. And though she put up a fight, Cecile ended up eating every bit of it as I took slow, arduous bites myself, my mind bouncing back and forth between Julien and Gracie.

For Cecile's part, she was mostly silent, texting throughout dinner with her clique of swim team friends, but at some point she leaned over the table and spoke to me in a conspiratorial voice. "So, are you like totally depressed because Droolian Poundwell's on a date right now?"

"What?" My fork dropped out of my hand and rattled onto the plate below it. "Oops!" I said, trying to act cool as I picked it back up. "I thought he said it was a work thing?"

"Nope. He totally didn't. I knew you would be sad. Look at your face." There she was—the old Cecile back in action.

I swallowed hard as my heart sank into a void. I had been barely treading water before, after Julien's hard-to-read behavior that afternoon and then my fight with Gracie, but now I was at risk of crying right there at the table. "I'm pretty sure he said it was a work thing," I repeated, my words clipped and defensive, painfully aware that I was blowing my cover.

"I heard him talking to her on the phone. Believe me, it's a date." She sounded more certain than I'd ever heard a fourteen-year-old sound before—her humorless tone of voice was bone-chilling.

I pushed some salmon aimlessly around my plate and fought the urge to ask her about the woman. I lasted about three seconds. "Who is it?" I said impatiently.

"That new professor lady, I don't know her name. She's visiting from New York. She's skinny and she wears all black. Much more his type."

"You saw her?" I couldn't help but jump on Cecile's every word. My knees were taking turns bouncing rapidly under the table.

"She came by to drop off a book a couple days ago."

"Oh." I nodded and took a miniscule bite of fish, choking it down even though my throat felt like it was closing up.

A new text alert sounded and Cecile refocused her attention on the phone in her hand.

"I'm sure it's nothing. Colleagues exchange books all the time," I said.

She looked up from her phone, one eyebrow raised. "He's on a date, Mischa. You should probably accept it. I have." Cecile went back to ignoring me while she sent a few more rapid-fire texts. "I told him about that text you know." She looked up and grinned, baring her silvery braces. "And you know what he said? 'Mischa's harmless.'"

"He said that?" I couldn't believe it. *Harmless?* It was the worst thing he could have called me—in my mind, in that moment.

A knock on the front door interrupted, at which point Cecile and I both rushed to the foyer. I got there first and boxed her out, peering into the peephole to find Gracie on the front stoop. Relieved to see my friend again, I swung the door open wide and embraced her so abruptly that she had no option but to hug back.

"I'm sorry," I said.

"I know, me too." She patted my back.

"Ugh, you guys are disgusting," Cecile said, then zoomed in on her phone as if some dire emergency had just come up. As she scampered upstairs, I was relieved to see her go.

I drew Gracie into the living room. "I gotta tell you something," I whispered.

"Me too," she said. I could tell from the look in her eye that whatever she had to say wasn't good.

"You first."

Gracie squinted, hesitating.

"Is it about your guy?"

She shook her head. "No, your guy."

"Did you see him or something? Cecile said he was on a date." I shoved an index finger into my mouth and started biting away at the nail.

Gracie pursed her lips together. "Yeah."

"Where?" I demanded, carelessly spitting a bit of nail onto the floor.

"At that bar by the movie theater. I went for a drink, and they were there, in a booth."

"Did he see you?"

"I don't think so. They were kind of…into each other."

"Oh my God." I collapsed onto the couch.

"You're cuter. And younger, obviously."

"I can't believe this," I said, burying my face in my hands. "Cecile told him about the text, and he said that I was 'harmless.'"

Gracie leaned over and situated the pillows behind me like a nurse attending to a terminally ill patient, which I suddenly felt like I was as she sat down at my side.

"I'm such an idiot," I whimpered.

"Don't beat yourself up."

"After seeing him this afternoon, I kept telling myself he must not be ready for a relationship. That if it doesn't work out, it's just bad timing. But no, he just didn't want *me*. Surprise, surprise."

"I know how you feel." Gracie took my hand. "We're in this together, okay? Guys suck."

"Well...at least the ones we find."

"Exactly."

"Oh my God. I don't even want to think about it!" I closed my eyes, wishing I could fall into a deep sleep and not wake up for a month. I had been doing so well just a couple of days ago. Why had Julien insisted on barging into my personal life and messing it all up? "I mean, I didn't even want him! He's the one who started this!"

"I know." Gracie looked up at the ceiling, seemingly searching her brain for something to cheer me up. Finally landing on an idea, she snapped her fingers. "Okay, here's what I'm thinking. I'm only here till tomorrow night, right? So I figure we have two options: go out and get drunk, or watch sappy movies in your bed and braid each other's hair."

"Movies and braids, please." I smiled, feeling my misery lift the tiniest bit as Gracie smiled like a deranged person and patted her knees, trying to get me to laugh.

"Let's do it, then!" she said, "Distraction, distraction, distraction—the name of the game."

I leaned my head on Gracie's shoulder and grabbed her arm. "I'm so glad you're here."

"Me too...me fuckin' too," she said.

* * *

Despite our grand plans for a late-night double feature, Gracie and I both passed out before the first movie was halfway through. We obviously needed the sleep, because we made it a full ten hours before either of us so much as stirred. Even more surprising was that when I awoke the next morning, my hair in a half-finished French braid, I felt oddly neutral. I even noticed the birds singing again, which seemed like a good sign. Maybe I had simply had enough of the ups and downs. The past few weeks had been so intense, my brain had finally overloaded and fizzled out. I was left with a strange sensation of blankness that helped when I saw the text from Liam on my phone: *How's it going?—L*

It was time-stamped 1:15 a.m. When I first saw it, Gracie was still sleeping, but I didn't need to consult her to know how to respond.

Things are good, I replied, then, *I can't be in touch with you. I hope you understand…*

It was harsh, perhaps, but I didn't know what else to say. I felt certain that no good would come from inviting the drama of Liam back into my life, and the fact that he had contacted me late at night seemed to speak for itself. When Gracie awoke, in a better mood herself, I didn't tell her about it. Instead, I invited her to come with me to Isabella's for my weekly visit and she happily accepted, having never met her before.

Not surprisingly, the two got along like old war buddies.

"Oh my God, why have you been keeping us apart?" Gracie demanded while passing Isabella's e-cigarette back to her. They were sitting at the patio table as I brought out a tray with six glasses.

"I haven't been keeping you apart. You were always too hungover to come with me, remember?" I said.

"That's my girl," Isabella cheered, giving Gracie a high five.

"Okay, here we go." I placed three glasses before each of them.

"Okay!" Gracie clapped her hands. "The Mischa Jones soon-to-be-patented juice cleanse!"

"That's right. So it's a juice in the morning, a juice in the afternoon, and a smoothie at night. Water all day. Herbal tea optional."

"Sounds like my own version of hell. Hit me!" Gracie picked up her first glass of juice and held it up to toast Isabella. "Here's to new friends."

"Yes, my dear, and to our dear Mischa." Isabella thrust her glass toward me. "May this juice not suck."

"Hear, hear!"

Before drinking, Gracie sniffed at the glass like a picky child. Isabella, on the other hand, downed hers quickly.

"I want you to be brutally honest," I said.

Gracie held up a finger. "I will reserve comment until I have finished all three."

"This one tastes like grass, but I do not hate it," Isabella declared before moving on to the next.

"So, let me tell you what my plan is—the idea came to me the other day, and I think it's a good one. I'm going to present this to Sasha as something she could sell at her spa. Like have them in a refrigerator by the front desk. People go in, they get a massage and a facial—they feel all clean, then bam! Clean living, at their fingertips, upon checkout."

"That's kind of genius," Gracie said, sipping from her second glass.

"I figure I'll make a few batches at the beginning of the week, put them in glass bottles. They'll be expensive, but the clientele is rich..."

Isabella tried the smoothie, which was a slight deviation on the peanut butter smoothies I had been making her. "Delicious," she said.

Gracie looked up at me after trying the smoothie. "Mischa?"

"Gracie?"

She pounded the table. "Five thumbs up!"

"Seriously?"

"Yum! And the juices have kick! And I have a distinct sense that they're doing something for me. I'm buzzing."

I blew the hair out of my face demonstratively. "Phew."

"I wanna take this shit to Washington. Straight to the top!"

"I know it's not a future plan, per se, but at least it's something, right? I mean, I still have to figure out my life."

"Don't we all?" Gracie said, suddenly wan.

"Oh, you girls have such a flair for the dramatic. Call me when you're incontinent like Carl over there," she said, pointing to a house across the street.

Gracie and I burst into laughter at the same time and Isabella raised her smoothie for another toast. "To Carl!"

"To Carl," we all said in unison.

In two hours, I would be sharing a tearful goodbye with Gracie, but the fact that she was here now felt like a small miracle. As we left Isabella's, I thanked her so many times for coming to Oceanside, she threatened to knock me out. But I truly felt like she had saved me that weekend—she may as well have shown up with little angel wings jutting out from her vintage acid-washed jean jacket. Even though she had come to Oceanside needing me, I had needed her right back.

* * *

Monday morning was like a cold splash of water to the head. I felt as though I had just returned from a long, exotic vacation—except the "vacation" had been nothing but heart-wrenching drama. Despite the emotional hangover, I was ready to get back to the grind and face the good, the bad, and the ugly of my life. In a way, I was back to where I'd started in June, when I'd first been faced with the existential questions about my plans for the future, or lack thereof. Only now, I was eight pounds lighter and actively heartbroken. *Oh well,* was all I could think. Time to switch into survivor mode.

First thing after I woke up, I sent an e-mail to Sasha about the juice cleanse, asking if she'd be open to a presentation. It had to be worded just right—this was a woman who liked to be fooled into things, and luckily I knew how to make Sasha feel like I was trying to help *her* instead of the other way around. Writing the e-mail also bought me some time so I wouldn't run into Julien in the kitchen; he had recently established a pattern of leaving for the office before nine a.m., while I had started showing up to campus around ten. I had been so frustrated, initially, when he'd started sending me off to the library to spend entire days at the Xerox machine. But now, having to face Julien alone for the first time since our kiss, I could not have been more relieved by my little hardship post. It meant I would only have to endure a few awkward minutes of niceties with him before retreating to the library where I could mope in peace if need be.

After breakfast, I packed my lunch, which consisted of green salad and grilled chicken. At some point I was going to need to get more creative about my healthy diet instead of eating the same boring things over and over again, but not today. Like they often said in OA: baby steps!

A punishing heat wave had descended early that morning and my car was sweltering when I got inside. It must have been 110 degrees in there. Feeling the first trickles of sweat spotting my T-shirt, I rolled the windows down and cranked the air-conditioning self-indulgently as I mentally prepared for a face-to-face with Julien.

The drive to campus went by too quickly for my liking, thanks to the empty roads and stoplights that seemed permanently green. It was as if everyone had gone out of town just in time to escape the weather. Arriving at the Lit building, I climbed the front steps and another flight of stairs to the second floor where Julien's office was tucked away at the end of the hall. The trek was not enough to warrant how out of breath I was by the time I appeared in his open doorway. Nerves had taken over and I was nearly panicked, but I tried my hardest to look indifferent. The truth was, I had no interest in talking about things; I didn't need him to tell me that he was seeing somebody, for I knew now that whatever we had had was over before it even began. "Knock, knock!" I announced myself, my feet stopping at the wooden divider between the hardwood floors of his office and the granite-tiled hallway.

"Mischa. Can you come in for a second?" Julien looked up from his laptop and placed his hands on his lap. He seemed grave.

Nope. Not a good time, is what I wanted to say, but as I tried to come up with a proper excuse, I heard myself practically gasping for air. "Sorry, I'm a little winded from climbing those stairs. I was just stopping to check in actually. I have plenty of copying left to do from Friday, so—"

"Why don't you sit down?" He gestured to the chair across from his desk. "It won't take long."

"Well, there's nothing for me really to go over. I just wanted to make sure you didn't have anything else that needed prioritizing before I went to the library." I added a nonchalant wave of the hand to make clear how absolutely indifferent I was as my cheeks burned bright red.

"If you don't mind, Mischa, I think we should talk." He nodded to the seat across from him, and I looked at it for a few seconds as my feet seesawed on the wooden divider. I tried, and failed, to come up with some reason why I couldn't stay, then finally relented.

"Do you mind closing the door?" he said after I'd started to move inside.

Glancing behind me at the open door, I feared that once it was closed, Julien would launch into some insufferable speech about how we could never be together and how absolutely perfect this visiting professor was for him and all the ways that she outshined me. Perhaps he would stick a few extra nails in the coffin by using phrases like "I don't know what I was thinking," or "It's not you, it's me." But at the end of the day he was still my boss, so I closed it like he asked.

"So!" I sat down with a freshly applied fake grin, placing my hands on my knees in a solicitous pose. "What's up?"

Julien leaned forward in his chair and snapped his computer shut. "We need to talk about what happened between us."

Right. That. "No, we really don't," I said. "I've seriously totally forgotten about it."

"Mischa—"

"Seriously! I'd tell you if I wanted to talk about it. I'm not really a big talker, in general."

"Cecile mentioned you were upset when you heard about my date on Saturday. I didn't even tell her I had gone on a date, and I certainly didn't want you to hear it that way. I can't imagine how it must have felt, after what we shared on Friday."

Tears started to well in the corners of my eyes. I licked my lips and squinted, squeezed my thighs with my hands, anything to keep from crying. Tears would make it look like I cared about him more. He would get the wrong idea. But nothing could stop the determined little droplets as they started to trickle down my cheeks. "I didn't tell Cecile about us, if that's what you're worried about," I said. "And whatever she told you about that text…it's not what it sounds like."

"I know. I'm not worried about Cecile right now. I'm worried about you."

"Well don't be worried. I'm fine. Believe it or not, you're not my real heartbreak of the summer." I wanted to sound harsh and dismissive, but my cracking voice and dampened cheeks betrayed me. "I wish nothing had ever happened so we wouldn't have to have this conversation," I said, succumbing further to my heaving breaths that bordered on sobs.

As I worked to even out my breathing, I noticed his eyebrows had scrunched up toward the middle of his forehead, and he was biting his lip. It seemed like a studied look, one that he'd used before, no doubt, to beg forgiveness.

"Mischa, I just want you to know that I care about you, and I never meant for things to go as far as they did. You deserve to be with someone who's right for you, someone who's not your teacher."

"Were. You *were* my teacher."

"It's more than that. There's a lot of reasons we can't be together. For one thing, I'm leaving. I took a new position in New York."

"What?" I braced the sides of my chair, rocked by the news. Regardless of what had happened in the past few days, I had come to view Julien and Cecile as a sort of surrogate family in Oceanside. The thought of them up and leaving felt like a betrayal.

"I'll be here through fall semester. We'll move in the winter. Cecile doesn't even know yet."

I shook my head in disbelief. A million questions swirled through my mind. How long had he known? Was it going to be a permanent move? Would he sell his house? "Does *she* know?" I finally asked, sounding unintentionally jealous.

"Who?" he said.

"The woman you're dating."

"Andrea? She's from New York, actually. She's only here as a visiting professor."

"Well, that's perfect," I said. It was like some bitter ex-girlfriend of Julien's had taken over my body. It wasn't that I was so hurt by him, specifically, just that everything with Liam and Julien combined had left me so disillusioned.

"Mischa, listen to me. You have an amazing life ahead of you, and I have no interest in bogging you down. Yes, we were drawn to each other, but that doesn't mean it makes sense."

"Right, like another professor makes sense," I said, still digging in, unable to stop myself fighting for something I hadn't even wanted in the first place. "Because we should all be with people who are exactly like us. What about all the great love stories that we read about, the ones that you teach? What about… what about Janie and Tea Cake from *Their Eyes Were Watching God*?" I was grasping at straws, still trying to impress him with literary references.

"Because we're not living in a novel, Mischa! Because Tea Cake got rabies and had to be shot!" Julien's voice had become stern and loud and he was leaning forward in his seat impatiently.

"Fine." I stood up from my chair, my eyes searching the ground as if my pride were something I had accidentally dropped there and just needed to be picked back up. "I shouldn't be here. I'm gonna go to the library. I'll find another place to stay as soon as possible—"

His face softened. "What are you talking about?"

"If you don't mind, I want to keep the job until I find something else."

"You don't have to move out. You're welcome to stay through the fall if you want. Cecile loves having you there, and so do I."

"Yeah, it's been real convenient for you, hasn't it?"

"Mischa, that's not fair."

"I have to move, Julien. I have to move on with my life." I wiped my face with the backs of my hands and walked slowly to the door, careful not to trip or do something else embarrassing in my fragile state.

As I opened the door, Julien called out to me and I turned to look back. "Mischa, I wanted to be a mentor to you, but I screwed up. I'm sorry, okay?"

I nodded, tacitly accepting his apology but offering nothing in return.

He smiled and bit his lip again—this time, not so studied. "See you back at the house."

I looked at Julien a few more seconds before leaving. This was the face that sent butterflies aflutter in my stomach a mere forty-eight hours ago. Now it just made me sad, and I couldn't bring myself to return his awkward smile.

Chapter 18

I made my way down the second-floor hallway of the Lit building like a convict who'd just been released from prison, with no idea where to go. I was thankful, at least, that the building was completely empty. All summer, I had only seen one other professor there, an older white-haired woman named Dr. Dixon who taught Russian literature. I had never had a class with her, but I'd heard she was tough. As a person, though, she seemed nice enough, and I always smiled and waved into her office when she was in. Passing by her office, I saw it was closed and figured she had finally gone on vacation, but then, in the stairwell, I heard a set of footsteps coming and realized it must be her. I didn't want to be spotted with my puffy eyes and wet cheeks, but unless I turned and ran at that very moment, there would be no avoiding her.

"Oh, dear," I heard her say when we crossed paths on the landing between the first and second floors. Much to my chagrin, Professor Dixon was staring at my face with a look of concern.

"Yes?" I said, pretending not to know why she had greeted me in such a way. Her face was pretty up close, artfully wrinkled and very pale for Florida.

"Come here," she said, motioning toward herself.

"I'm sorry, what?" I said. Although, before I knew it, I was obliging and walking into her arms to accept her embrace. I must have looked like one hell of a mess, or perhaps she had a heightened perception of other people's feelings and like many old people, couldn't care less about appearances. Either way I was surprised by how easily I fell into this stranger's arms, the chemical-y coconut scent of her sunscreen hitting my nose as I let my head rest on her shoulder. We stayed that way, huddled together on the landing, for what seemed like a long time but was probably less than a minute.

"Things seem so important when you're young, don't they?" she said, echoing Isabella as I finally pulled away.

I nodded, drying my cheeks with the backs of my hands. "I guess they do."

"I'm sure everything's going to be all right, whatever it is."

"Thank you," I said. A few fresh tears had collected in the corners of my eyes, and I was fighting them back.

"Good luck to you." Professor Dixon winked and patted my shoulder as I stood there frozen, waiting for her to inquire more—to ask what had caused the tears or offer her unsolicited opinion on Julien Maxwell. Most people wouldn't come upon a scene like this, I thought, and not have a morbid curiosity about it. But she didn't seem to have any curiosity at all. On the contrary, she waited only a few more seconds, then continued up the stairs without another word.

It was a bizarre experience to say the least. I kept thinking about it as I crossed the quad on my way to the library and wondered what it meant that I had become so pathetic-looking that old ladies were compelled to reach out and hug me in passing. The thought made me laugh. Instead of going straight to work, I decided to sit down on a bench to collect myself.

When I tried to go over what had just happened with Julien, I couldn't seem to recall the conversation very clearly, as if I had already blacked it out to save myself the embarrassment. I knew that he had told me he was moving to New York and that we weren't living in a novel. I could vaguely recall him saying something about "the amazing life I had ahead of me" and how he didn't want to "bog me down." *If you were so concerned with my future,* I thought, *then why did you complicate things by kissing me in the first place?* Part of me wished I had shouted at him back in his office and let him know it wasn't okay to toy with people's emotions, even though I knew it was better that I hadn't.

The fact of it was, I hadn't been initially attracted to Julien, probably for good reason. And now he had found somebody that sounded like a reasonable match, someone he could start a new life with in New York and forget all the dark history he left behind in Oceanside. It made all the sense in the world, whereas whatever brief little connection we shared seemed born out of mutual loneliness more than anything else. I thought about Isabella's story; how she had, at a young age, come to look at love as a business transaction. And then I thought about my good friend Gracie's currently jaded point of view, that guys are, more or less, inherently evil. I didn't want to feel either of those things, no matter what. I didn't want the sum total of my experiences—starting with Bradley and ending with this summer—to be perpetual bitterness, although it would be hard to shake the bitterness for a while. Eventually, though, I wanted to be a person who believed in love, even if I thought I might never find it.

Ten minutes passed before I stood up, calling an end to my pity party, partly because I'd had enough for the moment and partly because it was 103 degrees and climbing outside. Bypassing the library, I walked to the Plex and headed straight for the message boards in the lobby. I needed a place to stay and a new job, ideally, and needed them yesterday, but the notices I found were mostly old, with the exception of one pet-sitting gig that started the following week. I tore one tab from the posting, then all of them.

I was back outside, taking the path that cut directly from the Plex to the library, when my day took another bizarre turn: in the distance, running around the quad's periphery in short runner's shorts and a matching tank top, was Liam, or someone who looked just like him. I raised my hand to shelter my eyes and stared at the man pointedly as he jogged around the other end of the lawn. It was certainly his body—I could recognize that body anywhere—but the face was obscured at this distance and the outfit threw me off. The runner was decked out in a pretty serious-looking, neon-accented ensemble, which would have been an odd choice for Liam, someone I hadn't known to be a runner. Whoever it was, they eventually noticed me and politely waved from a distance. Embarrassed that I'd been caught staring, I turned and hurried toward the library, not bothering to wave back.

On my way to my favorite copy machine, sequestered in the corner of the library's third floor, I thought about what a strange summer it had been. I was ready for the wave that had washed me out into the abyss with Liam and gotten me caught up in the undertow with Julien to deposit me back on dry land. In fact, I started praying for it that night.

* * *

Second Tuesday in August: Oceanside Rec Center Meeting
Topic of discussion: "Sticking to Promises"
Calories imbibed: 1,550

I celebrated my first one-month chip as the designated speaker at the rec center meeting. Although I had begun sharing over a month ago, it was still daunting to plant myself onstage in front of everyone, stay there for a solid five minutes, and talk only about me. I had collaborated with the moderator, Sherrill, on the day's topic and had come prepared with a page full of notes in case I blanked, but I was still shaking like a leaf when she introduced me.

"Hi, everyone." I took a seat on the chair positioned in the middle of the low stage and placed my notes gingerly in my lap. "I'm Mischa, and I'm an overeater."

"Hi, Mischa," they all responded.

From this vantage point, I could see everyone in the room, but the looks on their faces were patient and accepting and I felt instantly reassured. I launched in, speaking quickly to avoid any awkward silences. "So, 'Sticking to Promises.' That's today's topic and very relevant to me as I am just receiving my one-month chip and feeling very happy that I've been sober this long. Four and a half weeks to be exact...But I'm still on the fence about the Twelve Steps. I'm not really sure why. At least for now it's important for me not to feel pressure either way. What's important is that I stick to the promises I make to myself, and I've been doing a pretty good job of it. I needed to get out of a weird living situation and I did that—I got hired to pet sit for a professor who's away until December. There're three cats and I'm kind of allergic, but other than that it's a pretty good deal. Also, I presented a product I developed to someone I used to work for, and she's thinking about investing, which is beyond what I'd hoped for. I'm trying not to get my hopes up too high but I've been thinking about it a lot and am feeling pretty excited about it. Something that helps me stay sober, too, is taking care of my friend Isabella. She, unlike me, has needed to gain a lot of weight lately, so I've been keeping a better eye on her, going by her house twice a week instead of just once, making sure the food I make her is really healthy but calorie-dense. Oh, and the big one, obviously: I promised myself I would stop binging and eating my trigger foods, which are basically everything that's not healthy—I'm kind of a kitchen-sink addict. So, for the last month, I have been sticking to that. It's been hard but it also feels really good…"

Coming up for air, I scanned the room, suddenly blanking on what to say next. I glanced at Sherrill for the time, hoping she would tell me I had run out of it.

"You have four more minutes," she said with a knowing smile.

"Really? Wow." The look of surprise on my face prompted sympathetic laughter around the room. But instead of bolting offstage like I wanted to, I hunkered down and felt something relax inside me. I started to talk about the hard stuff—about my expectations of other people and how I'd sometimes held others to higher standards than I'd held myself. I admitted to various obsessions over the years, starting with Bradley and leading up to Liam and (briefly) Julien that summer, and talked about the significance of my dad leaving. I said I knew it was cliché and people shook their heads kindly, reminding me that what I had to say was valid, even if it was their story too—maybe even more so because it was their story. I talked about my future and how grad school was still up in the air and how I felt I'd always ignored my own needs out of fear, choosing to focus on other people instead. By the end of it, I felt like a 500-pound weight had been lifted off my shoulders, and my heart swelled with pride when Sherrill turned the discussion open to the group and everyone who spoke thanked me for my honesty. I even stayed afterward for a few minutes, although part of me wanted to hide away and recover from all the exposure. And precisely because I stuck around, a pretty girl who looked around my age approached with an expectant smile on her face.

"Hi, I'm Monica." She offered her hand and I shook it.

"Hi! Mischa," I said, pointing to myself.

"Your share was great."

"Thanks! I really hate public speaking if you couldn't tell," I said.

"Yeah, me too. Hey, listen"—she glanced behind her, as if she had some big secret to tell me—"I know we're not supposed to do this since it's anonymous and all. I was actually here... well, this is my first time. I actually came for research for school. I told Sherrill, so it's all on the up and up."

"Sure, of course." I sounded uncertain as I wondered what Monica was getting at.

"Anyway, like I said, I know it's anonymous and all, but is there any way you can tell me if your last name is Jones?"

"Uh... who wants to know?" I answered, worried she might be Liam's longtime girlfriend or something equally terror-inducing.

Monica lowered her voice. "It's just that I've been working at the school, assisting in the Nutrition department, and you've been the first name on our waiting list for the grad program for a while now. And today we had someone drop out."

"Wait... what?" I shook my head like a cartoon character that had just been hit with an anvil. "I'm Mischa Jones. That's me! I'm her!" I cried it out too loudly, too un-anonymously, in a state of heart-pounding excitement. Everyone turned to look at me, but I didn't care.

"So, yeah, I got an e-mail tonight to call you first thing tomorrow... You're in. That is, if you're still interested."

"Are you kidding me? Yes! Beyond still interested. Oh my

God." I threw my arms around her—after my curious stairwell incident with Donna Dixon, I had become much less averse to hugging complete strangers in public—and bounced up and down. "Sorry," I apologized as I drew back. "This is just the best news I've heard all summer. Do I need to sign something? Of course I do, right?"

Monica laughed. "Yeah. Just stop by the office. I'll let the dean know first thing."

"Wait…is there a TA-ship?" I had almost forgotten to ask, but it was imperative. I wouldn't be able to swing graduate school otherwise.

"Yes. It's guaranteed for the first-years," she happily reported.

"Aah!" This time I actually jumped. "I have to go call my mom! Monica, you are an angel sent from heaven. Don't let anybody tell you different," I said.

In turn, she smiled big and shrugged modestly as I hurried out, waving and blowing her a melodramatic kiss.

* * *

I caught my mom sleeping—a rarity, since she was such a night owl. "Mom!" I cried into the phone after her groggy, drawn-out "hello."

"Honey! What a nice surprise," she cooed, sounding drugged.

"I woke you up, I know it. But it's worth it—listen, I got into Reid! I just found out! I go in tomorrow to sign!"

"Honey!" My mom gasped, rousing from her sleep state to join in my euphoria. "This is amazing! See? I told you it would work out."

"Thank you so much, Mom."

"Why are you thanking me? You're the one you should be thanking."

"No, I couldn't have done it without you. I love you so much. I'm gonna come home for Thanksgiving, okay?"

"I know, I know, I miss you too."

"And we're going to celebrate the fact that I'm gonna graduate and make something of myself before you're too old to care."

This made her laugh. "I'll never be too old for that, Fluffy."

There was that nickname again—back by unpopular demand. Instead of just letting it go this time, however, I decided to address it. "Hey, Mom? Why do you always call me that?"

"Call you what, hon?"

"Fluffy," I said, a hint of disdain in my voice.

"Oh, gosh. When did that start? Let's see...I guess it was back in Kenya," she said through a whimpery yawn. "Back when your dad was working at the consulate there. You were three or four maybe, and there was a bunny on the property. You called it 'Fluffy' and one day, you told me if you could be anything in the world, you would want to be that rabbit. I just thought that was so funny, I started calling you Fluffy."

"Wait, really? You were talking about a rabbit?"

"Yeah, why?"

I shook my head, utterly shocked. I had never once considered that the nickname could have anything to do with something other than my weight. Really, the way I had interpreted it spoke so much more about how I saw myself than what my mother ever thought. I had just assumed, because she was so skinny, that I had been a disappointment, which she needed to remind me of on a regular basis with a funny, nitpicking little nickname. But I had never asked about it, not until that very moment. So instead I had assumed the worst about my own mother. The realization made me sad and happy at the same time.

"Why?" she asked again.

"Oh, no reason," I said, making sure to pepper in a few more "I love yous" before letting her go back to sleep.

The next person I called, naturally, was Gracie, who indulged me in a marathon phone fest that kept us both up way later than we needed. But she was happy to celebrate with me, especially because she'd just been promoted to office manager, and with that came a paycheck slightly less laughable than her last.

"Look at us killin' it," she said.

"I know. If I wasn't covered in cat hair, I might not believe this was my life." I wiped my nose, which prompted another sneeze.

"You can always move back in with you-know-who."

"Ha! No, that chapter is closed."

"Hey, have you seen that other guy? What's-his-name?"

"Liam? No, not really. Although it's weird, I keep thinking I see him around town. The other day I thought he was two lanes over from me in traffic. And then I thought I saw him at the grocery store, but he was checking out with his back turned. A couple of weeks ago, I saw him on campus, running, and he waved. But I couldn't be sure it was him."

"Yeah, it's funny, I see Richard everywhere, but I'm usually wrong. I think that's just our brains working out the obsession."

"Cheers to that!" I laughed, holding up my glass of water as Gracie, inevitably, held up her nightcap on the other end. "Here's to our brains working out the obsessions."

"Amen, sister. Clink," she said.

"Clink," I repeated.

Chapter 19

Summer in Oceanside literally goes out with a bang. On the last Friday in August, the mayor sets off a cannon outside the courthouse, which marks the beginning of "Gator Gras," Oceanside's weeklong version of Mardi Gras featuring the world's biggest alligator cook-off among other things. This year I was sad to find myself sans Gracie, who had always dragged me out on opening night, and decided to venture out on my own in her honor. I couldn't remember the last time I'd had a drink or seen live music, and once classes began I could probably kiss a social life goodbye, at least for a while.

I wandered into town with no expectations. I just figured I'd catch the tail end of the parade, grab a beer, see whoever was playing at the pub, and call it a night. But when I wandered into the darkened bar that was hosting opening night festivities, I heard a familiar voice coming from the stage in back and nearly dropped when I realized it was Liam.

My first thought was that I should run, or risk getting drawn back into his vortex. But my body, seemingly disconnected from my mind, stayed planted at the back of the crowd. He was strumming an acoustic guitar, seated alone onstage and singing a ballad. Desperate for a better view, I stood on my tiptoes and peered between the heads of the couple in front of me. The spotlight emphasized Liam's late-summer golden perfection. He looked tan and healthy, but still just the right amount of brooding and complex to twist my heart into perplexed little knots. The sound of his voice was mesmerizing. I had never been a groupie, but at this moment I saw the appeal, watching his fingers expertly move from chord to chord and his face contort with emotion. I closed my eyes and listened to the chorus:

There goes that girl again
I'm in a whirl again
It takes an angel to wake the devil inside me
And now she's gone again
I've done her wrong again
It took an angel to slay the devil inside me—

I opened my eyes and watched him repeat the chorus once more, half hoping that he was singing about me, but half terrified as well. The song was beautiful and tragic, the guitar lines plaintive, his gravelly voice bittersweet. Liam's guitar eventually faded out and everyone around me started to applaud while I stood there in a trance. All the emotions I had felt when leaving his house that night I had put him to bed came rushing back. *If only, if only, if only,* I thought, imagining the perfect world in which we could be together. But then my reasoning kicked in, telling me that Liam looked this good and healthy after weeks of not seeing me. I was just as improved without him. It seemed obvious we were better off without each other, even if watching him bare his soul onstage made me ache with desire.

Liam looked out into the crowd, scanning the room, and I

panicked. A girl carrying two full beers knocked into me as she made her way toward the stage, and I felt a wet spot spreading on the back of my shirt. *It's a sign,* I thought. *Go now before he sees you.* Liam's gazed drifted to my section of the crowd, and I turned, bolting past the bar and through the open door to the sidewalk littered with confetti from the parade.

* * *

"Where are you taking me, Fluffy?" Isabella looked worried as she peered out the passenger window of my car at a row of dilapidated ranch houses.

"To my drug dealer's house," I joked.

She pushed up the large, Audrey Hepburn–style black sunglasses that had slid down her nose. "Oh, please, I'm officially too old for drugs and bad neighborhoods."

Isabella was looking far better on her eighty-sixth birthday than she had a month ago, and I was happy to know I'd had a hand in it. Ever since that champagne-drenched afternoon when I'd made her a peanut butter smoothie and left it on her nightstand, she had been requesting them regularly and had even learned how to make them herself. It had given me the idea for a counter-program to my cleanse that I was working on formulating—a smoothie-only regimen for older women like her who could stand to add a few pounds. Of course, my juices had just started selling at Sasha's spa, and expanding the brand wouldn't be an option until I saw how they were doing, but I needed something other than Liam to occupy my thoughts before fall semester began. I couldn't get that song out of my head, or the image of him onstage. I knew better than to act on it by now, but the crush had come creeping back all the same…

"Ooh…here we are," I said, spotting the address I'd been searching for on a hot pink mailbox and turning into the driveway.

Many things about my dear old friend still remained a mystery to me—her political beliefs, what kind of music she liked, how exactly she had ended up in Oceanside—but something she had been very clear about from day one were her many superstitions. Like any good girly-girl, Isabella loved astrology and psychics and crack theories about lunar cycles and their effects on the female brain. So when I found myself searching for the perfect gift for her eighty-sixth, I decided to book a session with Sasha's favorite psychic. The woman's name (doubtfully by birth) was Mimi Lamar, and she had easily the nicest house on her not-yet-gentrified block. The lawn stood out as freshly cut and very green against the dry, yellowed grasses that bordered it. The home was a single-story ranch, like the ones surrounding it, but the bricks were painted bright white and the shutters were a brilliant magenta. Hibiscus bushes with delicate white and pink flowers bordered the front walk.

"Well, hello there!" Mimi greeted us from the front door as I helped Isabella out of the car.

"Who is she?" Isabella whispered in my ear.

"She's a psychic!" I whispered back.

"What is she going to predict? The next five minutes before I keel over?"

"Stop it."

From the front stoop, Mimi ushered us inside, looking more Martha Stewart than Madame Zelda in her white capri pants and pink sweater set. We were directed to sit in her living room while she retrieved sweet teas for the three of us.

Isabella nudged me as we sat side by side on the couch and I noticed the wicked smirk on her face as she studied its peony-patterned upholstery. "It looks like a florist's shop exploded in here."

"Be nice!" I said, unable to stop myself from smiling at her snarky humor.

When she came back in and deposited our drinks on the coffee table, Mimi dragged a side chair up to Isabella's end of the couch and took a seat. "Do you mind if I take your hand for a moment?" she asked in a sweet, Southern lilt.

Feigning indifference, Isabella offered her right hand and the psychic set about with her reading. Not surprisingly, it was hardly any time before my friend had been won over by Sasha's soothsayer, and I was satisfied that my present was well chosen.

"You're going to have one last great love," Mimi announced midway through the session, after she'd brought out the tarot cards. "He's around you already. In your neighborhood."

"One of those old geezers? I don't think so." Isabella shook her head, disturbed. She came around, though, once Mimi identified the man as a younger "visitor" of the neighborhood, not an actual resident. Then Isabella happily jumped to the conclusion that her destined affair was with the Latino pool boy she'd been admiring from afar during her weekly water aerobics class. Mimi didn't seem so convinced of the pool boy theory, but Isabella was dead set on it.

"What about you?" Mimi glanced over at me at the end of the hour. "No reading for you today?"

I shook my head and smiled politely, thinking she was crazy to assume I had more than $100 lying around.

"Well, I can tell you're in love, anyway. I could see that the moment you stepped out of the car."

"No, I'm not, actually. Free and clear of all romantic entanglements, and feeling good about it." I smiled, hoping to convince both Mimi and myself. The "feeling good about it" part wasn't the most honest thing I'd ever said, but I was in fake-it-till-you-make-it mode.

Mimi cocked her head to one side and reached for my hand. When I didn't immediately offer it, Isabella picked it up from my lap and handed it over. Closing her eyes, Mimi clasped my hand between hers. "Ah…okay, I see. You've had a little heartache. But maybe something you didn't see as love actually was."

"Right." I rolled my eyes up to the pale pink ceiling, certain she was wrong.

"Who knows?" Isabella chimed in.

"I'm just warning you, I'm usually right about the love thing," Mimi said.

"The proof is in the pudding. If I get this pool boy, I'm calling you again." Isabella wagged a finger at Mimi, who chuckled and took a healthy swig of her iced tea.

Later, Isabella would speculate that the tea was drugged, because by the end of it, she had started to believe everything the woman said. I, on the other hand, felt pretty confident her speculations were wrong. After all, I was as far away from "in love" as I had ever been and almost certain that was a good thing.

* * *

When classes started back up, I had the inevitable run-in with Julien every once in a while, and thankfully our conversations got less and less awkward every time. I had officially come around to his logic about why he and I would never work, especially after I'd seen him eating lunch at the Plex with the woman he'd been dating. She was tall with the striking combination of straight, long, black hair and freckled, honey-toned skin. She seemed shy and quirky, and they fit together in a way that he and I never did. They were comfortable, a little boring perhaps. I envisioned them having this same lunch in a park in New York, and that made even more sense—a lively, urban backdrop for the staid couple of professors. At some point, Julien had appeared to catch me staring out of the corner of his eye, and like a spaz, I had snuck behind a tree, then run in the opposite direction.

Later that week, I saw him on his way to the Carver Lecture Hall, and he told me Cecile missed me and had been talking about me like I was an old, estranged confidant. I was surprised to hear it but flattered, and I promised to come watch one of her basketball games once the season started. It was a terribly normal, mature exchange, and I silently congratulated myself as we parted ways, knowing I had come a long way since stumbling out of his office in tears and into the arms of Professor Donna Dixon, a woman I'd never met before and had, mercifully, never seen again.

* * *

In my program, there were nine other students—four guys and five girls—and I was relieved to be the only one who had been at Reid for undergrad as well. Not only was I more comfortable from the get-go, but I also became the de facto Oceanside expert, arranging little outings here and there for the other students who had come from everywhere but Florida. Hearing this, Gracie had accused me of suddenly morphing into a social butterfly and complained she wasn't there to witness it. About a month into fall semester, my classmates and I decided to celebrate the end of our first big assignment by throwing a bonfire on the beach, something I hadn't done since freshman year.

"Look at these stars!" the Italian girl, Camilla, kept saying as she stood by the fire gazing upward, her marshmallow slowly petrifying on the end of the stick that dangled from her grip.

"What, they don't have stars like this in Italy?" I asked.

"Well, of course," she responded in her heavy, singsong accent. "They're better there, but I had low expectations for this place."

Inspired by Camilla's enthusiasm, we all took a moment, rolling our heads back to stare at the dark, silver-specked canvas above us. I couldn't remember feeling so content.

Then Rebecca, the easily distracted flirt from Mississippi, cried out, "Whoa, incoming!" and we all looked in the direction she was staring. Down the beach, an attractive male figure walked alongside the ocean, headed toward us.

"Wait—I know him," I said.

"From your dreams?" Rebecca replied with a chuckle.

"No, really." In a kind of daze, I dropped my marshmallow stick in the sand and made my way toward Liam at the water's edge. I couldn't ignore him this time.

"Bring him back here!" Rebecca called after me, sounding like she was only half kidding.

Liam recognized me as I approached—I could tell by his grin, a little nervous seeming. He pushed his hands inside his jeans pockets.

"Hey," I said, feeling my cheeks go red. Whether I liked it or not, he still had that effect on me.

"Hey." Liam kicked at the sand and glanced at me with a familiar twinkle in his eye. "I thought that was you. I was thinking about coming up, but I didn't know if you'd want to see me."

"You look really good," I said. And he did, just like he had onstage. His face was a little fuller even. He looked well rested, perhaps a few pounds heavier overall.

"Thanks. I've been staying healthy, working out, all the boring stuff. What about you? You look amazing."

I blushed. Liam's compliment was the best thing I'd heard in weeks, and it made me suddenly forget all the heartache he'd caused. In fact, standing there on the beach with him, our little fling felt like ancient history. "I'm sorry about that text I sent. I was just trying to focus on me," I said.

"Please, you don't have to explain anything. I just wanted to reach out. I didn't expect anything." Liam kicked at the sand again. He seemed awkward and human, and I remembered how emotionally raw he had been the last time I saw him.

"Hey, do you wanna join us?" I asked. "I'm just here with a bunch of other students in my program. Nutrition geeks. They'll love that you're a chef."

"I don't know…" He glanced back at the ocean, leading me to think, for a split second, that he might turn me down. "You got marshmallows over there?"

"You bet," I said, and held out my hand.

And then, like it was the most natural thing in the world, Liam took my hand and I led him back to the bonfire, where my new friends greeted him like he had just been named *People's* Sexiest Man Alive.

Ever the extrovert, Rebecca put words to what everyone was thinking. "I'm sorry, but I have never seen anyone as good-looking as you IRL. Do you actually exist?" She reached out to touch him, and Liam played along like a good sport.

"Last time I checked. What's your name again?"

"Rebecca."

"Hi, Rebecca." He reached out to shake her hand and she pretended to faint.

"Forget it. He's Australian, right?" Camilla looked at Liam

with an impish smile, and he nodded. "Never go to bed with an Australian man, Rebecca. They're brutes!"

"Oh right, because Italian men are soooo gentle," Rebecca countered, valiantly coming to Liam's defense.

I watched with amusement as the girls vied for Liam's attention and the guys ruffled at his presence. The old me would have been jealous, but now I was just entertained—proud, even. Eventually, the group normalized and one of the boys, Marcus, suggested we play a game called "Puppetmaster," which entailed inventing our own trivia questions and inflicting them on the group. The result was pretty hilarious, especially when the questions became more and more subjective and we were forced to answer things like: "What time did I wake up this morning?" or "Which world leader is the healthiest eater?" The game lasted until the marshmallows had run out and we finally declared the night over. Even then, nobody really wanted to go home.

When the last of the fire had been extinguished, Liam walked with me to the dark and desolate-looking parking lot and glanced around. "I don't see your car," he said.

"No, I rode with Camilla." I nodded toward her old VW and she waved, waiting patiently for us to say our goodbyes.

"Let me walk you home." Liam smiled and nudged my arm with his elbow. "What do you say?"

"What do I say? Hmm..." My instinct was to say yes, of course, but I was working on my impulsive tendencies. For some reason, I had kind of assumed we would part ways after the bonfire, like a couple of old lovers who were resigned to never see each other again. "Are you sure?" I finally asked. "I mean, I don't know what your situation is, but I don't want it to become some temptation. That's not to say I'm not assuming we would...I'm just remembering the last time—"

He stopped me, amused at my fumbling. "No, it's fine, I promise. Let me walk you, Mischa."

I smiled and scrunched up my nose, trying to fight the giddiness that threatened to overtake me. "Wait one second." I held up an index finger as I broke away from him.

At Camilla's car I informed her, very self-consciously, that I'd be walking home with my old friend. In turn, she teasingly warned me again about Australian men, but I promised I wouldn't fall prey to his brutish charms.

"Yeah, yeah, you guys have already slept together."

My jaw dropped. "How are you so sure?"

"Are you kidding me? The way he looks at you. With the eyes of a dog," she said.

I laughed at Camilla's odd choice of metaphor. It reminded me of one of Isabella's lost-in-translation moments.

She threw her car door open and slipped inside. "It's the truth!" she called out as she rolled down the window, waving goodbye.

I waved back and walked over to where Liam was waiting for me. I hadn't stopped giggling over Camilla's comment.

"What's so funny?" he asked.

"Camilla said you look at me 'with the eyes of a dog.'"

Smiling, he held out his arm and I took it. "Well I'm more polite than a dog, at least give me that."

We started to leave the parking lot headed in the wrong direction, but I corrected our path, explaining that I had moved. "We're actually closer to my new place than Julien's," I said, veering him in the right direction.

"So did you ever get off with that professor, then?" Liam tugged at my arm.

"Excuse me?" I glanced sideways at him, incredulous.

"I figured that was inevitable, no?"

"Why would you think that?" I was trying to act coy, but he had caught me off guard.

"Uh…maybe because he looked at you with the eyes of a dog? I dunno."

"Ha-ha, good one."

"So are you gonna answer me?"

I shook my head, smiling, knowing it would do neither of us any good to talk about Julien. Besides, I was too caught up in how invigorating it felt to walk with him like this, arm in arm. When I'd found him on the beach, he had immediately seemed like such a different person than the one I had met outside the Baptist church that fated night, so much more calm and vulnerable. "You've changed," I remarked.

"So have you," he said, drawing my arm in closer to his body.

As we moved inland, the air got balmier. I had been chilly at the beach, but now it felt like the perfect temperature outside. Passing through a strip mall parking lot, I gave Liam the short update on my life—how I'd started school and was selling my juice cleanse at Sasha's spa and how I was cat sitting for a math professor through the end of the year. He told me about the menu changes at his restaurant and said his band had licensed their song for a British car commercial, and he hadn't had another drink since that night I had come to his house. At some point, he lowered his arm and took my hand in his, and I felt a rush of emotions that I'd been trying to hold back.

"I thought I would never see you again," I confessed as we turned a corner onto a lamp-lit street lined with beautiful cypress trees. "I mean, not *see you*, see you. Actually, I did see you. That night you played at Gator Gras."

"Seriously?" Liam stopped in his tracks. "You were there?"

I nodded. "You were amazing. I should have stayed and told you that. I just…I guess I panicked, seeing you." I looked over at him. He shook his head, baffled, his eyes on the street ahead of us.

"I thought you might be there. I had this sense. There was this one song—I wasn't gonna play it, but I'd written it for you and I figured, if you heard it, you might forgive me." He laughed, his smile turning to a grimace. "Silly romantic idea, huh?"

"I did hear it," I said, knowing that the song he was talking about was the exact one I had heard. "It stayed in my head for days, Liam. It was beautiful."

He smiled and looked over at me, his eyes twinkling again. He tugged my arm and we started to walk. "The way I acted that last night you saw me was embarrassing. I wanted to reach out, even before I sent the text, but I had no idea what to say or how to say it. I missed you, but at the same time, I was in such a miserable place. I wish I could say that night was my rock bottom, but a couple years back I was even worse…if you can imagine." He chuckled. There was an anxiousness to his laugh. "I need to tell you something, though. I want to say that I'm sorry."

"It's okay," I rushed to answer.

"No, it's not. I dragged you into my shit and yelled at you for no reason. I hardly remember that night. I'm sure I don't even know the worst of it."

"I think the guitars got the worst of it," I joked.

Liam laced his fingers through mine, gripping my hand a little tighter. "I like you, Mischa."

"I like you, too…I think."

"You think?"

"I know." I leaned into him playfully, and he nudged me with his hip. "But where does that get us?"

"It gets us here, obviously," he said with a cryptic wink. "You know... I've told you things I never told anybody else."

"Ditto," I said, giving his hand a squeeze. It was a nice feeling, walking and talking like this after everything that had transpired between us, but suddenly the fear struck me that I knew where this conversation was going. "I don't think I can be your friend, Liam, if that's what you're thinking."

He glanced at me sideways, taken aback.

"As much as I'd like to say I could, I don't think I'd handle it very well." I gave him my best attempt at a smile and pointed to a street sign one block away. "That's my street."

There was a long gap of silence as we kept walking, the sound of our footsteps pattering against the sidewalk in unison. In another block and a half, we reached the house where I was staying and I lamented having to say goodbye. "I'd invite you inside, but there's three emotionally needy cats in there, and they are not interested in vying with anyone else for my attention."

"I wouldn't dream of coming in."

"Oh," I said. I pretended not to be hurt, but of course it stung a little to hear it. I still wanted him to want me.

Liam kept walking alongside me all the way to the front steps of the house, where he tapped lightly on my shoulder, and I turned to face him. "Listen, Mischa, I don't want to be your friend either."

I nodded, whisking a stray hair away from my face. "It was fun while it lasted, I guess. All two hours of it."

"No, that's not what I meant. I mean, I want to be something else to you. Something I haven't tried in a long time."

I blinked as if I hadn't heard him correctly. A million sensations rushed through me simultaneously as I stood across from him: exhilaration, happiness, terror, anxiety, even sadness. But the dominant voice inside my head was a hopeful one: *Is he saying what I think he's saying?*

"I'm not saying I've become a different person," Liam continued. "I'm still the same fucked up guy you met. But I'm really trying now." He paused for a breath, exhaling loudly. I couldn't believe this man could seem so nervous to tell me something. "You know that night at the spa? I felt like I really connected with someone for the first time in a long time, and it scared me to death. I felt like, what good is it when I have nothing to offer this girl? When I'm broken?"

I reached out for his hands and took them in mine. "You're not broken," I whispered.

"I haven't had sex since I was with you. I'm trying to make it till the New Year."

I nodded in encouragement. "That's great. I just don't know what you could want from me, then." In retrospect, it was a horribly insecure thing to say, but I couldn't see past our sexual history to what else might become of us.

"Here's what I want, Mischa. Tonight, I want to kiss you good night. And then next week, I want to take you on a proper date. And then I want to keep doing that. And we can get to know each other that way, with our clothes on. And then, hopefully, you'll see who I really am and hopefully it won't scare you. And as hard as it might be, we won't have sex for a while. What do you think about that?" Liam flashed the most brilliant smile I had ever seen, and I matched it.

"Umm…" My mind was all over the place. I could hardly think straight enough to answer. "I would like that," I finally said. "I just… I'm in a really good place right now, and I don't want to mess it up."

"I don't want to mess it up either." He pulled me toward him and gave my forehead a sweet little peck.

"No, but seriously," I insisted, trying to keep my wits about me as his magnetic pull worked its magic.

"I know, I know," he said. "Same with me. Listen, if it's not good, we cut bait. It's as easy as that."

I nodded. "Right. It feels good to be realistic about things every once in a while."

"Doesn't it?" He laughed, then pointed behind me, up at the sky. "Look! Do you see that? I swear that was a shooting star."

I turned to look but saw nothing. "Huh, no."

"Or a comet. Or a meteor shower. I don't know, but it was definitely something. We should make a wish," he said.

"Hey! We were just talking about being realistic!" I poked his chest playfully.

"Oh, c'mon." Liam closed his eyes and moved his lips as he made a silent wish.

"Fine." I closed my own eyes and searched my brain, only to realize that I had nothing to wish for in that moment. As I reopened my eyes and saw Liam standing before me, I felt woozy with affection. I figured his sudden reemergence into my life wasn't going to fully sink in for quite some time, but I wanted to revel in the newness of this moment for as long as I could. I drifted a little closer to him, and he leaned in to kiss me. As our lips met, the thrill of a thousand kisses flooded the synapses in my brain. Liam's hands found my waist as I reached up for his shoulders, and he leaned me backward as if he were about to dip me. I felt like the movie star version of myself. When our lips finally parted and our tongues met, everything was soft and sweet and perfect.

If someone were to hit a pause button on my life at that very moment, asking me to describe how I felt, I would have said something terribly melodramatic and clichéd, but it would have been true. I would have told them I felt like I was "walking on air" or like I had been "set free." I would have explained all the future plans that were running through my head, the things I wanted to do and see with Liam and all the late-night conversations I envisioned us having as we got to know each other with our clothes on. I would have said that for the first time since I was eight years old, everything in my life felt perfect and whole in a completely unexpected way that I couldn't have seen coming in a million years. I would have admitted that Mimi Lamar, Sasha's trusty psychic, had somehow diagnosed me correctly when she had said I was in love but that I didn't know it at the time, and maybe that meant Isabella was going to get her pool boy after all.

I could also describe my state in that very moment by saying how I didn't feel anymore—which was afraid. After twenty-two years, I had finally learned how to stand beside myself, to support myself and take comfort in my little army of one. In fact, for the first time that I could remember, I didn't feel like somebody or something else had this crazy power over me that I couldn't control. Whether or not things worked out with Liam, I knew it wouldn't be the end of the world because there was no more fear of abandonment in the deepest depths of my heart. At the end of the day, I wasn't hungry, or fragile, or wounded, or panicked. I wasn't anxious. I wasn't tragic. And best of all, I wasn't lonely... not because I had Liam, but because I had me.

Acknowledgments

Thank you to the beautiful and brilliant Rebecca Friedman for your guidance and friendship and to the lovely Michele Bidelspach for taking a chance on me and helping shape this book.

Thanks to my friends and family for your endless support and comic relief. And to anyone who's ever struggled with addiction or loved someone who has, thank you for making the world a better place by sharing your stories.

About the Author

Amelia Betts was born in the South, where she grew up on soap operas, sugar cereal, and Judy Blume. She learned the thrill of the secret crush when her older sisters started bringing boys home, and has been a hopeless romantic ever since. She now resides, and dreams up happily ever afters, in Los Angeles, California.

You Might Also Like...

Looking for more great romances?
Now available from Forever Yours

OPERATION
One Night Stand

Christine Hughes

IT'S TIME TO CHANGE HER SEXUAL KARMA

Caroline Frost had it all—until her boyfriend banged the super-skank intern, and *poof!* Caroline's happy little bubble disappeared. Now it's been six weeks of weeping, a mountain of ice cream, and a permanent butt-print on the couch. Enough is enough. She and her ladybits need an intervention—now.

Enter Operation: One Night Stand: Find a man who is

hotness personified and have some much-needed sexy time. The only problem is that Caroline is torn between a flirtatious, well-built guy and the ridiculously hot bartender serving her shots. This was supposed to be all fun and no games, but like the perfect scotch on the rocks, no good fling finishes without a twist...

HOT FOR TEACHER

As the new head of the English department, Dani doesn't have much time for anything but lesson planning and literature. Romance-or even sex? Forget about it. But then the principal introduces her to last-minute hire Nate Ryan. Finding time to mentor a new teacher won't be easy, especially when his incredible body and equally disarming charisma are enough to make her heart skip a beat...

Nate may be fresh out of school, but he's confident in his teaching skills—and in his feelings for Dani. But while she's everything he's ever wanted, he knows his place on her staff—and his age—may be problematic for his sexy boss. How can he convince her to ignore the gossip mill currently in full swing in the teacher's lounge and surrender to what's meant to be?

Love doesn't have to be perfect to be true...

Years ago, Tanner Green loved Sunny Letman. She was meant to be his first kiss, first love, first *everything*. Then their world spun upside-down and out of control.

Free-spirited Sunny doesn't do commitment. Sure, guys are great for a night or a week, but she *always* leaves first. That is, until professional skateboarder and town golden boy, Tanner Green, unexpectedly walks back into her life.

Despite their broken history, a fragile and undeniably electric connection still holds them together. Now Tanner has to convince Sunny that even though love isn't always perfect, it's worth sticking around for...